No After You

NICOLE PYLAND

No After You

Celebrities Series Book #1

Dani Wilder only intended to go to a fundraiser and donate money to a worthy cause. She had no idea that she'd meet the love of her life that night. There were only a couple of problems with that chance meeting. Dani had a boyfriend. That chance meeting – it was with Peyton Gloss, the world's most famous music star, who also happened to be a woman.

Peyton had only planned on performing that night. When she'd seen the most beautiful woman in the world in the crowd, she had to talk to her. Dani Wilder was a beautiful, kind, smart supermodel, who also happened to have a boyfriend. When the two women spend time together, though, it's clear to both of them that this is more than merely a close friendship.

In this prequel to **"All the Love Songs,"** find out what happened the night these two met, and discover how their relationship began.

To contact the author or for any additional information visit: **https://nicolepyland.com**

BY THE AUTHOR

Stand-alone books:

- The Fire
- The Moments
- The Disappeared

Chicago Series:

- Introduction – Fresh Start
- Book #1 – The Best Lines
- Book #2 – Just Tell Her
- Book #3 – Love Walked into The Lantern
- Series Finale – What Happened After

San Francisco Series:

- Book #1 – Checking the Right Box
- Book #2 – Macon's Heart
- Book #3 – This Above All
- Series Finale – What Happened After

Tahoe Series:

- Book #1 – Keep Tahoe Blue
- Book #2 – Time of Day

Celebrities Series:

CONTENTS

CHAPTER 1

WHEN DANIELLE Alexandria Wilder was born, her mother knew she was special. She probably had no reason to think so. All mothers thought their children were beautiful, brilliant, and talented. However, by the time *Danielle*, as she was then known, was eleven months old, her mother had entered her into a "Beautiful Baby" contest at their local mall. Danielle had won the contest. Her parents had gotten a gift card. They also earned themselves a contract with a local modeling agency that specialized in children. Danielle spent her third birthday at a photo shoot for a catalog. Her fifth birthday was spent at a commercial shoot for a local discount store. Her sixth birthday party had to be held three weeks after the date because she'd been cast in an independent film that was shot three towns over.

She was able to go to regular schools. Of that, she would always be grateful. She did miss a lot of it, though. Once she had entered high school, her modeling career took off. She wasn't doing local jobs anymore. She had become *Dani* by the time she was thirteen. Her then 5'9" height, long light-brown hair, and bright green eyes, along with her high cheekbones, made her a perfect runway model. One of her first runways was for an up-and-coming designer during New York Fashion Week. She would always remember that day because it was the first time she'd felt like a true model. But she would also remember it for another reason, later. On that day, the song she had walked down the runway to, was by a fresh new face on the country music scene. Her name was Peyton Gloss.

The song they'd played over the speakers as she'd walked, had fit the mood of the show perfectly. However, the song Dani was currently listening to, ten years later, was more pop than country and wasn't on speakers. Peyton Gloss was standing in front of Dani's table, alone on the stage. She had a guitar and a microphone. Her bright blue eyes flickered with the stage lights that were aimed all around her. Peyton's hair was just past her shoulders and in thick waves, and it had been strategically swept away from her face. The song she was singing was a slow one. It was beautiful. Peyton Gloss was beautiful.

"Hey, I'm going to get a drink," Steven said into her ear.

"Huh?" Dani shook herself out of the hypnosis she'd been in since the moment Peyton took the stage.

"Drink? The waiter hasn't been around since the performances started. I'm going to the bar. Do you want anything?"

"No," Dani replied somewhat gruffly before returning her attention to the stage.

"What's wrong?"

"Steven, she's performing. Shut up."

"Fine." Steven stood, slid his chair back under the table, and made his way to the bar.

Dani wasn't entirely sure where he ended up. Her eyes were back on Peyton. Peyton was wearing heels that made her appear even taller than she was. Dani knew Peyton Gloss was taller than most girls. As a woman that was now 6'1", Dani understood that. She also kind of liked that Peyton still wore heels. Steven was only 5'10". He often requested Dani wore flats when they went out together so that he wouldn't appear that much shorter than her. He'd even inserted lifts in his shoes sometimes so that they'd be about the same height. Dani had seen articles in magazines of Peyton out with her boyfriends or doing interviews on the red carpet. She'd always worn heels; even when her boyfriends were definitely shorter. Dani smiled at the thought before she glanced down at her own ballet flats.

"Thank you," Peyton said into the microphone the moment the sound from the final note strummed away and left the room in silence.

The room applauded the superstar who had been famous ever since that first album topped the country charts but had gotten even more notoriety recently, when she released a pop album that showed nearly no traces of her country roots. Dani had all the woman's songs on her phone, but she had never been able to make it to a show. Her career had always gotten in the way. But she wouldn't ever complain about that, of course. She'd been incredibly blessed in her life. She had sacrificed things, but she would do it all over again if she had to. She was happy in her life. Her parents and younger brother were taken care of. She had enough money to more than support herself. She had Steven, too. She had a good life. She nodded to herself at the thought as she applauded Peyton, who waved and left the stage.

"The bartender actually carded me," Steven said when Dani approached him at the bar moments later. "Can you believe that?" he asked without really asking.

"You're only twenty-four, Steven. He probably has to check. It's kind of his job," Dani replied.

"I got you a white wine." He handed her the glass Dani didn't actually want.

She watched him take a sip of his whiskey neat and place the glass on one of the high tables by the bar. He then pulled out his phone and started typing.

"It's after ten. Do you think you'll be ready to go soon?" he asked without looking up at her.

"The silent auction hasn't even started," Dani replied.

"I paid ten grand for the table, Dani. I think they got enough money out of us tonight."

"I wanted to bid, Steven. *You* gave them that money.

I haven't actually donated anything yet." She placed her wine glass on the table next to him. "If you want to go, though, that's fine. I can get a ride home from Jill," she said of her best friend, who'd joined them for the evening with her husband.

"No, it's fine." Steven shrugged. "I just have a ton of work to do." He finally looked up at her then. "Sorry, I'm taking my stress out on you. I shouldn't."

Steven was the youngest of three brothers. With his oldest one deciding to become a Catholic priest and his middle brother opting for a career in politics, Steven had been left to manage his family's real estate fortune. His father had passed away a few years prior. His mother had always stayed at home. It was all put on Steven's shoulders, and he was only twenty-four years old. He'd invested much of his trust fund into two tech start-ups that were doing very well, but that left him with three businesses that usually needed some kind of response from him.

"It's okay," Dani told him with a small smile. "You really can go if you want. Jill and Adam will take me home when I'm ready."

"It would be easier if you'd just move in with me, Dani." He slid his phone into his pocket.

"Where'd that come from? My place is closer to here than your place is," she said.

"Right. If you'd just finally move in with me, it would make things easier. Like, I can't ask Adam and Jill to take you all the way out to my place when your place is so much closer, but I was hoping you'd stay at my place tonight. You're leaving for Hawaii tomorrow, and I'm in Vancouver for the next week."

"Oh," she said. "We've talked about this, though."

"I know. I get it. We're young. We're busy. I know all that. Dani, we've been together for over two years."

"I know when our anniversary is, Steven." Dani crossed her arms over her chest. "I'm usually the one that reminds you."

"This isn't about that. It's just that – I don't know." He sighed rather loudly. "I feel like I'm always waiting on you, Dani."

Steven's phone rang in his pocket, and Dani felt somewhat grateful for a chance to delay this conversation for at least the length of a business call.

"Sorry, I have to take this," Steven told her when he glanced at the screen. "Hello?" He took a few steps away from her.

"That dress is amazing," a voice said from behind her.

Dani didn't want to be presumptuous. There was a great chance that compliment wasn't directed at her. The room was filled with beautiful women in beautiful dresses. This formal affair nearly always drew the highest of the high-end crowd, of which Dani was a member merely because of her relationship with Steven. She, likely, never would have been invited had he not bought the table each year. Dani turned around anyway, though, on the off chance that the comment had been directed at her.

"Whoa," she muttered mainly to herself when she caught sight of Peyton Gloss standing in front of her.

"She's right. It's a great color," the woman standing next to Peyton added. "Peyton, white or red?"

"Sparkling water," Peyton told her.

The woman walked off to join the line at the bar. Dani glanced behind her for a second to see that Steven was still on his phone.

"That's–"

"Lennox Owen," Peyton interrupted her.

"Right," Dani said. "And you're…"

"And you're Dani Wilder," Peyton said. "Peyton," she added, holding out her hand for Dani to shake with the widest, and also the whitest smile Dani had ever seen that wasn't photoshopped.

"You know who I am?" Dani asked. Then, she took Peyton's hand to shake. Her fingers slid against the softest skin she'd ever touched. "You play guitar?" she asked the dumbest question in the world but earned the continuation of that million-watt smile. "I mean, of course, you do. I just watched you do it." She shook her head rapidly from side to side as her cheeks warmed with embarrassment.

"What did you think?" Peyton asked.

"Just that your hands aren't callused at all," Dani said. "My friend Jill plays guitar. Not like you; she plays for fun, but she has calluses sometimes."

Peyton laughed and replied, "I meant about the playing. What did you think about the song?"

"It was great. I love all your songs, though." It was then that Dani realized she was still holding onto Peyton's hand. "Sorry." She let it go.

"Don't be." Peyton looked behind Dani to the line that her friend, Lennox, was still standing in. "Do you want to come over here?" she asked, pointing toward one of the tables.

"Oh, sure," Dani replied. "I don't want to keep you, though, if you have to go."

"I don't," Peyton offered softly.

They walked for a few seconds to find an empty table. Dani watched the people around them move aside as if the woman beside her had the power to part the Red Sea. For once, no eyes were on Dani; they were all on the pop star. Dani couldn't blame them. Peyton was gorgeous up-close. Dani was used to being surrounded by gorgeous women, but Peyton, right now, in those skinny jeans that had a little shine to them and that sleeveless black shirt, was doing something to her. Her heart was beating faster than she'd possibly ever felt it. Her skin felt clammy, including the hands she was trying to covertly wipe on her dress. Her breaths were coming in short and shallow, and going out the same way.

"Here's your sparkling water," Lennox said when she met them at the table.

"Thanks, Len." Peyton smiled at her. "Lennox, this is Dani Wilder. Dani, this is my bestie for life, Lennox Owen."

"Nice to meet you," Lennox said with an outstretched hand.

"You too," Dani replied, taking that hand, shaking it, returning it, and then wondering why shaking Lennox's hand had provided a completely different reaction than shaking Peyton's. "I like your movies," she added.

"Thanks," Lennox said with a smile that was nearly as white as Peyton's, but not quite as perfect. "So, you're here to donate some money like the rest of us, I take it?"

"It's a good cause," Dani said and glanced in Peyton's direction.

Peyton appeared to be staring at her over her glass of sparkling water. Her eyes glistened. Her skin was perfection, and Dani already knew how soft it was. She smiled at Peyton again, not knowing what else to say or do.

"Hey, you left your wine over there," Steven said, placing the glass of white wine on the table in front of Dani. "Oh, hi." He looked up to see she wasn't alone. "Steven."

"Peyton." Peyton pointed at herself. "Lennox." She pointed at Lennox.

"Nice to meet you," he replied, looking at Peyton, then Dani, then down at his phone, which beeped at the same time. "Sorry. I just need to respond to this."

"I saw you walk once, in Paris. I was there for Fashion Week," Lennox told Dani.

"Oh, yeah?"

"Yeah. I don't know how you guys do that. I'll take making a movie any day over walking down a runway in six-inch heels, wearing the things you do," Lennox added.

"You get used to it, I guess." Dani shrugged.

"You do it really well," Peyton said.

Dani smiled at her, and she knew she was blushing. She couldn't stop it even if she tried. So, she just lowered her head for a moment, to try to gather herself. Although she was used to famous people, she'd never had this kind of reaction to one before. She felt something on her hand, which was gripping the glass of wine she knew she wouldn't drink. When she looked back up, she noticed that Peyton's hand was an inch away from her own, but the woman's index finger had been the one touching her fingers only a moment ago. Peyton smiled a small smile now, and there was something about it. It was a shy smile. It wasn't the superstar smile Dani had seen in pictures and on stage. There was something very personal about this smile. Dani knew, somehow, that this smile was only for her.

CHAPTER 2

"Is it just me or is she really pretty?" Peyton asked Lennox.

"She's a supermodel, Peyton. I don't exactly think they make them in hideous," Lennox replied, smiling at her own joke.

"No, I mean, like, more than that." Peyton nodded in the direction of Dani Wilder, who was talking to Steven – the same guy who had so rudely interrupted them earlier. He was obviously her boyfriend. Peyton knew who he was. Steven English was a trust fund kid who'd invested in a few tech companies here and there. Peyton knew him because one of his start-ups wanted her to endorse a pair of noise-canceling headphones a couple of years ago. She had tried them, hadn't liked them, and then declined the offer. "It's weird. Sorry." She shook her head at herself. Then, she noticed Dani turning back around to them. "Should we leave you two alone?" she asked, cursed herself silently for even suggesting it, and took a drink of her now near-empty sparkling water.

"I'll grab you another," Lennox said, elbowing her with a smirk on her face.

Lennox started to walk off back toward the bar. Peyton would tell her what an asshole she was later, when they were alone. Right now, though, she was completely enamored with Dani Wilder, who appeared to not want that white wine in front of her at all.

"Hey, Len?"

"Yeah?" Lennox turned.

"What do you want?" Peyton asked Dani.

"Sorry?"

"To drink," Peyton told her.

"Oh, I'm—"

"Not interested in drinking white wine right now?"

Dani smiled and said, "Red would be great."

"Coming up," Lennox said and continued on her quest.

"Thank you," Dani told Peyton.

"Not a white wine drinker?" Peyton asked her, leaning a little over the table.

"Sometimes. I just didn't want it tonight. Every now and then, it gives me a headache. And I'm on a flight tomorrow, so I didn't want to wake up with one." Dani leaned in as well, matching Peyton's posture.

The table wasn't all that large. It was a cocktail party high-top table that could fit drinks and some small plates but definitely wasn't made for a crowd. With the two of them leaning over it now, Peyton could almost feel Dani's breath on her skin.

"Where are you going?" Peyton asked.

"Seven o'clock flight to Maui. I have a shoot there the following morning. I'm only staying the night. Then, I come home."

"And home is New York?"

"Yes. You?"

"My plans for tomorrow?" Peyton asked, confused by the question.

"Sorry. And I *did* recognize you earlier, Peyton." Steven approached the table, setting his phone down next to Dani's still full glass. "I had a few emails I need to answer."

"No problem," Peyton said.

She then watched as Steven put his hand on the small of Dani's back. Dani didn't look at Steven, though. Her eyes remained on Peyton's.

"I'm staying in town for a while," Peyton offered, referring them back to their conversation.

"New York?"

"I'll be here for the next few months while I work on the next album," she replied. "I usually record in LA, but I wanted to do something different for this next album."

"So, you'll be hanging out in New York?" Dani asked with a growing smile on her face.

"I will be, yes." Peyton's smile matched Dani's. "Are you going to Hawaii with her, Steven?" she asked but didn't take her eyes off Dani's remarkable green ones.

"No, I have a couple of investor meetings tomorrow. I'm in Canada the rest of the week," he replied, removing his hand from Dani's back when his phone chimed again. "That's my mom." He shrugged a shoulder. "Sorry, babe. Give me a minute."

"Tell her hi for me." Dani watched as Steven walked off.

"He's a busy guy," Peyton said.

"That he is," Dani agreed.

"Seven in the morning, huh?"

"What?" Dani asked, leaning in even further.

"Tomorrow morning? Your flight." Peyton leaned in as well.

"Oh, right."

"What airline?"

"Hawaiian."

"Do you like Hawaiian?" Peyton asked with what she knew was a slight smirk on her face.

"It's okay." Dani smiled back at her. "Why?"

"I have a plane. You could use it," Peyton offered.

"You just have a plane that I can use?" Dani laughed.

Peyton nearly burst with joy at the sound of it. What the hell was that? Dani's smile, Dani's laugh – Dani's everything right now – was making her heart race harder than her first performance in front of a record executive all those years ago.

"I have a plane, yes. You can use it."

"And why would I want to do that?" Dani asked. "I've got my first-class window seat."

"Is it next to my aisle seat?" Peyton asked.

"I don't know. Are you on a flight 638 to Maui tomorrow morning?"

"No," Peyton said seriously.

"Do you want to go to Hawaii, Peyton?"

"Yes."

She watched as Dani gulped. Lennox returned. A glass of red wine was placed in front of Dani. A glass of sparkling water was placed in front of Peyton.

"What did I miss?" Lennox asked.

"Dani, can I borrow you?" Steven approached and asked.

"Sure." Dani left the table reluctantly and walked off with Steven.

Peyton's eyes followed her until she said, "Thanks for the refill."

"No problem. You two seem to be getting cozy," Lennox said.

"Cozy?" Peyton asked, looking over at her friend.

"Yes, cozy." Lennox laughed. "Pey, you're someone that has a lot of friends. I'm used to you meeting someone, liking them, and inviting them to your next show or event or something. But I have no idea what's going on here."

"Sorry, I should probably be going," Dani delivered upon her return.

"Everything okay?" Peyton asked.

"Steven's mom needs him to stop by. She's a diabetic and is having problems with her insulin pump," Dani replied. "He knows how to fix it. And I told him I'd go with him since she likes me, and I have a way of calming her down when she's anxious."

"I'm sure you do," Peyton said. "Sorry, I just meant that..."

"It was nice meeting you," Lennox told Dani.

"You too."

Dani then looked at Peyton. Her green eyes met Peyton's blue ones. Peyton knew then that something had transpired tonight. She wasn't sure she could identify it if asked, but something had occurred.

"I meant what I said, Dani. Can I borrow your phone?" she asked.

"Babe, we've got to go," Steven said, staring down at his phone again.

"Sure." Dani passed her cell phone to Peyton after unlocking it.

Peyton quickly entered her phone number. Then, thinking that she didn't want to chance not talking to Dani Wilder again, she sent a text to her own phone from Dani's, in order to capture the woman's number. She passed it back to Dani after that.

"There you go," she said.

"Thanks," Dani replied with a shy smile. "I have to–"

"Go. I know."

"Bid on something good for me in my absence?" Dani asked.

"No problem." Peyton smiled at her.

Dani gave one more smile, turned, took Steven's hand, and walked away. Peyton felt it deep down in her soul then. She couldn't name it right away, but she'd try to do that later, when she cloistered herself in her music room at home and tried to find lyrics that would explain how she was feeling right now. She watched Dani, hand in hand with her boyfriend, leave the gala. Instead of feeling like she wanted to stay at the party with Lennox and enjoy themselves, Peyton knew all she wanted was to go home and spend some quality time with her guitar and her notebook. She had told Dani she would do something, though. And she would keep her word.

"What should we bid on?" she asked Lennox.

CHAPTER 3

DANI SAT ON THE SOFA in Steven's living room later that night. It was technically morning now. They'd spent about an hour at Steven's mother's house, making sure she had what she needed. Steven also made sure to call the nurse they had checking in on his mother whenever he was out of town, to set up the appointment for her to come by and check the pump and insulin supplies for tomorrow before he had to leave for the week. His mother had always been a diabetic, but it had gotten worse after his father's death. She had stopped taking care of herself then. It was a constant battle these days, to get her to eat right and exercise appropriately. His brothers did what they could. Steven did, too. But they relied on staff to help when they couldn't.

It was after one in the morning by the time they made it back to his place. Steven had fallen asleep near instantly. Dani, however, couldn't. Because she was now staying at Steven's place, she would have to go out of her way tomorrow morning to pick up her stuff before heading to the airport for her flight. It wasn't as if she had never done that before. It just made things unnecessarily complicated. Her phone buzzed from its position on the table. She looked down at the readout and smiled immediately.

"Hey," she greeted.

"Hi. Did I wake you?"

"No, I'm still up."

"Did I wake Steven?"

"No, he's in bed; asleep."

"And you are where?"

"In the living room; not asleep," Dani said as her smile widened.

"I just left the party."

"Yeah?" She leaned back into the couch.

"I bid on something for you."

"You did?"

"I did."

"And what is it?" Dani asked with quiet laughter because she didn't want to wake Steven.

"It's a surprise."

"A surprise?"

"Yes."

"And when will you surprise me?"

"Tomorrow. If you get on the plane with me."

"What?" Dani laughed a little louder.

"I don't have any plans for the next two days. I was just going to write, but I can do that anywhere. Let me fly you to Hawaii."

"Peyton…"

"I'm sure your boyfriend has a fancy plane, as well," Peyton said.

"He does."

"And why isn't he using it to fly you to Hawaii?"

"I didn't ask him to."

"Ask me," Peyton said softly.

Dani had to think about it for a moment. She had no idea what was happening. She'd heard stories about how generous Peyton was with her friends. There were several annual parties where the woman went all out. There were gifts that weren't about money but were personal to the ones she gave them to. Peyton was a kind friend. Of that, Dani was certain.

"Okay."

"Tomorrow morning… at maybe eight instead of seven?"

"Now, you're negotiating?" Dani laughed again.

"You'll come to find out, Dani Wilder, that I am *not* a morning person."

"Eight is fine," Dani agreed.

"I'll have a car pick you up. Text me Steven's address?"

"I wasn't planning on staying here. My stuff is at my place."

"Then, text me Steven's address, and the car will take you there first."

"I can get a–"

"Dani?"

"Yeah?"

"Just text me the address, okay?" she asked sweetly.

"Okay."

"I'll see you tomorrow," Peyton said.

They hung up after that. Dani still had a ridiculous smile on her face. She stood, made her way into Steven's bedroom, and moved into the bathroom to take care of a few things. Then, she slid under the blanket and lay on her back, facing the ceiling. Moments later, Steven shifted in bed, sliding over to encourage her to rest against his chest. Dani did so because it was what they typically did when she slept over at his townhouse. Her eyes closed after a few minutes of listening to his slow, even breathing. Instead of thinking about the boyfriend she was snuggled up against, though, she was thinking about Peyton Gloss, America's sweetheart and maybe the most beautiful woman in the world.

***

"Peyton?" Dani questioned.

"Hey! I'm here to pick up Miss Danielle Wilder for her flight," Peyton said with a smile.

"Dani?" Steven's voice came from behind her.

Dani turned from the spot where she was holding open the front door of Steven's house for Peyton. She'd thought the driver would be at the door; she'd thought wrong. Instead, she found Peyton Gloss standing in front of her, looking like someone who was definitely a morning person. Peyton had her hair pulled back in a ponytail. She had on just a little makeup, but it was enough that Dani could tell she was wearing it. She had on a comfortable-looking hooded sweatshirt, with NYU on the front in white letters, and a pair of well-worn jeans with all-white tennis shoes.

"Morning," Peyton said in Steven's direction as he came up behind Dani.

"Good morning. What are you doing here?" Steven asked, wrapping his arms possessively around Dani's middle and kissing her cheek.

"He doesn't know?"

"He was asleep, remember?" Dani said to Peyton and then turned to face Steven to add, "Peyton is flying me to the photo shoot today."

"Why?" he asked her, looking confused as he stood there in a pair of dark-green boxers and a white undershirt.

"Because she wanted to," Dani replied. "Anyway, I've got to go so that we can run by my place and get my stuff."

"If she's flying you there, what's the hurry?" he asked.

"I've kind of got the plane and the crew on standby. We really should get going," Peyton interjected politely.

"Dani, I could have flown you there," he said softly to her.

"She offered, Steven. You're busy today anyway. I didn't want to give you one more thing to worry about."

"It's my job to worry about you. I'm the boyfriend."

Dani kissed Steven's cheek and said, "I know. She offered last night. I should go, though. I'll see you next weekend when you get back?"

"Sure." He leaned in and kissed her on the lips gently. "I love you."

Dani felt strange then. She'd been with Steven for over two years. They'd said those three words to one another thousands of times by now. It was also easy to say those words to him. When they'd met, she was sixteen. He was seventeen. They began as friends and remained that way for years before he finally worked up the courage to ask her out on a date. They'd dated for several months before Dani had finally called him her boyfriend. He had told her he loved her the night they had their first time together. It had been her first time ever, and she was only his second. She had said it a few weeks later. Then, she had moved her primary residence to New York. He'd bought the townhouse from his father and had asked her to move in. She had declined then, citing their young age and her evolving career. He'd asked her at least once every few months if she was ready. Each time, she had said no. But she had promised that, one day, she would be ready for those steps with him. It was now over two years since their first date. And, currently, Dani wasn't sure if she would ever be ready for everything he wanted with her. Steven was only twenty-four years old, yet he was talking about moving in together, engagement, marriage, and children. She just wanted to focus on the next photo shoot.

"You too," Dani replied in a near whisper for some reason.

She turned around, grabbed her purse, smiled at Peyton, who was standing in the doorway, patiently waiting for her, and headed out, closing the door behind her.

"Sorry, I guess I should have just waited in the car." Peyton ushered her to the black SUV that was waiting for them outside Steven's building.

"No, it's okay. I still can't believe we're flying on your private plane, and that you've come all the way over here to get me."

The driver opened the back door for them. Peyton motioned for Dani to climb in first. Dani slid over, allowing Peyton to slide in next to her. The driver closed the door. For a moment, they were alone. Dani realized it was the first time that had been the case. She looked over to see that

Peyton was looking back at her. Peyton smiled shyly. Then, she yawned.

"Sorry, I didn't get to sleep until after three."

"What? Why?" Dani asked, turning to her side to face the woman just as the driver climbed in and started up the car.

"Well, I stayed at the party until about midnight, because I needed to know if I won that auction. Then, I dropped Len off at home, headed home myself, called you, and stayed up for a bit, writing." Peyton leaned back against the seat.

"Peyton, why did you come all the way to pick me up? If you wanted to come with me to Maui, you could have just met me at the airport."

"I wanted to come," Peyton replied, turning her face toward Dani. "I'm used to late nights. It's kind of part of the job. There are always things going on after shows. Even if I finish at nine or ten, I have to get changed, do a meet and greet or two, have a meeting with a sponsor or someone else who thinks they're important, get back on the bus, and head to the hotel. Sometimes, it's one in the morning before I'm even close to being calmed down. Performing is such a rush. I usually have to drink chamomile tea or something to help me get to sleep."

"It's not the same thing, but walking a runway does that to me. The whole experience is such a rush." Dani leaned in a little closer to Peyton. "When you show up, there are hours of getting ready ahead of you. People are moving all around you while you're half-naked, trying to put a necklace or a bracelet on you, while someone else is doing your makeup or hair. Someone else is kneeling in front of you, trying to get the heels to buckle. Then, you actually have to walk out there. Cameras flash everywhere. People whisper. The music is always so loud. When you get back, you do it all over again. It's like that until the show's over. Then, you feel like you can finally breathe, but there's an after-party. Then, there's another after-party at someone's house after that. When you finally get done with everything, you're exhausted, but you can't actually sleep because–"

"You're totally wired?" Peyton suggested.

"Yeah," Dani replied excitedly. "Your entire body just wants to crash, but your mind can't stop."

"I know how that goes."

"I guess you would," Dani said.

They talked more about their respective careers until the SUV pulled in front of Dani's apartment. The driver opened the door on Peyton's side. They both slid out of the car.

"I'll just be a minute. I packed last night, before the party."

"Oh, sure," Peyton said, clearly disappointed.

"I'm sorry. I thought it would…" Dani then stopped herself. "Come on up, Peyton."

"I don't–"

Dani grabbed Peyton's hand after she removed her keys from her purse. She pulled the woman with her through the main door and toward the elevator. When they moved inside it, and Dani pressed the button, she looked down and realized that her hand was still clutching Peyton's. Peyton hadn't said anything. Dani decided to just leave things the way they were. Why not? Peyton must be a touchy-feely kind of friend. Dani could be that way, too, sometimes. She enjoyed the feel of Peyton's hand in her own. They stood that way in silence until the ding of the elevator. The doors opening caused Dani to snap out of it, and she dropped Peyton's hand. Once inside the apartment, Peyton stood off to the side as Dani went to grab her suitcase.

"How long have you lived here?" Peyton asked.

"About a year and a half. I was in a smaller place, but a friend of mine needed to sublet, so I moved in and then took over the lease when her lease ended."

"So, you don't own?" Peyton asked when Dani returned to the small foyer with her small carry-on roller.

"Not yet. Someday, though. Why? Think I'm throwing my money away on rent?"

"No." Peyton laughed and rubbed the back of her neck for a second. "I was just wondering if you, owning this place, and Steven owning his, was the reason you two didn't live together. Sorry, that's incredibly personal."

"It's okay," Dani said. "Do you want the tour? It will take about fifteen seconds."

"Sure," Peyton replied with a smile.

"O-k-a-y." Dani moved toward the kitchen. "This is where I don't cook anything because I'm hardly ever here." She moved them into the living room. "This is where I don't entertain people or even myself because I'm hardly ever here." She moved them to the guest bathroom, the dining room, and then into the bedroom. "This is where I never sleep because I'm hardly ever here."

"Well, Steven's house is pretty nice." Peyton shrugged.

"I'm just usually working," Dani replied, watching Peyton's reaction.

"Right. We should probably get going. I do like your place, though," Peyton stated.

"I'm sure it's not nearly as nice as your place."

"Which one?" Peyton asked and seemed to genuinely want to know.

"How many do you have?"

"A few," Peyton said.

CHAPTER 4

DANI WILDER smelled like a meadow. She smelled like every flower in that meadow that had just experienced the first rain of the spring. Dani's head was pressed against the window of the plane. The woman was staring out at the ocean below, but Peyton couldn't care less about the ocean. She'd seen the ocean a million times; in every kind of weather in almost every part of the world. She'd never seen Dani Wilder staring out the window and looking down at it with such reverence, even though she'd probably seen the ocean just as much as Peyton had. Come to think of it, Peyton had never been in a meadow. She had no idea how meadows smelled.

"It's always so cool, flying over it," Dani said, turning her head toward Peyton.

"It is," Peyton agreed, suddenly feeling the awe for the view thanks to Dani's reaction to it.

"Thank you for this. First class is nice, but nothing beats private."

"Anytime," Peyton said. "I mean it. Anytime." She then smiled at Dani. "Do you want some breakfast or something?"

"I'm okay," Dani replied softly, resting against the comfortable chair.

"I was thinking about going over there." Peyton pointed to the sofa that lined part of the left side of the ten-seater plane. "I usually sit there. It's more comfortable. Just have to sit here for the take-off and landing."

"Oh, okay." Dani nodded.

"Do you want to join me?" Peyton asked.

"I might just stay here and keep looking out the window. You don't have to worry about me. I've got my music and a book if I need something to occupy me; if you want to work on something."

"Work?"

"Yeah, like, if you want to write or do whatever else it is musicians do." Dani chuckled. "Sorry, I don't know what musicians do."

Peyton smiled at her and said, "I'm not working today, Dani. I'm here because I wanted to get to know you. I thought we could talk."

"Oh," Dani replied. "Are you sure?"

Peyton wanted to ask if Dani was used to Steven working all the time. She didn't think that would be appropriate, though. Steven was Dani's boyfriend. Dani had been with him for a long time. She obviously loved the guy. Besides, Peyton couldn't fault anyone for working hard or long hours. She did the same thing, and she loved her job.

"Come over here." Peyton stood and made her way over to the sofa. She sat with her legs under her and motioned for Dani to join her.

"Miss Gloss, your usual?" the flight attendant asked when he made his way over toward them just as Dani sat down next to her.

"I normally eat an egg white omelet if I'm flying in the morning. Red and green peppers with cheese. Want one?"

"If it's not too much trouble," Dani replied, settling into the sofa only about a foot away from Peyton.

"Two of the usual. And I'll have OJ this morning. Dani?"

"OJ is fine."

"Coffee, too?" Peyton asked her.

"If you're having some," Dani said.

Peyton laughed at how adorable her new friend was and said to the attendant, "Coffee for both of us would be awesome."

The flight attendant nodded with a polite smile and walked off, leaving them alone again. Peyton turned her attention to Dani, who was staring out the window that was now behind her. Peyton smiled again, finding Dani adorable. She wasn't sure she had ever referred to a friend, old *or* new, as *adorable*, but that was how Peyton would describe Dani in this moment. She had turned to the side, placed her socked feet on the sofa bench, placed both arms on top of her knees, and was staring out the window at the clouds just on the other side of it. There was another word Peyton thought would be perfect in this moment. Dani Wilder was *beautiful*. Her eyes were open but slightly closed due to the intense light from the sun. The green looked even greener today; if that was even possible. Her lips weren't what Peyton would call full, but they were perfect for Dani's face. Her nose was just the right shape for those eyes and those cheekbones. Dani's neck was extended, long and smooth. Her hair was pulled back. It was just this side of brown, but Peyton could also see someone describing Dani as a blonde if her hair caught the light just so. Yes, Dani Wilder was beautiful.

"Tell me everything about you," Dani said when she turned, suddenly wide-eyed, toward Peyton.

"Everything?"

"Yes, everything. Start with childhood. We've got about a million hours before we get to Maui."

"Are we flying around the universe a couple of times?" Peyton asked.

"If you've got the time," Dani said with a smile.

Peyton laughed lightly, settled into the sofa, and said, "I've got the time."

A few hours into the flight, they'd enjoyed breakfast and conversation. Dani had relaxed more into the comfort of the private plane. Peyton had suggested they watch a movie when Dani, yet again, had proved herself to be adorable and had moved to the seats they had previously occupied, expecting a screen on the back of the seat in front of her. Peyton had discovered then that, despite the fact that Steven's family did own a private plane, Dani had never flown in it. She had never flown private before this very flight. There was something nice about that to Peyton.

Peyton called the plane her own, but, technically, it wasn't her plane, of course. It belonged to a company who specialized in dealing with people like her. They had a few plane models she could choose from and were always on call for her. This one was a long-haul plane. It came complete with a small bedroom, a bathroom at the back, and a full kitchen that the attendants used to prepare meals.

Peyton opened the door to the back, after letting the flight attendant know they'd be watching a movie. She felt incredibly lucky in that moment. She was on a private plane with a new friend whom she was totally enamored with and wanted to get to know more and more every time Dani said anything. Dani sat on the end of the full bed; apparently, awaiting instructions on what to do next.

"You can lie down. Do you want popcorn?" Peyton asked, placing two bottles of water on the table next to the side of the bed she usually rested on.

"No, I'm not much of a popcorn fan."

Peyton lay back on the bed after moving back to the door to close it for some privacy. She grabbed the remote from the table, turned the TV on, and patted the spot beside herself. Dani smiled, taking the hint, and moved to lie down next to Peyton. They chose a movie to watch on the modest flat screen in front of the bed, and settled in. They also talked here and there as the movie went on. Peyton noticed, eventually, that Dani wasn't talking as fast or as often as she had been. She glanced over to see a woman with heavy eyes.

"Nap?" Peyton asked, pausing the movie.

"No, I'm okay." Dani rolled onto her side, facing Peyton, which argued against her point.

"Dani, sleep. I could use a nap myself. It's a long flight."

"Yeah?"

Peyton turned off the TV, sank into the bed, and replied, "Yeah. Do you want to be under the blanket?"

"I'm okay," Dani said softly.

Peyton lay down next to her then. She rolled onto her side, watching Dani, who now had her eyes closed. After a few minutes, Peyton could tell the woman was asleep. She slid just an inch closer to Dani because of the great need to be closer to her, then tried not to think about what that meant as she closed her own eyes and fell asleep.

CHAPTER 5

"I COMPLETELY FORGOT to ask you if you had a place to stay," Dani said the moment they walked into the hotel. "You can stay in my room, obviously."

"I made a reservation when you agreed to let me take you here," Peyton informed. "I called their front desk at, like, two in the morning. I have the suite."

"Suite, huh? The magazine is paying for a king bed for me, and I felt special." Dani made her way to the front desk, pulling her roller behind her.

"You could stay with me," Peyton suggested. "It's a king, too. But it's a suite. I've got a full kitchen, a living room, and I think they even said there's a hot tub in it. I don't know; I was tired when I called."

"You don't have people to do that for you?"

"Not at two in the morning, Dani." Peyton smiled at her again.

"Reservation for Dani Wilder," Dani told the agent at the desk.

"Reservation for Jane Smith." Dani looked over to see Peyton talking to the agent to her right. "I booked it last night."

"Ah, yes." The agent that was serving Peyton found the reservation. "You have the aloha suite for just one night, correct?"

"That's correct."

"Aloha suite?" Dani asked with a little bit of envy in her expression.

"Cancel your reservation, Wilder. The magazine can eat the money. Stay with me. I'm great at ordering room service."

"One of your many talents, apparently," Dani replied. She turned to the woman in front of her and said, "Actually, can I cancel this?"

***

She had spent nearly the past twenty-four hours with Peyton Gloss. The flight had been long but pleasant in the privacy of the plane. They had napped for a couple of hours. They'd woken and chugged water so as to avoid jet lag. They had eaten a small lunch and a slightly larger dinner. They'd watched another movie, and they'd talked. It was the best flight Dani had ever been on in her life, and she had been on many.

They had checked into Peyton's suite, which was beautiful. Peyton ordered them a late dinner since, with the time difference, they had gained six hours back. Dani felt the same way she did when she was walking down a runway: she was exhausted and ready for bed but knew she wouldn't be able to sleep at the same time. She was wired. Peyton Gloss had her wired. Peyton Gloss also had her gawking.

"How is it?" Peyton asked around nine o'clock, when she moved to climb into the in-room hot tub.

Dani was already enjoying the heat from the water on her very tired muscles. She swallowed hard at the sight of Peyton in a bikini. It was a pale pink, and with Peyton's just barely tanned skin, it looked perfect. Dani had been around hundreds of half-naked women before. She had seen all of them in underwear, lingerie, and bathing suits a lot smaller than the one Peyton was currently wearing. All the same, Dani swallowed again, as Peyton settled right in front of her.

"You tell me," she replied finally.

"It feels amazing," Peyton said with her eyes closed.

"So, Jane Smith is because of security, right?" Dani asked.

"I change it up, but, yeah. It's just easier."

"I read somewhere that you usually travel with security," Dani said.

Peyton opened her eyes and replied, "I do, when people expect me places. I had a couple of them hanging around last night, and they drove both Len and I home. It was a scheduled appearance. The driver this morning was security, technically. But no one knew I was coming here, and I'm only staying the night, so I decided to leave them at home."

"What's that like?" Dani asked, running her fingertips along the water where she watched the steam fade into the air.

"Well, I wish I didn't have to do it, obviously. But I love my career. I wouldn't change that for anything. If that means I have to give up a few things, so be it." Peyton paused. "I do wish I had a little more privacy. And the press always wanting to talk about who I'm dating or not dating or maybe dating is annoying, but I try not to complain." Peyton looked around the overly large bathroom. "I mean, look how lucky I am. I'm twenty-five years old. I have the only job I've ever wanted. My friends are amazing; yourself included." She smiled at Dani. "My family is happy and healthy. I flew on a private plane today, and I'm in a hotel room enjoying a hot tub with you tonight. It doesn't get much better than this."

"It doesn't?"

"I don't think so, no. Why? Think I'm missing something?" Peyton sent a small splash of bubbling water Dani's way.

"Last I heard, you weren't dating anyone," Dani said, feeling like maybe she shouldn't bring that up but needing to know all the same.

"I am single, yes," Peyton confirmed. "I don't think I

need to be in a relationship to be whole, but I would like to fall in love. I'm a hopeless romantic, I guess." She shrugged those perfectly toned shoulders.

"Have you ever been before?"

"In love?"

"I don't want to assume I know anything about your life because I read some article," Dani said.

"Thank you," Peyton replied genuinely and softly. "And I thought I had." She seemed to consider what to say next. "I've dated a lot, according to the media. But there was one guy I thought I would be with for a while."

"Which one?" Dani asked with a smile.

"Trevor," Peyton replied with another shrug. "We were together for over a year. He was a great guy; until he wasn't. In the beginning, though, it was a great relationship. He was supportive of my career and how busy I was. He didn't mind that I have a ridiculous obsession with certain guilty pleasure TV shows. He was nice."

"And then he wasn't?" Dani guessed.

"It wasn't like that. It just got harder. I went on tour. He's a regular guy, you know? He's not someone anyone knew until he started dating me. He worked for a law firm in New Jersey. He did the best he could, but it had gotten to be too much."

"You need someone who can keep up with you," Dani said.

"I think I just need someone who understands that my career isn't a choice."

"It's a calling," Dani said.

Peyton's facial expression had been serious, but it turned even more so with Dani's words. She nodded, with a small smile appearing. And her cheeks started to blush a darker shade of red.

"Is it for you?"

"Modeling? I don't think anyone would agree with modeling being a calling."

"But is it?" Peyton persisted. "Is it to you?"

"I've never done anything else," Dani said.

"Is there something else you'd like to be doing?" Peyton asked.

Dani thought about that question. The answer was yes. The thing she *would like* to do, though, was not something she *could* do. It was something she had never done before. It was something that made no sense. It was something that she had no idea how to handle. It was something that would change her entire life if she did it. So, instead, she *thought* about doing it. She thought about what it would feel like. She thought about how Peyton might react. She thought Peyton might like it. I mean, it's her fantasy we are talking about here. Dani could assume Peyton would like it, right? In that thought, that fantasy, Peyton *did* like it. Peyton liked it so much, she continued it. *They* continued it until they were no longer in the hot tub. They were in that king-sized bed. They were touching one another, holding onto one another, whispering to one another, enjoying one another, and not thinking about the consequences.

"I guess I'd like to be on the other side," Dani offered something up. "Of the camera, I mean."

"Photography?" Peyton smiled knowingly.

"I take pictures here and there. I have a nice camera. Steven—" Dani stopped at the mention of her boyfriend's name.

"He bought it for you," Peyton stated, appearing to be disappointed.

"For Christmas, a couple of years ago. I brought it with me, actually."

"Where?" Peyton asked.

"In my carry-on. I don't need to pack many clothes. They dress me at the shoots. I only have stuff to sleep in and stuff to wear there and back. That's all I need. Usually, I don't even bother bringing makeup or using a dryer on my hair. There's no point. They would just change it all anyway. I'm a pretty low-maintenance model."

"Supermodel," Peyton corrected.

"I don't usually call myself that."

"You should," Peyton said. Then, she stood up in the hot tub and added, "I'm going to hop in the shower. It's after one in the morning our time. I think I'm going to call it a night."

"Okay. Can I stay in here for another minute?"

"Stay in here as long as you want," Peyton said as she climbed out.

Peyton made her way out of the bathroom and into the bedroom. Another minute later, she entered the bathroom again, wearing a hotel robe. Dani watched as Peyton walked past her and into the shower stall. Her arm emerged a moment later, holding onto the robe, which she hung on the hook next to the shower. The shower started. Dani sat there, transfixed. The stall wasn't plain glass. It was frosted, but it wasn't frosted enough. Dani could make out the shape of Peyton's body as she rubbed soap and water over her skin. She didn't hover anywhere in particular, but Dani thought about how *she* would if she got the chance. Then, she shook her head, stood, and climbed out of the hot tub. All the heat must have gotten to her.

She made her way into the bedroom, with a towel over her bathing suit. As Peyton showered, Dani removed the suit and replaced it with the other bathrobe in the closet. She sat on the edge of the bed, waiting for her turn in the shower. Peyton emerged only moments later, wearing an identical robe, which caused Dani to smile. Her hair was down and wet. Peyton was running her brush through it when she sat on the bed next to Dani.

"Do you sleep on a particular side?" she asked.

Dani stood and replied, "Either one is fine with me. I'll be right out."

She made her way back into the bathroom, removed the robe, and climbed under the hot spray. She showered quickly and then turned the water to cold, hoping the shock of it would snap her back to reality. She made her way back into the bedroom, after brushing her hair and teeth, only to find Peyton wearing a cute pair of light-blue sleep shorts, with cat and dog cartoon images all over them, and a matching plain light-blue shirt. Dani, herself, had changed into a pair of light-gray sweats and a white tank top. When she caught Peyton's eyes drifting downward to her chest, she realized her mistake. She'd packed before the party. She'd planned to sleep alone. Peyton's eyes returned to her own. They were a little darker now than Dani remembered. Peyton's cheeks were also a little darker than she'd seen.

"Ready?" Peyton asked.

"Sure," she agreed.

They slid into bed at the same time, leaving plenty of space between themselves. Peyton turned off the light. They remained silent for several moments.

"Good night," Peyton finally said so softly, Dani almost didn't hear her.

"Yeah, you too," Dani replied.

CHAPTER 6

PEYTON WATCHED DANI work and did her best not to stare. That was hard, given the fact that Dani was lying on her back in about six inches of water, staring seductively into the camera. Her hair was that sexy kind of half-wet. Her makeup was subtly understated. Her eyes were electric. The photographer kept coaching her into doing whatever he needed her to do, and Dani listened. She listened well, according to Peyton, who was pretending to read a copy of the same magazine Dani was going to be on the cover of soon.

She needed to talk to Lennox. This definitely wasn't normal. Peyton had at least a hundred female friends. Ten or fifteen of them she would call her close friends. Four or five of them were her closest friends in the world. She'd never thought about *any* of those friends the way she was thinking about Dani Wilder.

When they broke for lunch, Peyton was hopeful Dani would join her at one of the tables they had set up. Unfortunately, Dani had a meeting with the photographer, and she ate her lunch while sitting in front of the computer, looking at some of the pictures they had already taken. Peyton sat on her own for much of the day. People in the business were used to famous people, so she wasn't special here. It was nice, not being the focal point of a photo shoot like this. Dani could steal the spotlight anytime she wanted. And, damn, this woman could really steal the spotlight.

Peyton caught a glimpse of Dani in the third suit of the day when she emerged from the curtained-off area. It was silver. It was a silver bikini against Dani's tanned skin.

"Jesus," Peyton whispered to herself.

***

When the photo shoot wrapped, Dani grabbed her own stuff from the van she'd stowed it in earlier, and also grabbed Peyton's. Then, she pulled both bags toward the car that was waiting to take them to the airport for their overnight flight back to New York.

Peyton watched Dani load their things with the help of the driver. She smiled when the woman slid into the seat next to her, and she instantly rested her head against Dani's shoulder. Peyton was more than exhausted. It had been a long day, even though she had just been sitting there, watching Dani work. The sun was out in full force and had gotten to her. All she wanted to do was get on that plane and fall into a deep sleep. Well, all Peyton really wanted was to get on that plane and fall into a deep sleep next to Dani Wilder. That was wrong. Dani had a boyfriend. Peyton had *only* had boyfriends. None of this was right. If she didn't knock it off soon, she knew she would regret it. Yet, she couldn't resist the comfort of Dani's shoulder. When Dani didn't question it or pull away, Peyton closed her eyes until they arrived at the airport.

They climbed on board, grabbed a couple of bottles of water, and Peyton pulled on Dani's hand to signal that she wanted to go to the bedroom. Dani followed without words. They changed in separate rooms and climbed into a much smaller bed than the one they had shared the night before. Peyton turned off the light, and Dani rolled to face her. Peyton did the same. Without words, they both fell asleep.

***

"Oh, I forgot to ask you," Dani said when Peyton's SUV pulled up in front of her own apartment.

"About?" Peyton asked, looking at a woman she had woken up next to on the plane when they had stopped to refuel, and the woman she had fallen right back asleep next to moments later.

"The surprise; the thing you bid on the other night," Dani said as the driver opened the door of the car to let her out.

"Oh…" Peyton rolled her eyes at herself. "I completely forgot. Do you know Gibson Shaw?"

"I think I met him once, at a fundraiser. Why?" Dani asked.

"I bid on photography lessons with him," Peyton replied with a smile. "For you."

"You did?" Dani asked, getting somewhat serious in that moment. "That's-"

"A coincidence, huh?" Peyton laughed lightly. "Three lessons are included. I thought you might like them. I honestly had no idea you were actually interested in photography. The other options were vacations, mainly. That didn't seem appropriate. There was a boat… I guess I could have bid on that."

"You don't already own a boat?" Dani asked with a smile.

"I don't, no," Peyton replied. "I rent one, occasionally. But I'm not someone that likes being out on the water every day. And I can't exactly take a boat to my next tour stop."

"I guess that's true," Dani replied and looked out the window to the street. "I should probably go. I'm sure you have a busy day."

"I don't. I'm off today. Well, I'm never really off; I'm writing. But I don't have anything else planned. Do you?" Peyton asked, swallowing right after.

"I'm supposed to check on Steven's mom around lunch, but that's it," Dani answered, reaching for her purse.

"Want to do dinner later?" Peyton asked. "I mean, if

you're sick of me by now, I totally–"

"I'm not sick of you," Dani interjected quickly. "I'm not," she added softly.

"Dinner?"

Dani nodded and replied, "Okay."

"Text me later," Peyton said.

Dani nodded one more time, slid out of the car, and said, "Thank you."

"For what?"

"All of it," Dani said.

Peyton sat in the car until the door was closed behind Dani. Then, she shifted over a little in order to see Dani for just a few more seconds. She watched as Dani entered the apartment building and then disappeared behind the door. Peyton sighed to herself. The driver started up the car and entered Manhattan traffic. Peyton rested her head against the seat and closed her eyes. It was only a minute later when her phone buzzed. She pulled it out of her purse and glanced at the readout. She smiled when she saw Dani's name on the screen.

Dani Wilder: Is it later yet?

Peyton couldn't stop her smile. The driver made a few turns, and it was still there. It was still there when she made her way inside her house. A few cameras caught a glimpse of her, but none of the people behind them shouted questions at her, which was a nice change. This house was one of a few that she owned. It was the first property she'd ever bought without the help of her parents, though, so it carried special meaning to her. It also wasn't completely finished in her mind, but it was done enough that Peyton could call it home when she stayed in New York. It was four stories, had six bedrooms, five baths, a small indoor pool and hot tub, and a loft space where she had a pool table and a poker table that provided her friends with entertainment when they spent time here. She had a small theater, too, with four reclining chairs and a sofa resting in front of a giant screen. Lennox had even bought her one of those popcorn makers as a housewarming present to go in the room.

It was in that room that Peyton first went after she showered and changed for her day. She felt rested, despite having flown over the country, entered a different time zone, and slept on a plane the night before. Peyton had slept on planes a lot over the past decade or so. She wasn't sure, though, that she had ever had a better night sleep on a plane. Maybe she'd never had a better night sleep in her life. When the plane had stopped to fuel up, to be able to make the rest of its journey, the flight attendant had allowed them to remain in the bedroom instead of buckling up for safety. The descent, though, always woke Peyton. Dani didn't wake until they were taking off again only a few minutes later. The woman was a little scared, apparently, which Peyton again, found adorable. Peyton had let Dani know that they were merely taking off again, but her hand had ended up on Dani's lower back. It had remained there, running smooth circles on Dani's skin under her shirt. Peyton had touched Dani's actual skin. It was soft and warm. It had Peyton looking away from the woman next to her then, because she had wanted to slide her hand up higher. She had comforted Dani in the brief moment. Then, Dani smiled at her and flopped back onto the bed. Peyton had been forced to remove her hand. They'd both fallen back to sleep after that.

Peyton sat in her favored recliner, lowered it to her favored position, and turned on the big screen. She toggled with her remote over to the Internet and used it to search for Dani. For some reason, the screen on her phone was too small to glimpse a photo of Dani. Hell, her laptop and giant monitor she had in her office were far too small. Peyton wanted the biggest screen she could find to take in the beauty of Dani Wilder. She clicked on the first few images of the woman when she was younger. Dani was an adorable kid, too. Her print work from when she was maybe four or five had her dressed for the times complete with nice, big hair. The look had Peyton laughing. She moved onto the images of Dani as a pre-teen and then teenager. She then came across a few videos of Dani walking a runway. She clicked on one or two and admired how the woman could walk in heels like that so gracefully. The fourth video Peyton clicked on made her gasp a little. She read the description beneath and found out it was her first major runway show. The song that was playing in the background as Dani walked was one Peyton knew well. It would be, though. It was hers.

CHAPTER 7

"YOUR HOUSE IS amazing," Dani said later that night.

"Thank you," Peyton replied.

Peyton had given her the tour of the place, and Dani had taken it all in with wonder. It was so different than Steven's place or the other places his family owned. Dani hadn't grown up rich. Both of her parents had always worked and still did to this day. Her mother was a high school principal. Her father was an accountant. As a kid, Dani's money had helped them on the important things, like food and the mortgage. It wasn't until Dani was in her teens that the real money started coming in. She had helped them pay off the house and put money away for her brother's college education should he have chosen to go. Then, she moved out on her own at seventeen. It was just easier that way. She loved her family dearly and visited as often as she could, but she didn't get back home nearly as often as she would have liked.

Peyton's wealth was on par with that of Steven's family, but the way the woman chose to decorate her townhouse was completely different. Peyton's house was bright, where Steven's was dark. It was soft, where Steven's was all hard edges. It was also welcoming, where Steven's was more displeasing – likely, for those people that didn't quite belong. His space was filled with browns and blacks with dark grays as accents. Peyton's had been filled with whites and yellows with accents of golds and a few reds here and there. Dani loved it.

"I made a vegetarian dish. I hope that's okay?" Peyton asked after making her way into the kitchen, with Dani following close behind.

"You cooked? Peyton, you didn't have to cook. I thought we would just go out or order in," Dani replied, standing on the opposite side of the expansive and pristine kitchen island.

"I noticed you didn't eat meat in any of the meals we've had so far… And I may have looked it up to confirm my suspicions."

"I'm a vegetarian, yes." Dani smiled at her. "I went vegan for a bit, but I actually had a hard time with it. I lost a bunch of weight, and the doctor said I needed to take supplements just to get back up to what I was before. I actually lost a couple of jobs because of it. Back then, it looked like I had an eating disorder. The industry is really trying to stay away from that stigma these days. So, I stuck with not eating meat, at least, and got healthy again."

"I read that, yeah." Peyton nodded as she removed a pan from the stove.

"You read it?" Dani asked, confused.

"In some article. You gave an interview about it." She placed the pan on top of an oven mitt on the island. "It's a Spanish dish. I hope that's okay."

"I thought we'd be eating from cartons, so this is more than okay," Dani said with a smile as she stared down at the dish that smelled delicious. "And, of course, you can cook. You can sing, play, write, act, direct, decorate, and cook. What else can you do?"

Peyton gave her a confused look.

"What? I'm not allowed to do my own research on you?" Dani asked with a smile.

"I directed one of my own music videos; that hardly

counts. I've had a few bit parts in some movies, but nothing I would actually call real acting. I did decorate this place myself, so I'll take that compliment. And my mom taught me to cook. That compliment goes to her. I set the table already. Red tonight, right?"

"Yes," Dani said, loving that Peyton remembered.

"Good. It goes great with this." She spooned the dish into a large bowl.

"Can I help with anything?" Dani asked, stepping back from the island.

"Pour the wine?"

"Of course."

They made their way into Peyton's informal dining room. Yes, she had a formal one, too. It wasn't as stuffy as Steven's, but Dani could tell that Peyton rarely used it. The informal room was a round table with only four chairs. There were placemats in lieu of a tablecloth. The silverware was nice, but not overly fancy. The window behind them had a pale-yellow curtain and a shade that had been drawn. Dani guessed that most of the shades had to be drawn in this house due to the proximity of the woman's neighbors and the fact that everyone knew Peyton owned the house. It made her sad, but only for a moment, because the food in front of her was delicious. The wine matched perfectly with the flavors. The conversation was even better. They laughed often and spoke of their friends and families. They talked about the things they loved about their jobs, along with the things that came with them but were less appealing.

"And that's when you started getting into photography?" Peyton asked. "When Steven bought you the camera?"

"I guess I must have mentioned it before that, since he gave it to me as a gift. I don't remember calling any attention to it, but there is was. It's a nice camera. I'm not sure I know how to use all the features on it. It's hard to find the time, honestly."

"Then, you'll like the photography lessons," Peyton

suggested. "I'm sure Gibson Shaw can go over all the settings for you. Maybe he'll even suggest a different camera for you. It's been a couple of years since you got that one. I'm sure they've got better models now." She sipped on her wine.

Dani watched as Peyton lowered her glass and glanced down at the half-finished meal on her plate.

"Probably," Dani agreed. "I wouldn't know. I've been so busy with work that I've hardly taken the thing out of its bag. I was in Hawaii, but for less than twenty-four hours. And when I wasn't sleeping, I was working."

Peyton then stood and left the room without a word, leaving Dani wondering what she had said. When Peyton returned, she carried a manila envelope, which she placed next to Dani on the table before sitting back down.

"Those are the details of the package I won."

"Peyton, I was only kidding when I said you should bid on something for me. You should take these." Dani moved to slide the envelope over to Peyton.

Peyton's hand topped her own. The feeling of a spark – as if a bolt of lightning had touched Dani's fingertips – took over her entire being for a moment. She wanted to live in that moment. She glanced down to see the hairs on her arm stand at attention, as if *she* should be paying attention. She looked up, met Peyton's endless blue eyes, and inhaled a deep breath.

"Dani, I got them for you. I don't know… Maybe I knew, somehow, that you were interested in photography."

Peyton's fingers remained on top of hers. Neither of them moved. It was as if Peyton wanted to remain in this moment with her. It was as if they were in this together; this unspoken thing between them. Dani needed to move. She didn't *want* to move, but she *needed* to move. Steven was in Vancouver. He was her boyfriend of two-plus years, who would be calling her later tonight to say goodnight. Steven was the one she had been planning a life with, despite the fact that she was always making him wait.

"Maybe we could share them," Dani suggested, finally pulling her hand back from Peyton's. "You could come with me."

Peyton pulled her hand back into her own lap and replied, "Sure. If it works out with our schedules, that could be fun."

"Do you own a camera?"

"Does my phone count?"

"I'm pretty sure Gibson Shaw would tell you no and then go on and on about how camera phones are going to bring about the end to good photography."

Peyton laughed at that as she slid her nearly empty wine glass over the table; back and forth, and back and forth. Transfixed, Dani watched the woman's arm move; Peyton's fingers gripped the glass and then let it go before repeating the action all over again. Dani watched her in this private, somber moment. Peyton's blue eyes looked a little sad. The waves in her light-blonde hair had fallen a bit. Her makeup wasn't as perfect as it had been when Dani had first arrived. She was completely gorgeous.

"Do you want to watch a movie or something?" Peyton asked.

Dani should've said no. Instead, she replied, "Okay."

***

Dani sat down on the sofa next to Peyton in the middle of the theater room. She could have chosen one of the many recliners. She could have chosen one on the opposite side of the room, far from Peyton. But she didn't. She sat down right next to the woman, who then took the remote and aimed it at the large screen.

"You're not much for popcorn, but Lennox bought me that." Peyton nodded to the machine to the right. "It makes pretty good stuff. There are seasoning mixes and stuff on the shelf under it if you're interested. She also stocked the cart with candy and stuff. I replace it every so often. My friends, despite the fact that many are actresses and models, go through that crap like crazy." She chuckled. "What kind of movie do you want–" Peyton stopped herself abruptly and turned to Dani. "I haven't seen this one yet." She nodded toward the movie title she'd highlighted.

"The one with about a million ghosts?" Dani asked.

"I've heard it's really good," Peyton replied, clicking into the movie to get the details. "Come on. It'll be fun. When was the last time you watched a scary movie?"

Dani thought about that for a second. Steven wasn't much of a scary movie kind of guy. He wasn't much of a movie kind of guy, period. She would also never watch a scary movie alone, because she was a coward. She turned to Peyton and nodded at her.

"Go for it," she replied with a challenging smile.

"You should know, I'm terrified of scary movies," Peyton said.

"Then, why are we going to watch it?" Dani asked through a laugh.

"Because it's fun," Peyton replied.

"Okay." Dani turned forward on the sofa and stared at the screen as Peyton started the movie.

Within minutes, Peyton had screamed three times. Dani had laughed at it each time. Then, Peyton had reached for Dani's arm and wrapped it around her own shoulders. Dani had stopped laughing then. Peyton's head was on her shoulder. Every so often, when Dani would turn away, Peyton would move even closer to her body. Peyton's arm went over her stomach. She'd squeeze every few minutes when a particularly terrifying moment would happen. Dani got scared herself, a few times, but wanted her strength to help Peyton through the movie. She resolved not to flinch or scream. She just held onto Peyton and allowed her own heart to race in her chest. Toward the end of the movie, Peyton must have realized Dani had been hiding her fear well. She lifted her head and looked into Dani's eyes.

"Are you scared right now?"

"About the movie?" Dani questioned in a voice that was a slightly higher pitch than her usual.

"Yes."

"I'm okay."

Peyton shifted slightly, in order to take Dani in better, and asked, "Is there anything that scares you that *I* can protect *you* from?"

Dani stared back at her, forgetting the movie playing in front of them and focusing only on Peyton's worried expression and Peyton's hand that was currently on her thigh.

"Yes," Dani said with a hard swallow that caused Peyton to recognize her intent. "But, maybe tonight, let's just stick to the movie."

Peyton gave her a slow, barely-there nod, and shifted back into her seat, removing all the parts of her own body that had been touching Dani.

Dani felt the loss but also knew it needed to happen. They had just acknowledged it. They had acknowledged whatever it was that was going on between them. Dani could hardly breathe. The room suddenly felt small and dangerous. She stood abruptly from the sofa.

"Dani–"

"I'm going to run to the bathroom. I'll be right back."

Dani left without waiting for Peyton's response. She made her way to the closest bathroom, pressed her hands fully to the counter, and leaned over it, breathing hard as she glanced up at the mirror in front of herself. She didn't recognize the woman looking back at her.

CHAPTER 8

PEYTON REGRETTED IT the moment it happened. When she'd seen Dani's startled and terrified reaction, that was when it really clicked. Dani was just as scared as Peyton was, but Dani had another reason to be. Dani had a boyfriend. Peyton continued to remind herself of this very fact for the next several days. She would wake up in the morning and say it out loud. Then, she'd go into her music room, strum her guitar for a bit, and sing it along with the melody. She had even written it down on random pieces of notepaper strewn about the room she let almost no one into. It was really more of a den than a music room, but Peyton liked the smallness of it. It was comforting to her. It had an overstuffed loveseat lining one wall. A huge window, that usually had to be kept covered, lined another one. Her guitars rested on stands in front of it. Her desk was on the third wall with the door, and the fourth wall had some of her platinum and gold records hanging there. They reminded her of how far she had come and, somehow, also challenged her to always try to do more.

"Hey, sorry I only have time for dinner while I'm in town. I have to run back to LA for some re-shoots," Lennox said, kissing Peyton on the cheek before she sat down at their table at their favorite restaurant in the city.

"I know how busy you are, Len." Peyton took a sip of her water. "I'm just glad you could make it."

"You sounded upset on the phone. What's going on, Pey?" Lennox asked, sliding a napkin over her lap. "And we could have stayed in tonight."

"I don't mind them," Peyton replied, knowing Lennox was referring to the cameras aimed at them through the window outside. "I've kind of gotten used to ignoring them."

"Peyton, are you okay?"

"I'm fine." Peyton picked up the menu, knowing what she would order already but needing the distraction. "How's the movie biz?"

"Fine."

"Fine, huh?"

"I'm tired, but I'm used to it," Lennox replied as the waiter approached. "We'll have two sparkling waters and a shrimp appetizer."

"Extra sauce," Peyton said. "You always forget the extra sauce, Len."

"Sorry." Lennox smiled at her. "Extra garlic sauce, please."

The waiter, who had waited on them before, nodded politely and walked off.

"How's Jamie?" Peyton asked of Lennox's younger sister.

"She's okay. We're at that age, though."

"She's a teenager." Peyton shrugged. "You and I have both been one. It's rough."

"It's worse with the autism. She's talking to someone once a week now. That seems to be helping."

"That's good. Is there anything I can do?"

"No. She's tested out of all the math classes at her school." Lennox met Peyton's eyes. "All of them. They say she's ready for some college-level stuff, but the school doesn't provide that. She's taking classes from a professor on the side and really seems to be enjoying it."

"That's amazing," Peyton replied, knowing how difficult it was for Lennox to care for her baby sister sometimes. "Tell her if she wants to do my taxes for me next year, she's more than willing to give it a try."

"I won't, because she will." Lennox winked at her best friend, who was five years her junior but had always been more like a sister to her than sometimes Jamie could be. It wasn't because of Jamie's autism. It was because she and Jamie were so far apart in age that it was often difficult for Lennox to see her as a sibling and not as a child she was basically raising. Peyton knew that and did her best to be someone Lennox could count on and talk to. "Anyway, how's the new record coming along?"

"It's not," Peyton said.

"Writer's block?"

"No, the opposite."

The waiter brought over their waters and stepped away.

"How does that work?" Lennox asked, taking a sip.

"I have too many songs."

"Couldn't you just use the extras on another album?" Lennox asked.

"It doesn't really work like that. When you're putting together an album – it's a story, you know?"

"What story are you telling with this one?" Lennox asked.

"I don't know yet."

"So, that's the real problem? You don't know the story?"

"I have about twenty new songs. I've written the lyrics at least."

"Peyton, that's amazing."

"It is. I have some others I wrote on the road. Those, at least, have the music to them, too."

"Wait... Twenty new songs? New as of when? Last time I saw you, you hadn't written anything new *since* the road. That was, like, a week ago."

"At the party; I remember." Peyton nodded, took a sip of her water, and glanced at the photographers gawking at them through the window. "They're all new. Most are very rough."

"You've written lyrics to twenty songs in a week? What's gotten into you?" Lennox chuckled lightly.

"I don't know," Peyton lied.

"I don't understand… Why do you seem sad if you've managed to write twenty new songs, Pey? I've seen you when you're blocked – and it's bad, but this version of you seems depressed."

"I'm not depressed." Their shrimp appetizer was placed between them. "I don't know… I guess I'm still blocked on what the story of the album is going to be. So, no matter how many songs I write, until I figure that out, I'm stuck."

"What are some of the ideas?" Lennox asked, sliding a few shrimp over to her plate.

"I don't have any."

"How about love?"

"Cliché."

"Pop revolution?" Peyton glared at her. "Okay. Okay." Lennox laughed. "How about starting over?"

"What do you mean?"

"You're full-on pop now; no more country. You've moved to this city since your last album and tour. You're single for the first time in a long time. Trevor left, like, six months ago… Have you written a good breakup song? Maybe there's a good song about finding love in your mix of new ones? You could put that one first, follow it with a good breakup anthem, then focus on all the new stuff that's happened in your life."

Peyton considered Lennox's question. She did have several good love songs in the mix, she thought. None of them were about Trevor.

"Yeah, maybe. I'll think about it. Tell me about the re-shoots," Peyton said, changing the subject.

***

Peyton hated not telling Lennox everything. Over the course of their friendship, she had always confided in her. This week, though, had been a whirlwind of events and emotions. She wasn't ready to process them out loud with her friend. She hadn't even told her sisters, of which she had three. That made sense, though. Emily, Erica, and Elizabeth were all younger than her. They were triplets. Her parents had had difficulty conceiving before Peyton, and the world had yet to find out Peyton's secret. The media seemed to know all the details of her love life, personal life, and her professional life; except for maybe the biggest one: Peyton had been adopted at four months old. Her birth mother and father had given her up. She, herself, had been told when she was twelve years old.

Her mother had gotten pregnant when Peyton was five. Her parents had been so happy at the thought of welcoming another child. They had gotten a surprise when they had discovered they had ended up with triplets by way of fertility treatments. It had been interesting, growing up the older sibling to triplets. From the moment the girls were born, they were inseparable. They were more than siblings to one another, which meant they had their own language, their own secrets, their own bond that Peyton would never be able to share.

Because they were only twenty years old and had all chosen the same university in the Midwest, Peyton didn't get to see them all that often. Lennox became her closest friend in the world. And, even though it sounded terrible, she also became more of a sister to Peyton than her actual sisters. Lennox was the only person, outside of Peyton's immediate family, that knew of the private adoption. Peyton had planned to keep it that way not out of shame, but out of worry. If the press ever discovered it, they would do everything they could to find her birth parents. And she didn't want that. Peyton had asked her parents about them once they had told her of the adoption. They had told her who they were, she had made her peace with their decision, and after understanding their circumstances, had to agree with it. Her parents loved her and her sisters more than anything. Her mother was the one that taught her how to play the piano. Her father taught her about the Rolling

Stones and the Beatles. They had given Peyton the love of music she still had today. And she wouldn't change that for anything.

She sat on the floor of her music room, staring down at handwritten lyrics on multiple pieces of notebook paper. She crossed some out. She circled some and moved some lyrics to another song entirely. Then, she grabbed her favorite guitar for writing and strummed a melody she had been working on. She knew it would never make the final cut, but she couldn't get it out of her head. In fact, she'd likely never show it to anyone. It was in her mind, however. Peyton had no choice but to finish it first. Once she did, her brain might let her move onto the next song that actually had a chance of making it on the album. The song she was working on already, had a title. It wasn't a well-thought-out one or anything. It wasn't even good. It was just what she wrote down first so that she knew what it was later. As if she could ever forget what she was writing about... She would never forget the emotions that brought forth the words she'd written down for no one else to see. The title of the song was, "Dani." And the soft acoustic guitar was all the song needed.

Peyton played what she had already written a few times, adding words and notes here and there. She sang the feelings themselves more than the words and closed her eyes to let the full effect sink in. Then, she lowered the guitar to the floor and sighed.

"Dani Wilder has a boyfriend," she said to herself.

Her phone lit up from its position on the floor next to the guitar. Peyton always left it on silent when she was in this room, but that didn't stop the screen from lighting up with a message. This one made her smile and then repeat the words she'd just uttered before she read it.

Dani Wilder: What are you doing tomorrow?

CHAPTER 9

"I CAN'T. I INVITED PEYTON OVER today," Dani said.

"I just got back from Vancouver, Dani. I thought we could have dinner tonight."

"I told her she could come over whenever after I got done with my workout this morning," she replied.

"I got in at, like, two in the morning. And you had to wake up at five to go do that. We've had, like, an hour together. And now you're leaving?" Steven asked.

They were in Dani's bedroom. Dani was getting dressed to go out to pick up a few things. Steven was lying in bed, with messy bed head and his laptop. He had shown up in the middle of the night, letting himself in with his key and giving Dani a mild heart attack in the process. She hadn't gotten much sleep after that. He'd made an attempt to do a little more than sleep. Dani hadn't rebuffed him to be cruel, but he was supposed to get in around ten, and they were going to go to sleep together. She was not in the mood to do anything other than sleep after he'd scared her nearly to death. He'd taken the hint, rolled off her, and had fallen asleep soon after. She had waited until her usual alarm at five to get out of bed officially. She had gone to the gym and worked out a lot of tension and some anger at Steven for just assuming it was okay to climb into bed with her after not letting her know he was coming over and then trying to have sex after doing so. She'd returned home to find him still asleep, showered, and made herself some breakfast, leaving extra coffee for him, since she knew he wasn't much of a breakfast guy.

"Steven, it's not my fault you were late last night. I work out at five most days. You knew that before you came over here."

"I know." He closed the laptop. "I don't understand why you're getting dressed to go out when Peyton's coming here at some point during the day. Is she so famous she requires some kind of special red carpet everywhere she goes, and you have to go pick it up and install it?" He laughed at his attempt at a joke.

"Steven, I'm going grocery shopping. She's coming over around lunch, according to the text she just sent me. I'm buying us stuff to eat for that lunch, and–"

"So, you *will* be free for dinner, then."

"No," Dani said as she tied her tennis shoe. "I've worked every day this week; I have one day off. I'm sorry I made plans with my friend because I thought you'd be working."

"I am working," Steven replied. "I'm talking about dinner, Dani." He ran his hand through his slightly curly hair.

"Peyton and I are having dinner together."

"What about Jill?"

"Jill? What about her?" She stood straight, having finished with her shoes.

"Isn't she your best friend?"

"Yes."

"When was the last time you saw her?" he asked.

"The night of the party."

"But you're hanging out with Peyton all the time?"

"All the time? I haven't seen her since right after we got back from Hawaii."

"You went to Hawaii with someone you just met.

That's a little weird, Dani."

"I went to Hawaii for work. She went with me. We had fun." Dani sat on the edge of the bed. "I'm allowed to have more than one friend, Steven. In fact, I'm allowed to have as many friends as I want."

"I know that." He leaned forward. "I didn't mean it like that. I guess I'm just surprised."

"By the fact that I can make friends?" She lifted an eyebrow at him.

"Dani, I've always worked. Since you and I met, I've had one job or another. For years, you've always made time for me. And now, it just doesn't seem like you're interested. Do you not want to spend time with me?"

"I do, Steven." Dani placed a hand on top of his. "But I made plans today. I don't want to cancel them. That would be rude."

"Okay." Steven ran his hands over his five o'clock shadow. "I understand. I'm sorry. I shouldn't just assume you'll drop things for me. I don't do that for you most of the time. It's unfair of me."

"Thank you," she said, reminding herself that her workaholic boyfriend was a good guy.

"I'll get some work done while you're out if that's okay," he said.

"That's fine." Dani sighed. "Can you be gone by the time she gets here, though?" she asked, not quite knowing why.

He nodded and said, "Girls' day." He nodded again. "I get it."

***

"Do these belong to you?" Peyton asked, holding up a pair of boxers between her thumb and forefinger.

"Oh, God." Dani dropped the grocery bag on the kitchen counter and moved to the living room where she took them from Peyton. "Sorry. Steven's."

"He's back from Vancouver, right?" Peyton asked, moving into the living room to sit on the sofa.

"He got back late last night." Dani heard the shower running. "And he was supposed to be gone already. I'm sorry. Hold on; I'll be right back."

Dani made her way into her bedroom and the master bath, where she saw Steven standing in the shower while he listened to a podcast on his phone, which was on the sink. She pressed the pause button, causing him to turn in the shower.

"Oh, hey. I didn't hear you come in."

"I just got back. I thought you'd be gone by now," she said.

"I got stuck on a conference call and decided to take a quick shower before I head out. I'll be gone before Peyton gets here," he replied.

"She's already here." Dani crossed her arms over her chest, knowing her anger at him was irrational. "She ran into me outside with the groceries."

"I thought I had enough time. I'm sorry. Let me finish up, and I'll leave you two alone, okay?" he asked.

"Your boxers were in the living room, Steven." Dani held them up and then placed them on the counter. "You knew I had a guest coming over today. You couldn't try to be a little cleaner?"

He opened the shower door and said, "Dani, I got in late last night; got, like, no sleep; found out my girlfriend didn't want to touch me or be around me at all, apparently; and I rummaged through my bag to shower and change as quickly as I could so that I could get out of her hair. I'm sorry if my boxers ended up on a chair or something. The rest of my stuff is in my bag that I've already packed, by the way."

"Okay," she replied, not knowing what else to say.

"Do you need to yell at me some more or can I finish my shower?" Steven asked, clearly agitated.

"Sorry, I'll go."

Dani left the bathroom, returned to the living room, and found Peyton still sitting on the sofa, typing on her phone.

"I got a lyric idea," Peyton explained and lowered her phone. "I type the random ones into my phone until I know what to do with them," she added. "Everything okay?"

"He's in the shower. He'll be out in a minute."

"Did you guys have a good night?" Peyton asked then, lowering her eyes to the floor.

Dani moved into the kitchen to begin unloading the groceries.

"He got in late," she answered without giving any more details. "I told him you were coming over for lunch. He'd planned to be gone, but you surprised me early." She smiled over at Peyton.

"Sorry. I thought there would be traffic, but we got here pretty quickly." Peyton stood and moved into the kitchen. "Can I help?"

"I thought we'd have sandwiches for lunch. Want to make yours?" Dani asked.

"Depends… Does it have to be vegetarian?" Peyton asked with a lifted eyebrow.

"No." Dani laughed at her. "I got turkey, ham, roast beef, and salami. I have no idea what you like."

"Well, now I have to eat all of it so it doesn't go to waste," Peyton replied with a laugh.

"I'll eat the leftovers," Steven commented when he emerged buttoning up his shirt. "Am I allowed to make a sandwich to-go?" he asked Dani.

"Of course," she told him, wishing the tension between the two of them wasn't so apparent with Peyton in the room.

Steven moved to the counter, kissed Dani on the lips quickly, and began making his sandwich while Dani stood next to him, motionless. Peyton appeared to be watching the whole exchange with an unreadable expression on her face.

"Thanks, babe. This is my favorite," Steven remarked in Peyton's direction about the roast beef that was, indeed, his favorite brand. He reached into the drawer behind him, pulled out a sandwich bag, and slid his creation inside it. "I'll eat in the car to get out of your way."

He kissed Dani on the cheek this time, glanced over at Peyton for some reason, and moved back into the living room to grab his bag. Then, he was gone.

"Sorry about that," Dani said.

"About what?"

"He's... I don't know."

"You guys have been together for a long time, huh?" Peyton asked, moving to make her own lunch.

"Over two years, but it feels like a lot longer. We've known each other forever."

"That's crazy to me."

"Why?" Dani asked, standing next to Peyton now, making her own sandwich.

"For starters, you're two years younger than me; and the longest relationship I've ever had was a little over a year."

"I guess." Dani shrugged. "We met when I was a teenager, obviously. Started dating years later. He's a year older."

"What's next for you guys?" Peyton asked, finishing up her sandwich with mustard.

"What do you mean?"

"Two years, Dani. That's a long time," Peyton said, licking some rogue mustard off her finger.

"I guess."

"You guess? Trevor wanted us to move in together at the one-year mark."

"But you didn't."

"No, I didn't." Peyton sat at the stool at the island.

"Why not?" Dani joined her.

"I don't know. I guess I just knew he wasn't the one."

"The one?"

"I know you know what I'm talking about," Peyton said through a laugh and a sideways glance at Dani.

"I know you write a lot of love songs, Miss Gloss," Dani replied with a lifted eyebrow.

"I do. That's correct."

"And you believe there's one guy out there for you?" Dani asked with a swallow.

Peyton lowered the sandwich she'd only just picked up and said, "I guess I hope there's one person out there for me, yes."

Dani caught the use of the word *person* in Peyton's response. She also caught the use of the word *hope*. Dani swallowed again.

"Me too," she then replied.

Peyton turned to catch her eye at that.

CHAPTER 10

Peyton sat next to Dani on the sofa. They were watching an episode of one of Peyton's favorite reality TV shows. They had shared lunch together, spent some time shopping down the street at some of the local shops, and then had returned to Dani's place to enjoy a quiet dinner in. They'd cooked together. Dani wasn't the world's greatest chef, according to her own words, but Peyton had to disagree. Of course, it could have been the fact that they had cooked the food together. Maybe Peyton's own skills had improved the cuisine. Or maybe it only tasted better because they had eaten it together.

"I can't believe she's going to choose him!" Dani exclaimed in the direction of the TV.

"She likes him," Peyton replied.

"But he's dating, like, ten other women at the same time. I don't even know why women go on shows like this," Dani said, shifting a little closer to Peyton on the small sofa.

"The trick is knowing that 99 % of it is completely fake and just enjoying it for entertainment and not thinking at all about the lack of lasting relationships likely to come out of the show," Peyton said, shifting closer to Dani as well.

"I don't think I could ever go on a show like this," Dani said after a moment.

"Well, you don't need to. You *have* a boyfriend."

"You'd consider going on a show like this?" Dani asked. "To find your person," she added.

Peyton looked over at her and met Dani's eyes. She gave her a small smile. Then, she noticed that their thighs were pressed against each other. Neither one of them had moved to part them. There was plenty of room on either side of their bodies. Peyton could pull back and still have more than enough room to be comfortable. She just hadn't yet. She would. She'd do it now. No, she'd do it now. She'd move over, stretching her legs at the same time so it didn't look suspicious. Now. Okay. Now. She stared into Dani's green eyes and stayed exactly where she was.

"No, I don't think I'll be finding that person on a reality show," Peyton finally said.

***

A few hours later, Peyton's head was once again on Dani's shoulder. Her eyes were heavy. It was late. She was tired. She had stayed up nearly the entire night last night, in her music room, trying to get music to the lyrics she'd already written. She had also stayed up late, if she was being honest with herself, because she knew Steven was back in town. Dani had told her as much during their text exchange to make their plans for today. Peyton had known he was going to go to Dani's place last night. She'd also known the couple hadn't seen one another in more than a week. They'd likely have some catching up to do. That kind of catching up had Peyton wanting to vomit. That was wrong. She knew it. Dani was in love with Steven. Steven made her happy. Peyton needed to go on a date; a date with a man. She would talk to Lennox to see if she had anyone she could maybe set her up with. Lennox knew a lot of people in the industry. And the one thing Peyton had learned after her breakup with Trevor, was that she would likely need to find someone who understood what it was like – working in the public eye like she did.

Then, she felt it. Dani's arm wrapped around her and pulled her in. Peyton didn't move at first. She didn't want to spook her. No, she should spook her. She should remove herself from Dani's magical embrace. Yes, it was *magical.* What made it even more magical was the fact that Dani was now playing with Peyton's hair. She was pulling the strands through her fingertips. Peyton closed her eyes fully to take in how good it felt to be held by this woman. She knew it was wrong. She didn't care. Dani pulled her in tighter. Peyton placed her arm over Dani's stomach, pulling the woman back into herself even closer. She both heard and felt Dani let out a deep sigh. Then, the fingers in Peyton's hair were gone. The arm around her shoulders was back on the sofa, not touching Peyton at all. Peyton opened her eyes. She shifted from her position, stretched, and stood.

"I should get going. It's late," Peyton said. "I've kept Steven away for long enough," she added more for herself than for Dani.

"He's staying at his place tonight," Dani replied softly.

Peyton tried not to smile, because smiling at that would be wrong. So, instead, she reached for the jacket she had left hanging over the chair next to the sofa, and slid it over her shoulders.

"I had a great time today, Dani," she said with a small smile.

"So did I," Dani replied, sitting up on the sofa and then moving to stand.

The woman made her way toward Peyton, and it was only then that Peyton really noticed their height difference. Dani was two inches taller than her. When she made her way closer, Dani's arms went around Peyton's neck, and she pulled her in. Peyton wrapped her own around Dani's waist and rested her head on Dani's shoulder.

"Get home safe, okay?" Dani said.

"I will," Peyton replied.

She took in the scent of Dani, the feel of her against her own skin, the warmth of this woman against her. She reached for the hem of Dani's shirt and lifted it just enough to rest her hands on the small of Dani's back, needing to touch her.

"Dani…" she muttered against Dani's neck.

Dani didn't pull away at first. She let Peyton hold onto her. She let Peyton slide her fingers up and down the small of her back. Then, she pulled away.

"I'll walk you down," Dani said without meeting Peyton's eyes.

When they arrived at the front door to the building, Peyton saw security waiting in front of the SUV. She turned back to Dani and gave her a likely unconvincing smile.

"Hey, I was going to go home this weekend." Peyton passed her purse to the security guy standing next to her. "Do you want to come?"

"To meet your parents?" Dani asked, clearly surprised.

"Not exactly," Peyton said. "They're not there. They're visiting my sisters for parents' weekend at college. I was going to stay at the place I rent nearby, though. I go there at least once a year on my own. It's a great place to get away from it all. I stay on Lake Superior."

"Michigan? I thought you grew up in Wisconsin," Dani said, crossing her arms over her chest and leaning against the doorframe.

"Nope. Michigan. I was born in Wisconsin, though. We lived there until I was about five. Once my parents had the trips, we moved to Michigan to be closer to my grandparents. That's really where I grew up. It's beautiful this time of year. I wrote a song about it, actually." Peyton smiled at the memory.

"The kaleidoscope of red, orange, and gold hues makes it worth missing all the news," Dani said while staring at her.

"It was one of my early songs. I hope I've gotten better since then. I was using a rhyming dictionary when I was thirteen." Peyton chuckled. "It's really beautiful, though. There are these colorful tunnels across winding two-lane roads. And there are close to a hundred waterfalls in Porcupine State Park."

"And you go there every year?" Dani asked her.

"I do. I was planning on taking Lennox this year, but she called me this morning to say she can't come. She's stuck in LA."

"So, it would be just the two of us?"

"Only if you agree to go," Peyton reminded.

"I can't. I'm supposed to go to the vineyard with Steven this weekend," Dani replied.

Peyton nodded and said, "It's pretty beautiful there, too, I guess. Good night, Dani."

"Night," Dani replied. "Take care of her, please," she added to the security officer that was helping Peyton into the SUV. "She's very special." Dani smiled widely at Peyton before she disappeared inside the building.

***

"Hey, Pey," Emily greeted. "Mom and Dad said you were thinking about skipping your annual retreat thing and coming to parents' weekend with them?"

"I was," Peyton replied as she tucked her phone between her ear and her shoulder and poured the hot water from the kettle into the mug with the tea bag.

"Hey, sis," Erica greeted.

"Am I on speaker?" Peyton asked.

"Yes. It's just Erica and I, though. Lizzy is out."

"Hey, Erica."

"Hi, Pey."

"So, what's up?" Peyton asked.

"We were wondering if maybe you'd come another weekend instead," Emily said after a moment.

"Why?"

"It's just a big weekend. Mom and Dad will already be here. Plus, it's the three of us, and we want to go to the football game."

"It's kind of a mess, sometimes, you know?" Erica added.

"Because of me." Peyton set the kettle back down and moved to sit on a stool. "You're worried I'll cause problems."

"We're already your younger sisters, Pey. People know who we are. We're used to getting stares sometimes. But we want to kind of just have a chill weekend with Mom and Dad, if that's okay. Lizzy wants them to meet this guy she's been dating. I want to show them the project I'm working on for my sculpture class. Erica has a recital on Sunday night. As much as we'd love to see you—"

"Parents' weekend is a big deal. I get it. A lot more people on campus. I bring security and drama with me. I understand. How about I come up another weekend and get us a box at the stadium? We can all go to a game together then?"

"That would be awesome," Erica said.

"You sure you understand?" Emily asked.

"I didn't go to college. I'm living vicariously through you guys. I want you to have a normal experience, okay? I'll visit another weekend. I'll just keep my weekend at Porcupine."

"Have fun! Run under the falls for us, like old times," Erica said.

"I will," Peyton replied and laughed. "And tell this guy that Lizzy is seeing that he better not hurt my little sister, or I'll send my security after him."

"We will," Emily said while laughing. "Bye, Pey. Love you."

"Love you," Erica added.

"Love you both. Tell Lizzy, too."

Peyton had spoken to her parents the night before about maybe joining them to visit her sisters at school. She needed a break from the city, but she didn't want to go back home alone this year. She needed the people she loved around her, and she needed a distraction from thinking about Dani Wilder and her boyfriend, Steven English, who had likely spent most nights together since Peyton had said goodnight to Dani on her front stoop. She needed a distraction because thinking about Steven and Dani's romantic weekend in the vineyard made the bile rise in her throat.

"Dani has a boyfriend. Dani has a boyfriend. She's allowed to be happy. She's supposed to go on romantic weekends with the man she loves. Those romantic weekends involve sex. They'll definitely be having sex this weekend. That's normal. They should do that. Couples have sex." She picked up her mug. "Couples, that have been together for two years, go on these kinds of trips to–" She dropped the mug in her hand at the thought. It clattered into the sink Peyton was standing over, breaking into, thankfully, only three large pieces. "Fuck!" she exclaimed. "He's going to propose to her."

Peyton picked up the remnants of the mug from the sink and tossed them into the trash can under the sink. She no longer had any need for herbal tea. She made her way into her music room to try to write a song about what it feels like – when you've fallen in love with someone that belongs to someone else.

The next day, Peyton hopped on a plane and headed to her rental house. She blared music in her headphones. She watched movies. She read books. She wrote songs. She played her guitar outside as she watched the sunset over the water. She did everything she could to try to get the idea of Dani and Steven's big weekend out of her mind. At the end of Friday night, though, as she tucked herself into the bed, she could only think about how crazy it was that she had met the person she had been hoping for all along and that that person had hoped for someone else.

CHAPTER 11

SHE WATCHED STEVEN as he stood out on the balcony of the house his family owned, talking on his phone. They were supposed to arrive yesterday, but Steven had a last-minute meeting pop up. They had arrived this morning instead. Well, it was more, like, Saturday afternoon when they'd arrived. Steven had spent the entire time since then on one of his many devices. Dani had watched him for the last five minutes or so, wondering why he'd even bothered bringing her here if he wasn't even going to be here himself.

"Sorry, babe." Steven slid the glass door closed behind him. "There's a problem with the data for the upcoming board meeting. That's what's causing all these problems."

"I understand," Dani said.

"It'll just be another hour or two, probably," he added, sitting down next to her.

"For how long?" she asked softly.

"What do you mean?"

"How long is this going to keep happening, Steven?" She looked over at him.

"It's the quarterly board meeting, Dani. It's—"

"This was our weekend away," she interrupted him. "I could have spent the weekend with Peyton at her place in Michigan."

"What are you talking about?"

"She invited me to spend the weekend with her," Dani explained.

"Who does that?"

"*You* did, Steven. And then you failed to spend any actual time with me," Dani reminded.

"I mean, who does that when they're just a friend, Dani? I'm your boyfriend; we are supposed to go on weekends away."

Dani swallowed and replied, "Steven, she was going there anyway, and wanted to know if I was interested. That's all. It's also not the point, though."

"You know how swamped I've been, Dani."

"I do. But you always are. I'm going to go for a run. I'll be back in about an hour, I guess." She stood.

"You ran this morning before we left," he said.

"And now I need to again because I'm upset, and running calms me down," she replied.

"*You're* upset?" Steven stood. "Why? Because the weekend I planned for us hasn't turned out exactly as you'd planned?"

"Because you're always busy, Steven."

"*I'm* always busy? Whenever I'm home, you're with Jill or now Peyton. I want to take you to a nice dinner – you have plans with Peyton. I want to surprise you and come to your place at night, when I haven't seen you in a week, and you can't even let me touch you. You practically pushed me away that night, Dani."

"You startled me, Steven," she returned.

"We haven't had sex since…" He threw his arms over his head. "Dani, I can't even remember the last time we had sex. You slept over last night but were too tired."

"You were on your computer all night. And when you're suddenly interested in doing something with me, it's sex, and it's at midnight. And I'm supposed to just what? Get myself in the mood?"

"You have to get yourself in the mood to want to have sex with me?" Steven asked, obviously hurt. "Dani…"

"It's not like that. I didn't mean it that way. Last night was just…"

"What is going on with you lately?" he asked.

"Nothing," she answered, running a hand through her hair.

"Dani, something's clearly going on with you. I get that I'm busy. But you are, too. Your work takes you all over the world for sometimes weeks at a time. I don't complain. I know my job is crazy right now, and has been for a while, but we've never had these kinds of problems before. What's changed?"

"You're right," Dani said, taking a deep breath. "You've always been this way. I'm expecting you to be different, and you aren't." She sighed. "I haven't talked to you about that, and I'm sorry."

"That I need to be different?" he asked.

"I don't know." Dani moved toward the sliding glass door. "I don't know, Steven."

"Dani, what the hell? I try to make an effort by bringing you–"

"I don't want you to make a damn effort, Steven!" Dani practically shouted as she turned around to face him again. "I want it to just be a part of who you are. Is that too much to ask? You have to go out of your way to even think about doing something like this. I'm convinced your mother put you up to it, since the only time you've mentioned a trip with me was after I spent time with her and mentioned I needed to get out of the city. I'm smart enough to put two and two together," she added.

"She mentioned it to me, yes. But that doesn't mean I wouldn't have asked you here," he replied. "She's coming for dinner tomorrow. Should I cancel?"

"You don't need to cancel." Dani moved to grab her

hoodie, which she had tossed over the bed. "I am going to go for that run, though."

"Dani, we need to talk."

"We can talk after my run, Steven."

***

Dani ran and ran. The weather outside wasn't ideal. The rain had come in that morning and blanketed the ground in slickness, making the run more difficult than it needed to be. That seemed to fit her mood, though. She hadn't meant to go off on Steven like that. He'd just annoyed her so much recently. When she thought about how Peyton was alone in Michigan, and how she would have probably had more fun there with Peyton than she had with her absent boyfriend recently, her strides hit the pavement harder and faster, until she had to stop running entirely. She bent over, breathing hard, and pressed her hands to her knees before she stood up and placed them over her head as she stared out at the water that hadn't offered much comfort to her.

They had been to the vineyard several times since they had been friends, and a few times since they had started dating. Dani had always enjoyed the trip, the time with Steven, and the beautiful landscapes. Today, however, she needed more than the beauty of this place to get her through. She reached for the phone that had been playing her running playlist, and dialed a number as she began walking back to the house.

"This is Peyton. Leave me a message."

"I've never gotten your voicemail before." She laughed to herself. "That's it? Really? Just, 'Leave a message?'" She sighed. "Okay. Can you call me when you get a second? I know you're in Michigan, trying to relax." Dani paused, running her hand over her sweaty forehead. "You know what? Never mind. You deserve a break from all the drama. And this is drama-related. I will talk to you when you get back in town on Tuesday. You're coming back on Tuesday, right? Okay. I don't know why I'm leaving a voicemail. I could just text you." She paused again, realizing how ridiculous she sounded. "I'm sorry. I'll just talk to you when you're back."

She hung up the phone, wishing she hadn't left the message at all. She should have just hung up and sent a damn text. She probably shouldn't have called Peyton at all. Peyton was supposed to be relaxing, writing, and having some alone time. Dani didn't want to interrupt that. She made her way back inside the house to find Steven sitting on the sofa in the living room. It was probably the first time she'd seen him without a device of some kind in his hand in weeks, maybe months.

"I'm sorry," he said.

"For what?" Dani asked, standing in front of him, removing her jacket.

"I've not been here. I get that," he replied. "I have a lot going on, but that shouldn't detract from you and me."

"Okay," she replied, moving to sit in the chair next to him.

"Do we need to keep talking?"

"I don't know." Dani sighed. "I can accept your apology, Steven. But I'm still not sure I can trust that anything is going to change. I mean, you own a company and invest heavily into two more. You have obligations."

"You do, too," Steven replied, motioning toward her. "You're busy."

"I am. I know that. I guess when I'm here with you, though, I'm actually here. When you're with me, you're on the phone or on the computer. I usually get about ten minutes with you before you're tired and ready to go to sleep. In the mornings, you're on your way out as soon as you wake up."

"So, what do I need to do?" he asked genuinely as he leaned back on the sofa.

"I don't know. I guess – figure out your priorities. I

mean, where do *I* fall on that list, Steven?"

"Dani…"

"What? It's an important question, don't you think?" Dani stood. "I'm going to take a long bath and soak my muscles. I think, tonight, I'd like to sleep in one of the guest rooms, though."

"Do you want to go back to the city?" he asked.

"No, I don't want to ruin your mom's plans. It took a lot to get her to come out here. She's getting in around lunchtime, though, right?"

"Around one, yeah."

"Okay."

"Will I see you before she gets here, Dani? It's like you're saying goodnight right now." Steven stood. "We need to keep talking."

"Not right now. I need to clean up, and – I don't know. I need to relax. I thought we were going to do that this weekend, but it's just been one stressful thing after another. I think I'll go read for a while."

Steven didn't say anything else as Dani left the room. She hoped he would use the time to think about what she just said to him, but she turned just before she left the room completely to see that he had picked up his phone once again. Dani lowered her head and walked to the master bathroom. She ran the bath, soaked for a bit, and dressed after she finished. She grabbed her bag and carried it into one of the many guest rooms. It wasn't late. She wasn't tired. She loved the view from the balcony, though, so she decided to sit outside and read a book she'd been meaning to finish for a while. Her phone rang just as she turned the page to chapter fifteen. Dani pulled it from her pocket, glanced at the readout, and smiled a small smile; but not one that met her eyes.

"Hey. Sorry for my frantic texts."

"Is everything okay?" Jill asked.

"It's just normal Steven drama," Dani replied, leaning back in the comfortable chair.

"Your texts said you two had a fight."

"We did. It's the same stuff, though. Although, this time, sex came up," Dani offered.

"What about it?" Jill asked.

"Are you in a place where you can talk about this stuff?"

"I'm at home alone. Hubs is out tonight," she said, referring to her husband by his pet name.

"We haven't done that in a while," Dani confessed.

"How long is a while?"

"I don't remember the last time."

"Damn. Really? What's up? You haven't been in the mood or something?"

"It's not just me. It's him, too. It's like when he's actually interested, I'm not. Most of the time, though, he's not even around."

"Oh, that happens."

"What do you mean?"

"Busy working professionals, Dani. You have to make time for the romance now. You guys are at the two-year mark now. Before, it was the honeymoon period."

"I don't think we've ever had the honeymoon period."

"When you just got together, you weren't tearing each other's clothes off?" Jill asked. "God, we didn't leave the bedroom for days when the hubs and I first started dating. After we got married, we had at least a month where we were barely clothed before reality set back in and we had to start working a little harder."

"Really?"

"You told me you and Steven had a good sex life," Jill replied.

"We did." Dani shrugged to herself. "I thought we did. It was regular, at least."

"And not anymore, I take it?"

"Non-existent now."

"Dani, do you ever maybe think that you guys were better as friends than as a couple?" Jill suggested.

"What?"

"Just that you two were friends forever before you started dating. I've kind of only heard you complain about Steven for, like, the last year. Even when you were telling me you were going to the vineyard, it was like an obligation you had to fulfill as a girlfriend," Jill added. "I don't know… It's your relationship. Steven's a good guy."

Dani thought for a moment before she said, "Yeah, he is."

"I hate to do this to you, but my sister is calling. She's on her own with the baby tonight. Can–"

"Oh, sure. Tell her I said hi."

"I will. Hey, you'll figure this out. If it's meant to be with Steven, it'll be. It's a bullshit sentence, I know, but I think that if it's meant to be, you're willing to work on it. I don't believe in that, 'It's just meant to be, so everything else falls in line' kind of stuff. I believe in the work."

"You're a wise woman," Dani said.

"Well, I'm nine years older than you; comes with the territory. Anyway, I love you. I've got to go. Call me tomorrow if you need to," Jill replied.

"I will. Love you, too."

Dani stared out at the fall leaves on the trees and the beautiful vineyard landscape, pondering Jill's unexpected question. She also pondered her own reaction from her best friend's phone call. When she had gotten the call, she had been excited because she thought it was Peyton returning her voicemail. She loved Jill to death. She did. They had been friends since Dani joined her current modeling agency when she was twenty-two. Jill was the sage, older model, who was at the stage in her career where she was expanding her empire, investing in other things to do with her time, and doing shoots on the side with the occasional runway. She also had a great husband and was planning a family one day. Dani always loved talking to Jill. But, tonight, more than anything, she had wanted to talk to Peyton.

CHAPTER 12

PEYTON WOKE on Sunday morning to a dead cell phone and on the floor of the room she used as her music room in the rental. She looked around, realizing she had fallen asleep with a piece of notebook paper pressed to her arm. She had spent much of the night writing and playing random notes on her guitar and on the piano that came in the rental. It wasn't as good as the one Peyton had in New York, but it did the job. She had worked out a few hooks, a couple of choruses, and an entire lively anthem she knew would be a single on the next album.

She stood, went into the bedroom, and plugged in her phone to charge while she showered and brushed her teeth. Then, she made her way into the kitchen to make some coffee and have some toast. Peyton wasn't all that hungry. She had been eating junk food for most of the night, trying to get Dani Wilder out of her head as she wrote music. Dani was beautiful. She was kind. She made Peyton laugh. She was ambitious and made no apologies for it. All of those things were attractive to Peyton. And while Peyton had met thousands of women in her life that possessed all those same traits, she wasn't sure what it was about Dani that made her wonder what kissing a woman would feel like.

Peyton finished her breakfast, walked back into the bedroom, and reached for her phone. She had three texts from her publicist, one from her agent, four from her lawyer, two from her mom, one from Emily, and a voicemail from Dani Wilder.

"I've never gotten your voicemail before." Dani

laughed softly, and Peyton heard a car driving past her in the background. "That's it? Really? Just, 'Leave a message?'" The woman sighed an adorable sigh, and it made Peyton smile. "Okay. Can you call me when you get a second? I know you're in Michigan, trying to relax." Dani paused for a moment. "You know what? Never mind. You deserve a break from all the drama. And this is drama-related. I will talk to you when you get back in town on Tuesday. You're coming back on Tuesday, right? Okay. I don't know why I'm leaving a voicemail. I could just text you." She paused again. "I'm sorry. I'll just talk to you when you're back."

Peyton listened to the message twice before she checked the time. It was after nine. Typically, Dani woke at five and either went for a run or went to the gym. After that, she usually took a shower, ate breakfast, and then went about her day. Her schedule was probably different, given the weekend away, though. Peyton hovered over Dani's name in her contacts. She bit her lower lip, thinking about how much she wanted to talk to Dani. She was also curious about what had been the cause of the phone call. Then, she recalled her earlier concern.

"He did it," Peyton muttered under her breath. "He asked her."

She tossed the phone on the bed and exhaled. Then, she picked the phone back up and dialed.

"Hey, Len."

"What's up? I'm on set."

"I don't know. I think I might be ready to date again."

"Yeah? Ready to move past Trevor?"

"I think I'm ready for someone new, yes." Peyton sat on the end of the bed. "I don't know. Never mind."

"Never mind?" Lennox asked with a chuckle. "Pey, I'm about to shoot my scene."

"I'm sorry. I'm fine. I'm just tired and–"

"Lonely?" Lennox guessed.

Peyton thought about that for a moment. She *was* lonely. She was lonely right now because Dani was with

Steven. They were likely engaged or, at very least, had spent the weekend all over one another in a beautiful vineyard home. Either way, Peyton was lonely. Whenever she was with Dani, however, Peyton was the opposite of lonely. She had this sensation of completeness that she had never experienced with anyone. That thought had her imagining Dani's lips on her own again. She had to stop picturing that. Dani was in love with her boyfriend.

"Yeah, I guess that's it," she replied half-heartedly.

"Do you want me to set you up with someone or something?" Lennox asked.

"No, I just didn't get enough sleep last night."

"Up late, writing love songs, and you got lonely, didn't you?"

"Yeah. Go, do your scene. I'll call you later, okay?"

"Okay, Pey. I am here if you need me, though."

"I know. Love you, Len."

"Love you, too."

Around noon, Peyton made it outside for a long hike. She needed the walk and the air. She took her phone and turned the music up loud in her headphones. She was alone, except for the security guys that were about a hundred yards behind her. The trail behind the house was only a few miles long and was abandoned nearly every time she came to this place.

She missed her family when she got a picture from her sister, Erica, of the triplets with her parents. The message said they missed her, but Peyton wasn't sold on that one. Being famous in a family of people who just wanted to be normal wasn't ideal. Her parents were amazing people who loved her dearly. They had never pushed her into a career in music. They supported her, though, every step of the way. They just didn't want the attention that came with her career. Neither, it seemed, did the triplets anymore. When they had been younger, in their early teens, they had enjoyed it. But now, they were interested in some of the perks but didn't want the attention. They each had their own interests, relationships, and lives to lead. Peyton, sometimes, felt like they'd be better off without her.

By Sunday night, she felt like the alone time she had been craving was a mistake. Peyton missed the hustle and bustle of the city. There was something about that part of New York that made it less lonely. She packed up her things, called for the plane for the following morning, and let her security know they would be leaving sooner than planned. Monday morning, Peyton took the quick two-hour flight back to the city. She unpacked. She called Lennox and her parents to let them all know of her return to New York.

In her bedroom, Monday night, she opened the curtain just a bit in order to look out at the street. There were no cameras – which was nice, but there were several people walking down the street that would notice her if she remained there for too long. Peyton had a momentary wish that it would all go away: that she could be anonymous again, that she'd never been successful in music, and that she'd never met Dani Wilder. Then, she closed the curtain and climbed in bed.

***

When Peyton's phone rang the following night, she wasn't sure she should answer the call. It was Dani. And Dani, most likely, had news that would only make Peyton feel worse. In fact, Peyton had spent the entire day in bed, watching TV and eating yet more junk food. She was wallowing as if she had just broken up with someone, when in reality, she had spent just a few days away from a new friend.

"Hey," she greeted softly.

"Hey," Dani said. "How are you? I haven't heard from you in a few days."

"I'm okay. I got your message. Sorry, I didn't call back. I guess I got caught up in the relaxation there. I did some writing and playing, and time kind of got away from me."

"Did you just get back?" Dani asked. "I can let you go. You sound tired."

"No, I–" Peyton stopped herself. "I'm okay. What's up?"

"Nothing. I just wanted to talk to you, I guess."

"About?" Peyton asked, rolling onto her side.

"Oh," Dani said. "I don't know. I don't think I had anything specific." She laughed. "Is everything okay?"

"You called the other day. Was everything okay then?" Peyton asked.

"No, not really." Dani must have shifted her position. "Where are you?"

"In bed. You?" Dani asked.

"Same. Are you… Are you at Steven's?"

"No, he had to catch a flight to Chicago earlier today. He'll be back in a couple of days."

"Oh," Peyton said.

"I'm sorry about the message. Steven and I had just gotten into a fight, and I needed someone to talk to."

Peyton's eyes went wide as she asked, "Is everything okay?"

"I don't know, honestly."

"I'm sorry. I usually have my phone on silent when I'm working. And then it died, so–"

"It's not your fault."

"Are you two okay?"

"We're not exactly good, but – I don't know." Dani let out another quick laugh. "His mom was there on Sunday."

"Yeah?"

"She doesn't leave the city a lot. To even convince her to go was a whole big thing to do, but she showed up. We went for a walk. She helped me cook dinner. It was nice."

"It sounds like it," Peyton replied, missing her family again.

"Steven went out to get some firewood. He took forever, but it gave her and I a chance to talk."

"What about?" Peyton moved to sit up in bed.

"She wants me to think about settling down."

"Oh."

"She told me she thought of me as the daughter she never had. And she knows Steven loves me. She said it was about time."

"About time?" Peyton asked. "Did he…"

"He had no idea this lecture was coming." Dani laughed. "Anyway, it was a weird weekend. We got back Monday morning. I had a couple of meetings yesterday at the agency and a photo shoot today. I don't know… I just wanted to talk to you. Is that weird? Me, wanting to recap my weekend with you?"

"No, it's not weird," Peyton replied. "What are you doing tomorrow?"

"Tomorrow, I'm packing. I leave for Paris on Thursday."

"That's right. I forgot," Peyton replied.

"Steven is shortening his trip so that he can join me there on Friday."

"Another romantic trip," Peyton said before she could stop herself.

"I don't know about that. I'll be working for most of it, and he has some company there that's interested in meeting with him, so… We'll see what happens. I think it's his way of trying to make up the weekend to me."

"That's good, Dani. He's making an effort."

"I guess," Dani said. "I could maybe do something, though, if you're interested and free. It won't take me that long to pack."

Peyton thought about how she had planned to spend the following day. She was going to write in the morning, go to the studio for a few hours in the afternoon, and then have dinner with a few family friends that were in town. Even though she would have dropped all of it for a chance to spend time with Dani, something told her that she needed to take some time and space away from the woman who had snuck into her heart.

"I'm working, and then I have a dinner."

"Oh, you just asked me what–"

"I'm sorry. I thought I could make something work, but we could get together when you get back."

"Are you sure everything's okay?" Dani asked. "You don't sound like yourself."

"I'm just tired."

"I'll let you go then."

"No, that's not–"

"I'm tired, too. I'll say goodnight. I'm sorry I…"

"Dani, please don't be sorry." Peyton closed her eyes for an instant. "*I'm* sorry. I'm in a weird mood, but it's not your fault. Can I call you tomorrow? And if we can make something work, we'll hang out?"

"It's okay. We can see each other when I get back. Have a good night, Peyton. Get some sleep."

With that, she was gone.

CHAPTER 13

DANI LOVED PARIS. She always had. She'd
seen it at least twenty times by now; probably more. As she
thought about that, she knew how unbelievably lucky she
was. How many people in the world get to go to Paris or
London or Hong Kong or Sydney repeatedly? Dani had
been to at least thirty beautiful islands for photo shoots.
She'd spent three days in Alaska doing a winter shoot once.
She knew how lucky she was. But she also had a little bit of
regret. As many places as she had been to, she had rarely
taken photos of her own while there.

Dani looked at the camera bag resting beside her and
hated herself for getting her hopes up yet again. Steven was
supposed to be back at the hotel by five. They were going
to catch the sunset together, walking around the city. She
was planning on taking some pictures that she could show
Gibson Shaw during one of the lessons that Peyton had
gotten for her. She thought about Peyton in that moment.
The woman had been off that night they'd spoken on the
phone. There was something different about it. Dani wasn't
sure she knew Peyton well enough to presume anything, but
she seemed sad. She also hadn't called Dani the next day as
she said she would. Dani had texted a couple of times.
Peyton had eventually replied that she couldn't make it work
after all and they could hang out when Dani returned from
Paris.

"Hey. Sorry," Steven said the moment he entered. "I
know I'm late. I'm sorry."

"It's after six," she replied.

"I know."

"We missed the sunset."

"Dani, I know. This time it wasn't my fault. I was in the car. There was an accident. I probably would have been better getting out of the damn car and walking here because of these roads that all curve together. Crappy cab drivers everywhere… Pedestrians all over the place... It's–"

"One of the most romantic places on earth, Steven. Everyone else thinks so," Dani interrupted.

"For some of us, it's just another city." He removed his tie and went to unbutton his shirt. "Give me ten minutes. When I realized I was going to be late, I made a reservation at a place I went to the last time I was here. I think you're really going to like it."

"We need a break," she said.

"That's why we're here, Dani. I know I'm late. I planned a whole night through," Steven reminded. "The reservation is for seven. I thought we could do a nighttime walk instead of a sunset one, and go to the tower. I know it's your favorite place here."

"I don't think I'm up for all that. I thought we were going to walk, take some pictures, grab something quick, and come back here."

"Oh. Did you have something else in mind?" he asked with a hopeful smirk.

"That's not exactly what I meant."

"Dani, I was going to take you out tomorrow night instead, but I moved the reservation up when I knew I'd let you down again. I made all these arrangements. Can you–"

"Arrangements for what? A reservation? It's dinner, Steven." Dani sighed and glanced out the window at Paris at night.

Then, Steven moved to reach inside his pocket. She watched him slowly pull out a small box. Her heart raced wildly. She knew what the arrangements were about then. She knew why his mother had talked to her about settling

83

down. She knew why her boyfriend had decided to join her in Paris for her work trip. Dani knew he was about to ask her the question most woman would love to hear. She also knew her answer.

"Steven–"

"Dani, just hold on a second, okay?" He knelt in front of her; his eyes wide open, and his smile wide. "I know I messed up again. I'm sorry I was late for something that was important to you. I made reservations and a big deal out of something you probably wanted to do in private. I should have known that."

"Steven, I think we should break up." Dani's own eyes went big the moment the words were out of her mouth. "Shit."

"You want to break up? Dani, I'm proposing."

She reached for his hands, which were still holding the ring box.

"We've known one another since I was sixteen years old. That's a long time, Steven. We were kids when we met. And even though we haven't officially been together this whole time, I think we can both agree that it feels like we've been together a lot longer than two years."

"Exactly," Steven said. "That's what I'm talking about. That's why I'm asking you to marry me, Dani. I love you. I've only ever loved you."

"Maybe that's the problem." Dani thought of Peyton in that moment for some reason. "I don't know, Steven. Neither of us has ever really dated anyone else."

"I dated Julia Downing when–"

"For three months," Dani interjected softly. "I've never been with anyone else." She shrugged. "Maybe we need to be with other people to see if this is what we really want." She motioned between the two of them with her index finger.

"You want to see other people, and I'm on my knees, asking you to be the only person I ever see again? Is this because I'm busy at work all the time? Because I was late again? Dani, there was an accident. I left the meeting in plenty of time to get–"

"Because I have feelings for someone else," Dani said louder than she had meant to.

"What?" Steven asked and stood up immediately. He stared down at her and asked, "Are you cheating on me?"

"What? No." Dani softened her tone. "Nothing has happened. I don't think anything can happen or will happen or… I don't know. I'm not a cheater, though, Steven. You know that about me."

"What the hell am I supposed to think when my girlfriend of two years says she wants to see someone else the moment I try to ask her to be my wife?"

"I suggested we see other people."

"I think it's clear what you meant," he argued, with his face turning red. "Fuck, Dani." He took a step back, needing the space. "You want to sleep with this guy? Is that why we haven't had sex recently? Am I allowed to know who is it that you're having feelings for? Wait…" He held up his hand. "I don't want to know any of that."

"Steven…" Dani tried to reach for his hand, but he pulled away.

"Dani, I need to go," he said, waving her off.

"We should talk more, Steven. I'm so sorry. I had no idea you were planning this. We just talked about living together, and I told you I wasn't ready. Now, you're asking me to marry you; your mom is talking to me about settling down with you and having kids. I keep trying to tell you that I'm not ready for all that and I think–"

"No, we don't need to talk anymore. You have feelings for someone else. That's pretty much the end, isn't it? I mean, what's the point?"

"Nothing's–"

"Nothing's happened; you're not a cheater. It doesn't change the fact that you're interested in being with someone that's not me and haven't been with me, apparently, since you started feeling these… feelings."

"Steven, we were friends before we started dating. Maybe we can get some space from this and talk about it another time?"

"Talk about you breaking up with me another time? This is the only time I want to talk about this, Dani."

"I know I'm hurting you right now, but I don't know what else to say." She wiped a tear from her cheek.

"Fuck, Dani." Steven ran his hand through his hair with one hand while shoving the ring box in his pocket with the other. "I thought this was what you wanted," he added a little more calmly.

"This, meaning…"

"The commitment."

"Steven, I told you specifically I wasn't ready for those things."

"Wasn't ready at all?"

"I don't understand."

"Are you not ready *at all*, Dani, or are you just not ready for those things with *me*?" he asked.

"I've been thinking a lot about us recently."

"Really? Seems like you've been thinking about some other guy more than me."

"It's not like that, Steven." Dani stood, made a move toward him, but stopped when he took a step back. "It's that I shouldn't be having feelings for anyone other than you if this is right. I believe that." She shrugged one shoulder. "If you and I were supposed to be getting engaged right now, I wouldn't be having any kind of feelings for someone else. I'd want to be in Paris with you. I'd want to head to that romantic restaurant just in the hopes that you were about to ask me to marry you."

"But you want to be with someone else, doing those things."

"No, that's not it." Dani sighed softly. "I just know I don't want to do those things with you. I'm sorry it came out this way. I'm sorry it happened tonight. It shouldn't have."

"I'm getting another room," he offered. "I'll see if I can fly out tomorrow instead of the day after. You'll have Paris all to yourself for the rest of your trip."

"You don't–"

"Just give me some time, okay? I have to figure out what to tell my mom and the family."

"Of course," she said. "Do you want–"

"No, I'll take care of it." He ran his hand over his five o'clock shadow. "Are you sure?" he asked softly.

Dani nodded just as softly and replied, "Yes. I'm sorry, but yes."

Dani watched him pack what little he had brought with him. Steven moved briskly, and she knew it was out of embarrassment. He didn't want to be in the same room with her anymore. Dani wanted to curl up into a ball on the bed and cry her eyes out for hurting him this much. The tears she'd already shed weren't enough. She wiped her cheeks again, holding in her sobs. She had done this to him. She didn't have any right to cry in front of him. She knew if she did, Steven would try to console her. He met her eyes after lifting the handle of his roller bag to his hip.

"I'm going to a different hotel," he remarked. "Dani, I–" He didn't say anything else; he just lowered his head for a moment, pulled the door open, dropped his room key on the table next to it, and met her eyes once more. "Good night."

CHAPTER 14

Dani Wilder: Can you call me?

PEYTON READ THE MESSAGE, closed the messaging app, then reopened it, and read it again. It had been four days since she'd last spoken to Dani. She missed her like crazy. Peyton especially missed her when Dani would send her pictures of her day via messages. She got one of a squirrel, eating something a tourist undoubtedly left behind, followed by a picture of Dani imitating that squirrel's eating habits. It had been so damn adorable, Peyton had replied with a heart emoji. Dani had sent one back. The next one she'd gotten was of the Eiffel tower and Dani in full-on model mode in front of it. That one had been less adorable and more... well, it was hot. Dani was wearing a light blue pea coat with overly large buttons in white. She had a matching white scarf wrapped around her long neck. Her hair was pulled up. Her smile – barely there. Her legs were long in the skinny jeans when added to the three-inch heels. Peyton had replied back with another heart emoji and no words. Dani had messaged asking if Peyton was okay. Peyton had lied and told her that she was.

While Dani explored Paris with her boyfriend, Peyton had been writing songs. Normally, she loved this part of the process. She thrived on creativity. Writing new songs for an album got her through the next two years of her life. Whatever twelve to fifteen songs ended up on the album, it would be her life until the tours ended. And then, she would start the process all over again. She couldn't get into the idea of a new album, though. Songs, yes. She had tons of songs. She always had songs. But the idea of going back on tour in a few months for the international leg and then releasing an album right after that wasn't as exciting as it had been previously. Peyton worried that maybe she was just over it all. She had been at it for a while. Maybe she was due a break from the business of it. Then, Peyton stared at the message again and knew her melancholy wasn't because of music. It was because her heart had decided to do something she wasn't ready to deal with.

"Hey," Peyton greeted softly.

"Okay… What's going on with you?" Dani asked.

"What? You asked me to call you. This is me calling. Did I get the time difference wrong?"

"Did I do something wrong?" Dani asked.

"What? Why would you think that?" Peyton asked, leaning forward in her chair.

"Because you're acting so weird, Peyton. What happened? I thought… I don't know what I thought." Dani sighed. "I thought we…"

"You thought we what?" Peyton asked, hopeful.

"I thought we were… I know we're new friends. I just thought we were getting close. And now, it feels like you're ignoring me or that something's changed."

Peyton rolled her eyes at herself and replied, "It's me. I'm sorry. You haven't done anything wrong. I'm just in a funk."

"With music?" Dani guessed.

"No. I mean, I don't know. Maybe." She lied. "I'm sorry if I've made you think you're doing something wrong."

"Are you okay?" Dani asked. "Is there anything I can do?"

Peyton wasn't sure how to respond to that. She could tell her how she felt utterly confused because she'd never thought about anyone the way she thought about Dani Wilder. Peyton was terrified by how strong her feelings were. She had tried to dissect them in songs and just in her thoughts. She wanted to kiss Dani. She wanted to do more than kiss Dani. More importantly, Peyton didn't just want to do those things. She wanted to have a life with Dani.

"You can't do anything. I'll be fine. I called you back, though. Is everything okay there?" Peyton changed the subject.

"Not exactly." Dani paused. "I don't know… Maybe it is. Maybe this is exactly what I need."

"What's exactly what you need?" Peyton asked.

"Well, Steven proposed," Dani said.

Peyton closed her eyes at that revelation. She couldn't control the impact of those words. Her eyes welled with tears. One managed its way through her closed eyes and moved slowly down her cheek. She wiped it away and avoided sniffling into the phone. It was in this moment that she realized how far gone she was when it came to her feelings for Dani. This whole time, she hadn't wanted to acknowledge how differently she'd felt when she'd met Dani. She had never experienced love at first sight. Peyton wasn't sure how to recognize it. But she knew now. She knew how to recognize it now. It was with the pain that came from knowing that person would never be yours because they belonged to someone else.

"Congratulations," Peyton mustered.

"I said no."

Peyton's eyes shot open; she waited a long moment and then asked, "Why?"

"Why?" Dani repeated.

"Is that the wrong question to ask here? I don't think I've known anyone to turn down a proposal, Dani. I thought–"

"I don't exactly know the right question to ask, either,"

Dani said. "I guess it just kind of surprised me, the 'why' question."

"Because you don't know?"

"I do know," Dani replied. "I guess I have this idea that when you're with someone, and you're about to take those important steps, you should be thinking about them all the time. You should want to know when they might ask that question so that you can prepare yourself. You should – I don't know – as my friend Jill says, want to tear their clothes off every minute." She let out a soft laugh. "I don't feel that way with Steven." She paused. "Peyton, I've sent you more messages than I've sent Steven lately. I've called you more times. I've talked to you more about my life and what I want out of it more than I have with my boyfriend. Well, ex-boyfriend now."

"You… You're not–"

"I ended it. It was the worst timing. He was on his knees, asking me to marry him, and I said I thought we should break up. I couldn't just say no without telling him why. And I couldn't say yes, because I don't want to marry him. I feel terrible."

"Breakups are hard." Peyton couldn't believe she'd just said that.

"It's not the breakup that's bothering me," Dani began. "In some ways, I've hardly had a boyfriend for the past year. I'm actually used to him not being around. It was when he started trying – like joining me in Paris, when I knew he's not who I want to spend my life with."

"You're feeling guilty, then," Peyton suggested.

"Yes."

"It's because you're a good person. You're an amazing person, actually." Peyton smiled at herself. "And I love the messages you send me. I like talking to you."

"You liked the squirrel?"

"I loved the one of *you* after the squirrel more," Peyton admitted.

"Yeah?"

"You had this cute expression on your face." Peyton smiled again. "I didn't see you post it anywhere, though. You normally post stuff like that."

"You mean online? Oh, that one was just for you."

"Just for me, huh?" Peyton teased.

"I wanted to cheer you up. You've seemed down lately."

"I'm not as down as I was, I think," Peyton confessed, wondering if Dani would pick up on her meaning.

"I'm back soon. Can we hang out?" Dani asked.

"Whenever you want," Peyton said.

"You're crazy busy with work, though. I don't want–"

"Dani, I'll make time for you," Peyton interjected. "I can pick you up from the airport if you want."

"Wouldn't that be an event?" Dani laughed.

"I'll stay in the car," Peyton replied with a laugh of her own, feeling instantly better.

"I'll call you when I'm back. We'll plan something."

"Dinner?"

"Depends. Are you cooking?"

"Yes," Peyton replied.

"Then, dinner at your place."

"And a movie?"

"Sure." Dani laughed again. "Nothing too scary, though."

"I'll be there to protect you, Dani," Peyton offered seriously.

***

Peyton should have asked more questions. She should have asked Dani what she had meant by saying she talked more to Peyton about her life or that she didn't think of tearing off Steven's clothes. Dani had mentioned those two things in the same speech; that must have meant something, right? Maybe she wasn't thinking about tearing off his clothes because she was thinking about doing that to

Peyton. No, that wasn't right. It definitely didn't mean that Dani was interested in dating her. Dani had just ended a two-year relationship. She would need time to process everything. Peyton could help with that. She could be a friend. Hell, she *needed* to be Dani's friend, because the thought of being more with Dani had her going crazy.

God, Dani's voice had been breathy and hot when she had said, "Then, dinner at your place."

Peyton hadn't called a woman hot and actually thought about sleeping with her before Dani Wilder. And she had thought about that. She had thought about touching Dani all over her body. She had never had thoughts like that about anyone. That, unfortunately, also included the men that she had dated. Sex had been good with her boyfriends. It had been great a few times, but she'd never craved it. Peyton wasn't certain how she had come to crave Dani's touch after only knowing the woman for a few weeks, but she had. She had been willing to allow herself the feelings Dani shook within her. She had written many of them down on paper. At the same time, though, Peyton was terrified of what this would all mean. If she could actually have Dani, what would that mean for her career? What would it mean for Dani's? How would she explain this to her fans? *Would* she even explain it to her fans? How would she tell her parents, her sisters, her grandparents? Peyton shook herself out of those kinds of thoughts. None of that mattered if she had misinterpreted Dani's rambling earlier. And all she had to do was ask a few more questions.

"Dani, what does that mean? When you think about me, what is it you're thinking about? Do you want me the way I want you? Isn't this the craziest thing ever? Can we even do this? *How* do we even do this? Have you ever done anything like this before? Why does it feel so good to be with you? When I met you, I knew something was different. Did you know that, too?"

Peyton stopped asking those questions inside her own head the moment she watched the black SUV pull up in front of her New York City townhouse. She had been checking the window for the past twenty minutes. It was dark out there, despite the fact that it was just after six in the evening.

The driver got out as Peyton watched through the curtains. She took a step away from the window to try to get her breathing to slow down. Then, she moved to the front door and waited. She pictured what would happen next in her head, even though she couldn't see outside anymore. The driver, one of her security guys, was walking around the car. He was opening Dani's door. She was climbing out, looking gorgeous, no doubt. He was then walking around to the back of the car to grab Dani's bag.

Peyton had been the one to insist on sending the car to Dani's place. Dani had relented after a few minutes, realizing there was no arguing with Peyton about it. Then, there was a knock at the door. The light from the lantern to her left gave Dani a bit of a glow behind her head that made her appear as an angel to Peyton. Maybe she'd always been that way in Peyton's eyes. Peyton's hand was still gripping the door handle, and she realized she had yet to invite Dani into the house.

"I'm sorry. Come in," she finally said.

"Thanks," Dani replied, moving into the house. "I feel like I should hug you. Why does it feel like I haven't seen you in a year?" She reached for Peyton and pulled her into her body.

"I don't know," Peyton replied. "But I say go with it," she added when she felt Dani pressed against her.

"Yeah?" Dani asked softly.

The woman's lips were so near Peyton's ear, it caused Peyton to close her eyes at just the sound of that one word.

"I'm glad I'm home," Dani continued.

"Me too." Peyton hugged her back hard. When Dani didn't resist, Peyton held onto her a moment longer. Then, she exhaled and released her from the hug. "Hungry?"

They spent some time in the kitchen. Dani helped

Peyton finish plating the meal Peyton had made for them. Peyton thought about just sitting in the living room, with plates in their laps, catching up on the things that they had missed, but she wanted tonight to be special. She'd prepared the table with two red candles – in honor of Dani's favorite color, which she had learned upon seeing Dani's closet for the first time. Half the woman's clothes were red. Peyton thought the color looked nice on her. She had prepared the wine before Dani had arrived, and had sparkling water there, too. She had even made a dessert she hoped Dani would enjoy. If she was ever going to try to figure out what the hell she was feeling for Dani, it was tonight.

They sat at the table. Peyton took Dani in from across it. The woman had her light-brown hair half up and half down. Her makeup was light and accentuated her high cheekbones. Her smile was bright and told Peyton she was happy to be there. She had worn comfortable jeans and a boyfriend-style sweater in gray that went over a plain white shirt. Earlier that night, she had kicked her tennis shoes off at the door in such a way that Peyton did believe Dani felt this place was home.

"So, tell me about what happened while I was gone," Dani said, taking her first bite. "God, you're a good cook." She smiled at Peyton.

"Yeah?"

"It's really good."

"Thanks." Peyton smiled back and dug into her own food.

"Tell me about what's been going on with you," Dani requested.

"I don't want to talk about that tonight, Dani. I thought we could talk about Paris and – I don't know, maybe my upcoming tour or something."

"Tour?" Dani asked, taking another bite.

"The international leg," Peyton replied. "It's in a few months."

"Oh," Dani said. "I guess I knew that."

"I don't think we've talked about it, but yeah, I'll be kind of all over the world for a while. I'll come back here and there, though."

"For how long?" Dani asked, looking concerned.

"It's about eight months in all."

"Eight months?" Dani asked, surprised. "That's almost a year."

"It's two-thirds of a year, yeah." Peyton laughed and took a sip of her water. "I wrapped the US tour already. I always find a place to hunker down, write and record the next album if I can, and then go on the international tour. I usually take a vacation or two during or come back home, depending on what I feel like doing. But yes, it's a long time."

"When will I see you?" Dani asked, looking even more concerned now.

"Whenever you want," Peyton replied, meaning it.

CHAPTER 15

DANI STARED AT PEYTON from across the table. Peyton was beautiful behind red candles. It was as if she had dressed for just the occasion of having them on her table. Her earrings had flecks of red in them. Her nails were painted the same shade, and her shirt had red stripes. Peyton looked like she had dressed up just to have dinner with her. Dani's cheeks blushed a little at the thought of Peyton Gloss, of all people, trying to look extra good for dinner with a friend. That was the thing, though… Dani didn't feel like a friend tonight. It didn't feel like a friendly dinner, either. The meal had been prepared expertly. The wine had been left out to breathe. There was even dessert in the kitchen, waiting for them to devour it. Peyton had the candles lit. She had soft music playing in the background.

"You look…" Dani started to say.

"What?" Peyton laughed. "Bad? I've been having trouble sleeping recently. Someone keeps texting me cute pictures at all hours of the night because she's on the other side of the world."

"I thought *I* was the only one sending you cute pictures," Dani replied in jest. "Tell me who is this woman, so I can find her and tell her to stop so that you can get some sleep?"

Peyton laughed again and replied, "She's back on American soil. I think I'll be okay now."

"You do?"

Peyton nodded as she sipped her wine.

"She wants you to get some sleep," Dani said. "And before, when I said that you looked…" She motioned with her hand. "I meant that you looked good." She swallowed. "You look nice tonight."

"Oh," Peyton said. "Thank you. So do you."

When dinner was finished, they retired to the theater. They both instinctively went to the sofa instead of separate recliners. Peyton scrolled through the options until they agreed on a movie to watch. Then, it happened. It happened so naturally, Dani almost didn't notice that it was different from anything they had done up until that moment. Dani lay down on the sofa, placing her head in Peyton's lap. Peyton played with Dani's hair. Then, she rested her arm over Dani's torso as they watched the movie in silence. All of that was new. All of that was exciting. All of that had Dani's heart going crazy, but what made it nearly burst out of her chest was when Peyton moved to lie down next to her, behind her. *Peyton Gloss* lay behind *Dani* on the sofa. Her arm wrapped over Dani's body protectively. Her head was resting on her hand behind Dani in order to still see the movie. Dani was being held by Peyton. She closed her eyes to let it all sink in.

She thought of Steven, worried about him, but only for a second before she brought herself back to the present. She didn't know what exactly was happening between them, but she knew she liked this. She liked whenever Peyton touched her. She liked when Peyton casually found a chance to graze Dani's skin with any part of her own. She didn't know the specifics of what Peyton was feeling, but she had spent the entire flight from Paris thinking about how much she liked Peyton. It was nuts. Dani knew that. She hadn't ever felt for anyone, though, what she had been feeling for this woman. She decided to trust it, trust herself, and let whatever happened between them happen. It was scary. She had never been held like this by a woman before.

"This is nice," Dani said when the movie was nearly over.

"Stay tonight," Peyton whispered near her ear.

"I can't," Dani replied reluctantly.

"Why not?"

"Because I have a photo shoot tomorrow. There's a car coming for me at four in the morning."

"Send the car here instead," Peyton suggested softly.

Dani felt Peyton's hand glide over her stomach on top of her shirt. The woman wasn't reaching for anything in particular. She was just touching Dani lightly, tentatively, and it was doing things to Dani that she wasn't prepared to deal with.

"Pey, it's already arranged." Dani closed her eyes in an attempt to think about anything other than how good it felt, to be touched by Peyton. "I should go soon, actually."

"Dani…"

"I know," Dani offered. "When the movie's over, I'm going to go home, Peyton."

"Okay," Peyton said, removing her hand from Dani's stomach.

Dani missed the contact but didn't attempt to put Peyton's hand back in place. Instead, she watched the rest of the movie, with Peyton lying behind her; wishing the hand would snake its way up under her shirt, touch her abdomen, her breasts, pull her shirt off and over her head, and slip beneath her jeans to cup her, slide between her wet folds, and take her.

She stood abruptly the moment the credits rolled. She straightened her shirt, her jeans, and then her hair for good measure. She stared down at Peyton, who was still lying on the sofa, looking up at her. Peyton's eyes raked over Dani's body. They were darker than usual. Her expression told Dani that Peyton wanted her to stay. She really wanted Dani to stay.

"I'll call you tomorrow after work?" Dani asked.

"Okay."

"Sleep well?"

"I'll walk you out," Peyton offered.

"No." Dani held up her palms facing Peyton. "Stay there. You look… good." She smiled at the woman.

"The car's out there," Peyton said.

"I know. They told me they were on call," Dani replied.

"Text me when you're home." Peyton straightened her own shirt.

"I will."

Dani wanted to lean down and kiss her. It seemed like the perfect end to the perfect date, but this wasn't a date. This was just two friends sharing dinner and a movie. Well, two very close friends, who sometimes hold onto one another a little too tightly. Dani smiled once more instead and made her way out of the theater. It hurt, leaving Peyton there, but she needed to get some air. She left the house, climbed into the waiting SUV, and took the short trip home. When she got inside her apartment, though, she felt stifled. She opened the windows in the living room, the bedroom, and the one in the kitchen. The view wasn't great, but the cool air felt good on her skin.

She took a long, hot shower, climbed out, and dressed for bed. She had an early call the following morning. She knew she should sleep, but she didn't think sleep would likely come. She closed the windows, moved back into the bedroom, and climbed into bed. She looked around the room that was still bathed in the light from the lamp on her table. It felt so small all of a sudden. Dani thought of the kitchen, the living room, the small bathroom – and it didn't feel right to her anymore. She'd never really meant to stay here this long.

When she had taken over the lease, it was always with the idea that someday, and likely someday soon, she'd be moving in with Steven. They would live together for a while. Then, they'd get engaged. They'd get married. She would have a few kids, and that would have a detrimental effect on her modeling career for a bit. That had been what everyone around her had told her would happen. It was what she just assumed *would* happen. However, just the thought of that happening now made her a little sick. She didn't want those things now. She may want them later, but Dani knew that if she did, she wouldn't want them with Steven. In fact, the more she thought about her relationship with him, as she snuggled into her comforter, she got the feeling that it had always been wrong. She and Steven had been wrong. They had been good friends – close friends, who cared deeply for one another, but the romantic aspect of their relationship just felt wrong to her. Maybe that was because it was wrong. But it might also had something to do with the fact that she just couldn't stop thinking about Peyton's hand on her abdomen, lightly rubbing and holding her from behind.

***

Texts and phone calls hadn't replaced how good it felt, to have Dani near her. They had known one another for such a short time, but having Dani in her life had changed it so dramatically. Peyton loved her career. She loved music; writing it, playing it, producing it, performing it, and everything else that went into her job. She had been doing it professionally for more than a decade. She'd only gotten busier, but her drive to do more and be better never slowed. In her previous relationships, this had not been an issue. Well, with Trevor, it was a problem, but that was because he wasn't in the business. He had taken all that on when he'd met and began dating Peyton. Peyton had been so surprised by him asking her out. She'd checked with him several times before that first date that he had intended it to be a date.

After, when it was clear that they both wanted to pursue a relationship, she had sat him down at her kitchen table. She described what had happened in her previous relationships when the public found out. She had warned him to the best of her ability that once everyone knew they were together, people that she had never met in her life would want to know more about this mystery man. That, in combination with the fact that they were rarely able to make their schedules work, had caused their breakup.

As the SUV pulled up in front of the studio, Peyton slid her sunglasses over her eyes and straightened her pants and shirt, running a hand to her head to make sure her high ponytail was still in place. Then, she put on her game face. The door opened. The flashes started. Peyton stepped out of the car. Two security guards stood on either side of her as she made her way inside the secure building. She heard several mentions of her name. She heard a few questions. The only thing that stood out to her, though, was the one comment that came just as the door was closed behind her.

"Deyton forever!"

Peyton moved into the studio to meet the producer she'd worked with on the past two albums. They exchanged a hug. As Peyton attempted to put the comment out of her mind, it only made her recall the articles online she'd seen just that morning, regarding her friendship with Dani Wilder. The rumors had already started. It seemed that whenever she spent any significant portion of time with another human – regardless of gender, people just assumed she was sleeping with them. She'd had other model friends that had fallen into the same media trap before, but Peyton hadn't slept with them or even remotely wanted to sleep with them. The media – mentioning that as a possibility for her and Dani in some random articles and giving them a nickname, only cheapened what they could have in Peyton's eyes. She sat on the floor of the booth, as was her custom. Matt sat on the small sofa in the room. He had a guitar in his lap. Peyton had pages from her notebook scattered on the floor.

"Where do you want to start?" Matt asked.

"I think I'm in the mood for a ballad today," she replied.

"Good or bad?" he asked with a small laugh.

"Something about love at first sight," Peyton said, moving papers into separate piles.

"Yeah?" he checked. "You don't normally like writing about that kind of thing. Didn't you tell me once you weren't really a believer in that?"

"That was at a New Year's Eve party, where I had no one to kiss, and all my friends had been paired off. I had also had several glasses of champagne." She laughed. "And it wasn't that I never believed it. I don't know... I just–"

"Who is it?"

"Who is who?" Peyton looked back behind her to glance at him quizzically.

"You're not back together with Trevor, are you? That's a mistake, Pey. That boy did not want the attention."

"I haven't talked to him since we broke up, Matt."

"Then, who has you thinking about love at first sight?"

Peyton sighed, turned back to her notes, and found the page she was looking for.

"This one." She held it up for him to see. "I've got verse one and the chorus. I need the rest. I have the melody locked in my head. I can't get it out. I'll play it for you, and you can tell me what you think. I want it to sound layered, heavy, really deep, if that makes any sense."

"Heavy, huh?" He laughed again, taking the piece of paper from her when offered.

"Yeah." Peyton shrugged.

"How heavy exactly? Like, this is the man of your dreams kind of heavy?"

"Like, this is the *woman* of my dreams kind of heavy." She turned back to the guy to see his wide-eyed expression. "Like, I met her, and nothing before her made sense, but everything does now. Like, she's at work right now, and all I want to do is be with her, but I'm here instead. Like, the only thing I can do to make that a little better is write a song about how she makes me feel. Like that kind of heavy."

"Damn, Pey. Really?"

"Yes."

"That's amazing, Peyton. It's Dani Wilder, right? I've heard the rumors. I try to stay away from that crap, but it's hard when you're holding a computer in your hand all the time these days."

"You can't tell anyone, Matt. This is the first time I've-"

"I wouldn't say anything to anyone ever." He nodded. "So, it's reciprocal, yeah? I've seen the photos. She looks pretty crazy about you. My guess is that's what the press is picking up on."

"We went to the gym together one time, and suddenly, we're a couple." Peyton leaned back against the sofa.

"So, you're not?"

"No, we haven't talked about it exactly. There are just these moments where it feels so good to be with her. She had a boyfriend up until recently."

"But not anymore?"

"No, not anymore. I'm going crazy. I've never felt like this for anyone, let alone another woman. I have no idea what I'm doing here. She just got out of a relationship, but all I want to do is tell her how I feel."

"Tell me." He smiled at her. "Tell me how it feels, since you can't tell her yet."

"It's the best." She smiled. "She's the best. I have no idea how this happened. One night, I'm performing at an event, and everything is normal. Then, I see her, and I'm suddenly a crazy person, falling in love with a woman I just met."

"You know how Beth and I met, right?" he asked of his wife.

"When you were in college." Peyton sat forward and turned to face him completely.

"Yes, at a gig. I was playing bass. She was in the crowd. I had a girlfriend at the time. We hadn't been together all that long, but I liked her enough to keep going out with her." Matt paused, sat back, and smiled while he strummed the guitar lightly, as if to offer a soundtrack to his own love story. "After the performance, I went out into the bar. My girlfriend was talking to a couple of her friends. The rest of the band was packing up. I needed to track down the owner, to get our tiny-ass paycheck that wouldn't even pay for our beer for that night when divided up." He met her eyes. "You never had to go through that phase in your career. You should feel lucky."

"Trust me, I do." She smiled back as he continued to strum.

"Beth was sitting at a barstool. She'd been waiting for her blind date to show up. He was very late. When I saw her, it was like the dark, dank, bar had disappeared completely. She was all I could see, Peyton. I walked up to her, offered to buy her a drink, and put my hand out for her to shake all in the same second, I think." He laughed at himself. "I was such an idiot."

"An idiot with a girlfriend," Peyton reminded.

"I broke up with her that night. I hadn't even gotten Beth's number yet. She had gone to the bathroom. I found my girlfriend. I told her I thought we should end things. She didn't put up much of an argument. I walked my dumb ass back over to that stool and sat there until she came out. I got her number and called her the following day. We've been together ever since." Matt's smile was wide. "I'm a little older than you. Beth and I have been a couple since I was twenty-one years old. We've grown together, changed together, fought together, made up together, and also made a pretty amazing kid together. I'm thirty-five years old, and I know for a fact that I don't want anyone else. I'll never find another woman who makes me feel how Beth made me feel that night. It's in my bones, Peyton." Matt paused as his kind eyes met Peyton's again. "Is Dani in your bones?"

"She's in my everything," Peyton said on a sigh.

CHAPTER 16

"How's life post Steven?" Jill asked after taking a drink of her strawberry lemonade, her favorite lunchtime beverage.

"It's oddly kind of the same," Dani replied, taking a bite of the mandarin orange slice in her Chinese chicken salad.

"I think that says a lot," Jill suggested. "I like Steven. I think he's a good enough guy. He's just not good enough for you, Dani. I don't think he realizes what he really wants for himself."

"What's that mean?" Dani asked, looking around the small, corner restaurant they'd been to a handful of times.

"Just that I think he wants a woman who – I don't know – stays at home, maybe."

Dani noticed a few phones pointed in their direction. She continued to eat, trying to avoid the attention.

"I don't know about that."

"How many times did you tell the man you didn't want to move in? How many times did he or someone in his family bring up that you two should be engaged by now? How many times did his mom ask you about grandchildren?"

"A few."

"A few? Really?"

"Okay. A lot." Dani chuckled. "I'm twenty-three years old. What is the damn hurry?"

"That's how people like Steven do things. You know how they are. They're old money. He's a lot more modern than the rest of them, but still. He wants a wife, Dani. I know he loves you. I think that's why it was always hard for you two, once you started dating. He loves you, but you're not that kind of woman. You don't just sit around, waiting for him to come home from a long workday, have dinner on the table, and have his slippers ready."

"He's not like that," Dani objected. "He's a little old-school, sometimes, but he's not that bad." She pointed her fork at Jill. "I do think you're partially right, though. He does want a wife. And he wants a wife that'll be there when he is, and who won't gripe at him all the time for being late. That's just not me."

"When you two first met, you were only really starting to pick up steam as a model. You had been doing it forever, but you were finally on a worldwide stage. You were still in high school, though. Once you really blew up, you two just kind of fell into this thing where people just assumed you were a couple. I think that's probably the main reason you two actually got together, to begin with."

"I did love him, Jill."

"I know you did, sweetie." Jill smiled softly at her. "But he's not the person you're supposed to be with. I knew it, and everyone else knew it. I'm just glad you figured it out before you committed your entire life to him."

"You never said this before," Dani replied.

"I said some of it. You just never heard me before," Jill countered. "That's kind of how I know this is the right time for you to make a clean break from Steven; find someone new."

Dani looked around the restaurant again, to see if anyone was close enough to hear what she was about to say. When she felt confident that the people who were still taking photos or videos on their phones couldn't hear what she and Jill were talking about, she leaned in further across the table, dropping the fork on top of her half-eaten salad.

"I need to tell you something, but you can't say a word to anyone, Jill. I mean it."

"Dani, I've never revealed any of your secrets before. I don't plan on starting now," Jill replied with a concerned expression on her face. She dropped her fork and leaned in to match Dani's posture. "What's wrong?"

"I think I might have already found someone," Dani replied in a near whisper.

"What? Really?"

"It's crazy." She shook her head at just the thought. "I'm not sure if I'm more scared of the fact that it might not happen at all, or if it's because it might actually happen."

"Who is it, Dani?" Jill whispered. "Someone we know?"

"Peyton," Dani offered.

"Gloss?" Jill practically mouthed the word. "As in…"

"Yes."

"And you two have–"

"Nothing. Nothing has happened." Dani glanced around again. "We touch sometimes. That's it, though."

"What does *that* mean?" Jill chuckled. "I touched your hand when we both went for a breadstick earlier. Does that count?"

"No, that doesn't count. Jill, I'm serious here."

"Okay. I'm sorry. Go on." She sat back in her chair a little.

"She holds me, or I hold her," Dani said.

"Holds?"

"We'll watch a movie and – I don't know – kind of snuggle up."

"Like how you've had your feet in my lap on the couch because you're, like, eight feet tall and need to sprawl out?" Jill asked with a smile.

"6'1". And you're not exactly a shorty, miss 6'0". No, that's not what I mean. That's stuff friends do. I'm talking about, like, really snuggling into each other. When I was at her house last week, we were lying down on the sofa together."

"Big sofa?" Jill lifted an eyebrow.

"No," Dani replied. "Small. We could barely fit."

"And you were close?"

"She had her arm around me," Dani answered.

"How'd that feel?"

"Amazing," Dani said, likely, with stars in her eyes and a blush on her face.

"Dani…" Jill leaned back in. "You're into her."

"It came out of nowhere," Dani said.

"Is this why you broke up with Steven?"

"No, that's about me. It's about Steven and I not being right together. It's not about her."

"But did she, maybe, help the decision come a little faster?" Jill suggested.

"I guess." Dani shrugged and leaned back in her chair. "I've never felt this way."

"About a woman?"

"No."

"Really?" Jill asked. "How long have you known her? Didn't you meet at that party we went to together?"

"Yes, it's crazy. I may have mentioned that before. I also keep telling myself that over and over again."

"Does she feel the same way? I mean, I assume she does. She's, apparently, holding you at night." Jill winked at her.

"We haven't talked about it exactly," Dani began. "We… allude to it sometimes. When I was there last, we almost talked about it for the first time. But I might have freaked out and left."

"The girl thing?" Jill asked.

"The *whole* thing." Dani lifted both of her perfectly shaped eyebrows. "Jill, I've only ever been with Steven. Right or not, he's the only real relationship I've ever had, outside of a few dates and a short-term thing here and there.

Plus, she's not exactly the *type* I thought I'd fall for."

"Fall for?" Jill questioned. "Already?"

"Maybe right away," Dani replied.

"Oh, sweetie." Jill reached across the table and squeezed Dani's hand. "Listen to me. If you like Peyton, if you're falling for her, I think that's amazing."

"It's terrifying."

"Good. It's supposed to be." Jill pulled back her hand. "Dani, it's supposed to be when it's just starting. When it's real, it kind of feels like you're always balancing on a wire like a freaking circus performer. You're scared it's going to start. You're scared it could end. You're scared it might just be the best thing that's ever happened to you while worrying that it could be the worst if it does ever end. I love my husband. We've been together for a long time. But there are days I still have those feelings. It's never really permanent, no matter what we try to convince ourselves by getting married or saying this is the only person we want forever. We all grow and change. It's work, and it's every single day. Steven wasn't willing to work for you. You weren't willing to work for him."

"Hey!" Dani objected.

"That's how you know it's not right," Jill asserted. "Peyton Gloss would be work, Dani."

"How do you–"

"Because of her job; not because of who she is. I don't know who she is. You haven't actually introduced me to her yet." She smiled at Dani again. "But she's one of the most famous people on the planet. You're well known, but she's famous, Dani. Have you thought about that?"

"Nothing's happened yet." Dani shrugged yet again. "I've just been thinking about how the hell I never noticed I could be attracted to a woman."

"Maybe you're not," Jill replied. "Maybe it's just her."

"Jill, I've seen how many women half-naked or even fully naked?" Dani asked the rhetorical question. "I've seen you naked at least a hundred times." She motioned to Jill, who laughed. "Beautiful, sexy women, who are paid to model clothing because of how they look. I've never even wanted to kiss one of them."

"Hey!" Jill glared mockingly.

"No offense."

"None taken." It was Jill's turn to shrug. "You want to kiss her?"

"More than that."

"Are you going to?"

"I don't know."

"Why not?"

"Because I don't know what she wants."

"Have you thought about asking her?"

"God, why would I do that?" Dani laughed lightly.

Jill sat there for a moment before she asked, "Right now, answer this for me. If you two did talk, what's the worst outcome? Is it that she returns your feelings and wants to go for it, or is it that she doesn't and won't?"

***

Dani made it home after lunch not feeling much better than before she had gone to talk to her friend. She had been hoping Jill would provide her with an answer. She didn't want more questions. Jill had been her older, wiser friend, who had married the man of her dreams and had the family and career she'd always wanted. Dani knew she wanted to take a similar path to Jill. She did want to get married someday. She wanted a family. She wanted her career to continue to thrive. She even wanted to do more than just model one day. She had plans for herself. She knew Steven didn't fit into them, but she wondered if Peyton could.

Jill had been right. If Dani told Peyton how she felt, Peyton might want to take the chance and go for it with Dani. If that happened, though, they'd have an uphill climb even at the beginning of their relationship. For starters, they were both women that had never been with another woman.

Secondly, they were both in the public eye. People were already starting to take notice of the fact that they were spending so much time together. They'd gone to the gym once. Cameras had followed. They had made a coffee run. Cameras were there. They had lunch in SoHo – Peyton was stopped for autographs when the security guys got caught behind them. Once the two girls realized it was Peyton with Dani, they asked for a picture with both of them. That was posted online. Now, they had people asking questions about their relationship. Dani wasn't sure if Peyton would want to go through that all over again, even if she felt strongly for Dani.

Dani flopped on her sofa, wondering what the hell she was going to do. Just as she had resigned herself to stop worrying about it and see what happened, her phone buzzed. She glanced at the screen and caught Peyton's name. Peyton's mom was coming for a surprise visit and would be staying with her, the message read. Peyton wanted to reschedule her plans with Dani for the following night. Dani's first feeling after reading that message told her all she needed to know. She wouldn't be seeing Peyton as soon as she had hoped, and that made her sad. It made her very sad.

CHAPTER 17

"PEYTON, WHAT ARE YOU planning on doing with it?"

"I haven't decided yet. It's just a guest room right now," Peyton replied.

"But you've got a lot of those already. You should turn this into an office," her mother suggested.

"Mom, I have an office."

"You have a music room. But your business isn't just writing songs anymore. You should have a place with a real desk and—"

"Mom, my music room is fine. I don't need a home office in the same way that Dad has a home office. Besides, I'm involved in my brand, but the business part of things is handled by people I pay. And those people have offices. My office is basically a tour bus."

"Fine. Fine." Her mother moved back out into the hallway. "I do like what you've done with this place, honey."

"Thanks, Mom," Peyton replied as they moved back downstairs.

Peyton's mom had decided on the impromptu visit only a couple of days prior. Peyton wasn't certain what had driven her mom to want to make the trip to New York on a whim, but she would never turn her mother away. Peyton had made a couple of changes to the house since the last time her parents were in town. They'd begun with dinner out after she'd picked her mom up at the airport. Now, it was a little after nine. Peyton was giving her the tour of the changes she had made. As they headed into the kitchen, Peyton put the kettle on, knowing her mother would prefer some tea before sleep. Her mom sat on the kitchen island stool and watched as Peyton worked to prepare two mugs.

"So, how are things?" she asked.

"How are things?" Peyton asked back with a laugh. "Things are fine with me. How are things with you?"

"Things are good. Work is good. Your father is good. Your sisters are in college," her mother replied.

Peyton laughed, sat down next to her mother, and said, "I caught that."

"What? They're good. They're just also in college."

"How was parents' weekend?" Peyton asked, placing her hands on the counter.

"It was nice. Erica's recital was great. She's not a featured lead or anything, but she seems to be enjoying dance more now than she did when she first got there. Her grades show that." Her mother scowled. "She's getting Cs in all her non-dance-related classes. Your father about went through the roof when he heard about that. The lecture he gave her was a good one. You would have liked it."

"Yeah?" Peyton chuckled.

"Yes. She'll need Bs next semester if she wants us to keep paying for her education. Emily's art classes are going well. Her sculpture won second prize at the show."

"It did? Why didn't she tell me? That's amazing."

"I don't know. When did you last talk to her?"

"A couple of weeks ago."

"Peyton, they're your sisters. You can't go a couple of weeks without talking to them," her mom chastised.

"I know. I've been busy."

"That's not an excuse."

"Mom, there are three of them. Plus, there's you and Dad. You guys outnumber me." Peyton stood when the kettle whistled at her.

"Peyton, we're all your family. We don't outnumber

you. You're one of our numbers, honey."

Peyton lowered her head, poured the hot water into the mugs, and tried to put on a smile.

"I just meant that I can't talk to everyone every day, that's all."

"I didn't ask for every day. I know your sisters are young. And there are three of them. Trust me, I gave birth to them. I know what three at once is like," she said.

"Right," Peyton replied.

"Lizzy's boyfriend is a college drop out. Did you know that?"

"No, I didn't." Peyton placed her mother's mug in front of her and moved back around to sit down next to her. "I take it, you're not a fan?"

"He's fine. He's just working at a car dealership as a receptionist or something. He's twenty-two, dropped out of school after three years, and doesn't plan on going back. Who drops out when you're that close to finishing?" she asked, swirling her spoon around in her mug.

"I don't know. I didn't go myself, so I can't judge, I guess."

"You didn't go because you couldn't. That's different."

"Well, maybe he couldn't, either, Mom. Maybe he couldn't afford it or something."

"I suppose that's a possibility. I didn't ask why. Lizzy was giving me that glare the trips perfected when they were little."

"Ah, *the* glare." Peyton lifted the mug to her lips to blow cool air on the steaming liquid.

"You could have come, Peyton."

"Huh?" Peyton looked over at her.

"To parents' weekend. It's parents' weekend, but it's really a family weekend."

"They asked me not to, Mom. I didn't want to cause any problems for them."

"Bullshit," her mother said. "They didn't want you to take the focus away from them. I understand that; it's their parents' weekend at their school. But they didn't have a problem with your fame and attention about five years ago, when you were spoiling them rotten with trips and new phones and laptops and–"

"They're adults now, though, Mom. They'd grown up with me being famous. They're kind of sick of it, I think."

"Then, cancel that trip you gave them for spring break this year."

"Mom." Peyton chuckled and took a drink.

"Honey, they didn't tell your father and I that they'd asked you not to come. We just assumed you couldn't. Had we known, we would have insisted you come with us."

"It's fine, Mom. It really is a parents' weekend. I'm just the lame older sister," Peyton said, trying to lighten the mood.

Her mother's hand moved to Peyton's back, and she asked, "Is everything okay with you?"

"Sure. Why?" Peyton asked, keeping her eyes down at the counter.

"You've seemed differently lately. Even your father noticed it when you two talked; and he's oblivious most of the time," she said with a little laugh at her husband's expense. "He wanted to come with me, but he couldn't get away from work."

"I'm okay, Mom."

"You were so excited when I talked to you a while ago. Now, I call, and you seem like you have no energy to talk. I guess, the other day, you seemed a little better, but I had already planned to visit."

"A while ago?" Peyton checked. "When?"

"It would have been, I guess, when you went to Hawaii or right after."

"Oh," Peyton looked at her mom for a moment and then back down at the island.

"Oh? Oh, what Peyton?"

"Nothing. I just liked Hawaii. That's why I was excited."

"You've been to Hawaii a million times. I don't remember you getting excited about it."

"Mom…"

"What? Peyton, what?" Her mother rubbed her back a little harder. "Talk to your mother."

Peyton took a deep breath and sat back in the chair, forcing her mom's hand away. Then, she looked over at her mother.

"Mom, I met someone."

Her mother smiled and asked, "You did, huh?"

"I met someone around that time, yes." She paused. "We've gotten close quickly, but nothing's happened."

"So, you were excited about a new guy in your life? Peyton, that's great. Why didn't you say anything?" Her mother took another drink. "Wait…" She set the mug down. "You got excited, and then you seemed distant. Did something happen? Does he not feel the same way or–"

Peyton knew this was one of those important moments in her life where she had to make a choice. She could tell her mother who had been on her mind. She could be honest with her. She could also lie. She could make up some guy that she liked for a minute, tell her mom a story about how he wasn't interested in her in the same way, and use that as an excuse for her recent discontent. She could then tell her mother that she had come out of the whole thing with good songs and that was the reason her mood had turned around.

"Do you remember my friend Dani?" she asked with a hard swallow immediately after.

"Yes, you hardly shut up about her, Peyton." The woman laughed. Then, she looked over at her daughter with wide eyes. "Peyton…"

"I met her the night before Hawaii, Mom. I haven't stopped thinking about her since," Peyton offered. "That's why I've been so off lately."

"Oh, honey." Her mother's hand went to her forearm. "Are you two…"

"No, Mom." Peyton shook her head. "Dani had a boyfriend up until very recently."

"So, Dani's… I don't know how to ask it."

"She's – I don't know. I guess she's straight. I mean, I thought I was, too."

"But you have feelings for her?"

"Mom, I don't know how else to describe it." She smiled at her mother hopefully. "I met her, and it's like it only makes sense to me that we should be together."

"Really?" Her mother's face lit up. "That's wonderful, Peyton."

"Wonderful?" Peyton questioned.

"Peyton, you seemed so happy. That's all I want for you. You know that."

"I do. I do. It's just that she was with someone. I was falling for someone I couldn't have."

"But she's not anymore. Do you think she feels the same way about you?" her mother asked as she used her hand to slide Peyton's rogue wave of hair behind her ear.

"I think so." Peyton enjoyed the feeling of her mother's touch. It always comforted her. "I don't know for sure. We haven't acknowledged that anything is happening."

"But something *is* happening?"

"It feels like it. It feels different than how it is with all my friends now. Some of them are a little on the touchy side. Like, they hold hands or hug each other a lot. I have a lot of European friends that do the cheek kissing thing."

"Okay?"

"I do that stuff, too, sometimes, which is why I wasn't sure at first. But now, how we are together is different to me. We've held hands a couple of times. We hug each other a lot, and we hold on, Mom. We hold onto each other like we don't want to let go. We hold each other sometimes. It's not just a friend thing."

"And you want more?"

"I do," Peyton admitted confidently for the first time out loud. "Mom, I want to be with her." Her eyes welled with tears. "I know this isn't what you expected or–"

"Peyton, don't." Her mother cupped her cheek. "Honey, you've always been way more than what I expected." She winked at her daughter. "And I mean that in the most amazing way possible. If you like this girl, you need to go for it, baby."

Peyton let a few tears fall and said, "What if she doesn't want to just go for it, Mom? I'm a lot to deal with."

"You are a beautiful, smart, kind, caring, funny person. Your job is a lot to deal with, but *you*'re not. If she doesn't want to be with you, Peyton, it won't be because of that. You won't know, though, until you talk to her, will you?"

"I don't want to lose her, though. What if it gets weird after she turns me down?"

"Why are you assuming she will?" her mother asked, removing her hand and taking another drink of her tea all while keeping her eyes on her daughter. She placed the mug back down and added, "You got excited again when she suddenly became single, didn't you?"

"Yes." Peyton laughed through her tears. "It was that obvious?"

"Now it is," her mother replied. "Honey, talk to the girl. Find out if she's in the right place to pursue another relationship. Sure, this one would definitely have its complications. But I don't think there's any complication out there that should prevent two people who care for one another from trying to be together."

CHAPTER 18

DANI WENT FOR her run in the park, but instead of doing it early, as usual, she had decided to sleep in, for once, and do it later in the afternoon. She had gone to the gym around eight and returned home to shower and change. After that, she had eaten a nice lunch she'd prepared herself, gone for the run, then returned home, showered for the second time that day, and decided she'd take her camera for a walk.

As she stared at the camera Steven had bought for her, she wondered about the protocol now. It was a gift. It was an expensive gift, but it was a gift. She knew he wouldn't take it back, but it also felt strange using it now to take pictures of her adventures. She decided she would go out and splurge on a new camera for herself and give this one to her parents. They could use it for their annual Christmas party or maybe give it to her brother. She packed it back up into the nice bag Steven had presented it to her in, and grabbed her purse and jacket.

She had looked up a few camera shops that were near her apartment and decided she would walk to the closest one first. She had no idea what questions to ask. All she knew was that she liked taking pictures, that she went to some of the most beautiful places on earth, thanks to her job, and that she couldn't use Steven's camera anymore. The first shop turned out to be closed, because someone was on a break and put a sign up saying they would be back in thirty minutes. So, she looked up the second closest store, hopped on the subway, and kept her head down once she sat in the car.

It was true that Dani had gotten recognized more recently, thanks to her relationship with Peyton. She wasn't in the mood to deal with that today, though. Today, she just wanted to buy a new camera and take it around the city to see what she could discover. She made her way back up to the street just in time to see a striking woman step out of a black SUV. She smiled at Peyton's overly large sunglasses, as if those would prevent people from recognizing her. She looked down at her own phone in her hand and quickly, without thinking, called her.

"Hey," Peyton greeted.

"Hey. What are you up to?" Dani asked, knowing the answer already after having watched Peyton enter a restaurant, likely for a late lunch or early dinner.

"Taking my mom to *linner*, as she calls it," Peyton answered with a laugh. "We had a brunch today. So, she's just now hungry for lunch."

"Oh, right. I forgot your mom was in town. Sorry." Dani started looking around for the camera shop that should be across the street.

"It's okay. What are you up to?" Peyton asked.

"Not stalking you, I promise." Dani laughed. "I just got out of the subway and saw you walk into the restaurant. That's why I called. I didn't see your mom."

"She's already here," Peyton replied. "One sec." There was a pause. "Mom, can you give me a second?" There was another pause. "You're here?" Peyton asked.

"I'll let you go. I–"

"Dani, join us," Peyton suggested softly.

"For linner?" Dani asked with a smile.

There was a moment where neither of them said anything. Dani held the phone to her face, continuing her smile. She heard some ruffling on the other end of the phone, which caused her smile to disappear.

"I miss you," Peyton said after the rustling died down.

Dani's smile returned, and she replied, "I miss you, too."

"My mom's here. She wants to meet you," Peyton added.

"She wants to meet me?"

"She knows about you," Peyton offered but didn't expound on exactly what her mother knew.

"I don't want to get in the way of your time with your mom, Peyton."

"Please," Peyton requested. "She's leaving tonight. She wants to meet you. She's pestering me right now, trying to get you here."

"Give me the phone," Dani heard another voice say on Peyton's end. "Dani?"

"Yes," Dani replied.

"I'm Peyton's mom."

"Oh, hello." Dani felt her cheeks suddenly blush for no reason.

"You're down the street?"

"I'm at the corner. I just happened to see Peyton get out of the car. I didn't mean to—"

"I'll change our reservation for three. We'll see in you a minute. Peyton?"

"Hey, I'm back," Peyton said through laughter. "Moms, huh?"

Dani laughed and started walking toward the restaurant.

"I'm on my way," Dani told her. "Hey, Pey?"

"Yeah?"

"You look cute in those sunglasses," Dani said with a wide smile and bright red cheeks.

***

"So, you've been modeling even longer than Peyton's been in music?" Peyton's mother asked.

"I've been doing it for as long as I can remember, but I think Peyton's been *in music* since birth from what she's told me." Dani smiled in Peyton's direction. "She showed me that picture of her at, like, a year old, with a wooden spoon and a pot on the kitchen floor."

"She was a terrible drummer," her mother said. "And

she showed you that picture, did she?"

"She did."

"It's not like I was hiding it, Mom. It's on a shelf."

"It's on a shelf in your music room, Peyton." Her mom smiled at her.

"So?"

"I think your mom is referring to the fact that you don't let many people into that room," Dani offered. "You told me that before you opened the door the night you let me see it for the first time."

***

Dani recalled that night. It had been one she'd always remember. After their dinner and before their movie, where she'd had to run out on Peyton for fear she might give herself away, Peyton had walked her down the hallway to the music room. It was the woman's most private place. Dani knew that. Peyton had already explained that only a few people had even seen it. To Peyton, her music was more personal than anything about her. And the space where she created it was more personal than her own bedroom. Dani understood that fact when Peyton opened the door, allowing Dani to walk in before her.

The room wasn't as large as Dani had imagined. It was clean, though, which had surprised her because Peyton had told her how she typically had pages and pages of lyrics all over the floor. That day, though, it was spotless. Dani had walked around the room, noting the instruments, the awards and accolades, but the items that stood out to her the most were the framed photos Peyton had chosen to display in this room out of all of her many, many rooms.

"My dad took that one," Peyton had told her, walking up behind her. "He said that's the first time I ever showed an interest in music."

"Beating a pan with a spoon?" Dani had asked through laughter.

"I had rhythm even back then, baby," Peyton had joked.

"I bet you did," Dani had said, still laughing. "You were cute."

"*Were?*" Peyton asked.

"You still are." Dani had turned to see that Peyton was standing so close, she could reach out and touch her. She could pull Peyton into her, hold her, and never let go. "Don't let it go to your head, though."

"So, I shouldn't let the gold, platinum, and uranium records go to my head?"

"You made up that last one," Dani had fired back.

"It would be cool to have a uranium record, though." Peyton had smiled.

"Couldn't that kill you?"

"Worth it, though, to go out on top," she had replied.

"What's gotten into you tonight?" Dani had asked.

"Nothing. I'm just glad you're here."

"Here for dinner and a movie?" Dani had asked.

"Here in this room, Dani." Peyton had looked around then before returning her eyes to Dani's.

"You seem extra funny tonight."

"Extra funny? Like I'm not normally funny?" Peyton had asked.

"You're normally funny." Dani had nodded. "You're just in a really good mood tonight, and you're extra funny. I like you like this."

"Did you not like me before?" Peyton asked with a lifted eyebrow.

"I liked you before just fine," Dani had said.

"But you like me more now because I'm extra funny?"

"Oh, my God." Dani had shoved at Peyton's shoulder. "Show me the rest of the damn room, Gloss."

***

They all climbed back into the SUV at Peyton's

insistence. Dani had objected, saying Peyton and her mom needed to head to the airport; she would just be getting in the way of their goodbye. But both Gloss women had insisted she join them. Peyton's mother rode shotgun because she got carsick. That left Dani and Peyton in the back of the SUV. As Peyton's mother talked to the driver about the traffic and how terrible it was, Dani and Peyton sat in silence. It was a mix between a comfortable silence and a tense one. Dani hadn't experienced that before and wasn't exactly sure what to do about it now.

"Hey," Peyton whispered close to her ear.

"Hey," Dani whispered back, turning her head to the side toward Peyton.

"My mom likes you. She told me when you went to the bathroom," Peyton whispered.

"She does?"

"She does."

Dani nodded and replied, "Good. I'm glad. I like her, too."

"That's good." Peyton turned to face front. "I like this dress."

The woman's hand found its way to Dani's thigh. Her fingers touched the hem of the dress Dani had chosen to wear on this particularly warm fall day.

"It's soft." Peyton's fingers were on the dress, but they were also grazing Dani's lower thigh near her knee.

"It is, yes." Dani gulped; her breathing sped up. "I got it at that place on fifth," she added.

"Oh, cool." Peyton's fingers were now less on the dress and more on Dani's skin. "It's nice. It looks good on you."

"Thanks. You can borrow it if you want. I think it'll be a little shorter on you." She looked in Peyton's direction, but Peyton was looking down at her own fingers dancing along Dani's skin. "But that could be good because then more of your legs would…"

Peyton's eyes met Dani's. Her fingers stopped moving,

but she didn't remove her hand away. Dani licked her lips, and she watched Peyton do the same in response. Dani's hand slid from the soft car seat between them, to cover the soft skin of Peyton's hand instead. They both continued to stare at one another. Then, Peyton's fingers laced between Dani's.

"So, Dani, what do you have planned for the rest of your evening?"

Peyton's mom's voice broke the moment. Peyton pulled her hand away. Dani straightened her dress with both of her own before placing them in her lap. Then, she looked up at Mrs. Gloss, who had turned just in time to see them separate conspicuously.

"I don't know yet," Dani replied. "I was planning on buying a new camera."

"You have a camera," Peyton pointed out.

"It's the one Steven gave me," Dani said, meeting Peyton's look of confusion. "I don't want to use that one anymore. I want to start over."

"Peyton, you should take her."

"Take her where?" Peyton asked, looking at her mother.

"To buy the camera. You two can go for a stroll and take pictures together."

"Mom, we can't just walk around the city taking pictures. Well, Dani might be able to."

"The shop's closed already anyway. I'm sure there's another one open somewhere, but I'm not really in the mood anymore."

"You're not?" Peyton asked.

"No. I was thinking I'd just have a quiet night in."

Peyton nodded. Dani watched as Peyton exchanged some kind of knowing glance with her mother. Then, the older Gloss woman turned back around to face the road.

"I'm sorry if we ruined your plans," Peyton said softly.

"Peyton, you could never ruin my plans." Dani turned a little to face her. "I was kind of thinking about just going home and doing some research."

"Research?" Peyton asked.

"I've been thinking a lot since I broke up with Steven. I think I always just assumed that one day, I'd move into his place, so I never bothered to find one of my own. I took over the lease on my place because I needed a place to live, but it's never really felt like home to me. I'm making good money now. I want to find something that's just for me." Dani smiled. "I was planning on going home after taking pictures of different neighborhoods I ended up in, and seeing if there were any listings I was interested in checking out later."

"You're going to buy something?"

"Probably. It makes more sense than renting if you can actually afford to do it. I don't know… I just feel like I want something new."

"Because you're starting over?" Peyton asked, but the excitement from earlier was gone from her voice.

Dani wondered where it had gone. The car pulled up at the private plane before she got a chance to ask. Peyton and her mother climbed out. Dani climbed out as well, hugging the woman who had been nothing but kind to her, goodbye before letting Peyton and her mother walk closer to the plane for their private goodbye. Dani watched them talk for a moment; then, she got back inside the car, offering one more wave as she did so. Peyton's mom waved back, gave her daughter another one of those knowing glances, and climbed the stairs to the plane. Peyton stood in the same spot for another moment before returning to the car and getting inside next to Dani.

"I'll take you back to your apartment," Peyton said.

"Do you want to come in when we get there?" Dani asked, hopeful.

"No, I'm kind of worn out from the mom whirlwind tour. I think I'll call it an early night."

CHAPTER 19

PEYTON HADN'T LISTENED to her mother. She had gone back to the studio to lay down some tracks with Matt and another producer she knew and liked. They had managed to knock out two songs in just a few days of work. There would still be some edits made, but Peyton was satisfied with what they had done so far. Her nights were spent talking on the phone to one of her sisters, Lennox, and Dani. It seemed so silly. People talked on the phone when they couldn't see the person they wanted to talk to in person. Peyton could see Dani. She lived a short drive away. They had both been busy, of course, but Peyton knew there was more to it than that.

Her mother had suggested again during their goodbye, that she tell Dani how she felt. Peyton had agreed, to get her mother on the plane, but there was something about hearing Dani talk about needing to find a new place just for herself and her brand-new start that had Peyton concerned. Dani had just gotten out of a long-term relationship. She was in that stage that many people entered post-breakup. Peyton, herself, had been there a few times. She had redone part of her house in Los Angeles once, along with the garden at her Hampton's estate. She had completely torn out the kitchen in her New York house after Trevor, and had it all redone. She had thrown out a lot of her clothes, decided she wanted light instead of dark furniture, and bought a car she had only driven two or three times that she then parked in the garage of her LA home. Dani was going through the same thing. She wanted everything in her life to be new. She wanted to be out there on her own, finding a home, taking her pictures, building her career, and enjoying her life as a single twenty-three-year-old supermodel. Now definitely wasn't the time for Peyton's feelings to get in the way of Dani's desire for change.

"You're quiet," Dani said to her as they entered the unit following the realtor Dani had hired.

"Tired, I guess. I was up late."

"Studio?" Dani asked.

"We got another song done."

"That's great, Pey."

"It's two bedrooms, one and a half bath," the agent said. "No terrace like the last place, but it still has a nice view from the living room windows."

"We'll just walk around for a few minutes." Dani pulled on Peyton's hand, moving them into the unfurnished bedroom. "What do you think?"

"It matters what you think; not me," Peyton replied, enjoying the feeling of Dani's hand in her own.

"You'll be hanging out here if I take this place. You should like it, too."

"Dani, it would be your home. I'd be a guest, at best."

"Please, you lost your guest status a long time ago, Gloss. I'd expect you to get your own damn drinks, help with the dishes, and clean up after yourself." She winked at Peyton.

"If I'm not a guest, then what am I?" Peyton asked through her laughter.

Dani stopped, turned to face her, and said, "You're my favorite person." She bit her lower lip. "And it's important to me that you like this place."

Peyton took a few steps toward her and asked, "Dani, why is it so important to you that I like it?"

"There's a competing offer... So, if you're interested, we should get an offer in sometime today," the agent interrupted.

Peyton's phone rang. She glanced at the readout and gave Dani an apologetic expression.

"Hey, Phil," she greeted her own agent.

"Hey there. So, you'll be happy to know that all your shows for the Asia leg are sold out. We added one more in Hong Kong, and it sold out within a few hours."

"That's great," Peyton replied, watching Dani and the agent continue to examine the apartment.

It was the third apartment she'd gone with Dani to see that day. Dani had asked her friend Jill to help as well, but Jill was out of town for the week, so Peyton had stepped in reluctantly. She didn't want to be a bad friend, but she had such a hard time being around Dani these days as the woman made all these changes. Peyton knew the changes were for the better, but to her, they represented Dani's new, single life. Peyton didn't want Dani to be single anymore. Peyton wanted Dani to be hers.

"The New Zealand and Australia shows are sold out, too. We were thinking about adding one more in Sydney but wanted to get your thoughts since we knew you were taking some time off after that," he said.

"Yeah, that's a few months non-stop," Peyton said, watching Dani turn to listen. "We can do one more, but I don't want to add any more shows after that, okay?"

"Sure, but what if–"

"No, Phil. No more after that. It's already eight months," she said, turning around away from Dani, who had given her an expression of disappointment Peyton couldn't take at the moment. "If we sell out everywhere else, we'll just enjoy that, okay?"

"Okay. But that won't stop the venues from requesting additional dates," he said.

"Tell them there are always other tours," she replied. "I've got to go."

"The tour?" Dani checked.

"Yeah, we sold out in some places. He wants to add a few shows."

"So, you'll be gone longer?" Dani asked.

Peyton followed her out into the living room and

replied, "No, same amount of time. I'll just take a shorter break between countries. It happens."

"Eight months?" Dani stopped at the kitchen sink, turned, and sighed.

"It's not all that long if you think about it," Peyton said, walking closer to her. "In the grand scheme of things, that is."

"It's almost a year."

"Didn't we do this already?" Peyton chuckled as she moved to stand only a foot away from Dani.

"When do you leave?"

"Not for a few months," she replied. "You'll probably be too busy moving into some kick-ass place to even miss me," she joked.

"Impossible," Dani offered softly. "Hey, when can you get away?"

"Away?"

"For the weekend?" Dani asked.

"I guess pretty much whenever right now. I'm in the studio a lot, but I don't have to be there on the weekend. Why?"

"Remember when you invited me to Michigan?"

"I do," Peyton said with a sideways grin. "I remember you turning me down for Martha's Vineyard."

"Can you blame me? Michigan or the vineyard?" Dani held out her hands, palms facing up to the ceiling.

"Steven or me," Peyton added before she could think to stop herself.

"You," Dani replied, placing her hand on Peyton's forearm.

"So, what do you think?" the agent asked from the living room.

"I think I'd like to see some other places." Dani stared into Peyton's eyes. "Have dinner with me tonight?"

"Okay," Peyton said. "Are you sure about this place, though?"

"It would take you, like, forty-five minutes to get here

from your place, even in one of those fancy SUVs of yours." Dani winked at her and moved toward the front door. "Oh, didn't you say Lennox was back in town this week?"

"She's back tomorrow, yeah."

"Jill's back tomorrow, too." Dani held open the door for Peyton. "Maybe the four of us could hang out."

"I'll text Len to see what she's up to," Peyton said, walking past Dani.

"So, are we going to the fourth place I have or…"

Peyton didn't hear the rest of what Dani's agent said because Dani had moved behind her, placing her hands on Peyton's hips, and ushered her in the direction of the elevator while imitating the annoying agent's high-pitched voice, causing Peyton to laugh over the agent's words.

***

"Hey, Pey."

"Hey, Len. What are you up to?"

"Just reading a script for some new pilot in my trailer. It's about zombies."

"Since when do you read scripts for shows about zombies?" Peyton laughed.

"I don't know… This one looks pretty good. They're hoping for a full season pick-up. It's been passed around by a few studios."

"Are you thinking about doing it?" Peyton asked.

"No, I just got a hold of the script. The script is pretty good, though. Hey, have you ever run into Kenzie Smyth on a red carpet?"

"No, I don't think so. Why?"

"No reason," Lennox answered. "I was just watching her show before the script arrived. She's really good."

"If the world only knew that Lennox Owen was just a TV whore," Peyton remarked.

"Please, does anyone know about *your* obsession with reality TV?" Lennox said.

"Your zombie show isn't reality TV?" Peyton joked.

"Not yet," Lennox replied with a laugh. "It's not just about zombies, though. It's about how people would react if—"

"Len, I'd love to talk to you about this like any other time, since I'm sure it's a great show, but I'm trying to invite you to hang out with Dani and I tomorrow night."

"Oh, sure."

"Yeah?"

"I'm free. What did you have in mind?"

"She and her friend Jill."

"I said I'm in, Peyton. Where and when?"

"Tomorrow night at my place?"

"We're not going out?"

"An actress, a singer, and two models out in the city?"

"Right," Lennox replied. "What's the occasion?"

"Why does there have to be an occasion? You know I throw random get-togethers with friends all the time."

"Peyton…"

"I just want you to meet her."

"Who? Jill?"

"No, Dani."

"I met Dani."

"For, like, five minutes."

"So, you want me to meet her for more than five minutes?"

"I want you to stop being such a pain in the ass right now and get to my place tomorrow by six for drinks."

"I'll be there." Lennox laughed.

CHAPTER 20

"DON'T MAKE A BIG DEAL about Lennox, okay? Peyton said she's super down-to-earth and doesn't like it when people make a big fuss."

"Is Peyton giving Lennox the same lecture about me?" Jill asked. "I am a Victoria's Secret supermodel, Dani."

"I don't know. Maybe she is," Dani replied.

"I think Lennox is a good actress, but I don't plan to fawn all over her."

"And don't say anything to Peyton that might tip her off about how I feel or—"

"Are you kidding me? If that girl doesn't know how you feel, she is blind."

"Don't ask to see her music room. If she wants to let you, she will."

"Danielle, I do not care about her music room." Jill paused as she took Dani's hand. "I only care about how she treats you."

"We're not…"

"Yes, you are." Jill rang the doorbell. "You just haven't admitted it yet."

"Hey," Peyton greeted just seconds later when she opened the door.

"Were you there waiting?" Dani teased.

"Maybe," Peyton answered with a smile. "Come on in. I'm still waiting on Lennox."

"She's here," Lennox said from behind Dani and Jill. "Sorry, the car had to park around the corner."

"Get inside before the cameras show up," Peyton said,

motioning for all three of them to enter.

"I just assumed you were staying here, Lennox," Dani said.

"Normally, I would. But I'm actually doing some reshoots in Jersey, so it's easier to stay over there."

"Lennox is not a morning person. She doesn't want to wake up any earlier than she has to," Peyton commented.

"Sounds like someone else I know," Dani said to her as they walked through the foyer in the direction of the kitchen.

"You're only a morning person because you work out," Peyton shot back.

"I *choose* to work out in the morning. I could work out whenever I want. *That* makes me a morning person."

"A morning person is defined by the attitude they possess in the morning," Lennox joined in. "How's your morning attitude?"

"She's just as happy, bright, and chipper as always," Peyton answered on her behalf.

"And I'm not supposed to make a comment about that?" Jill asked Dani in a whisper as they all gathered around the kitchen island.

"Shut up," Dani whispered back.

Peyton moved to stand next to Dani. They went through the basic introductions. Each woman gave the other compliments about their body of work. Dani noticed how Peyton poured her a glass of wine first, sliding it in her direction, before she poured one for herself. Then, she noticed how Peyton sat down on the stool at the island very close to Dani. The other two women talked while standing and snacking on the appetizers Peyton had prepared for several minutes. When they finally moved to the table, it was as a unit, with each woman carrying their own plate. They ate, talked, laughed, and enjoyed the vegetarian meal Peyton had prepared clearly with Dani in mind.

It was easy, Dani thought, to see how someone could fall in love with Peyton Gloss. This woman was one of the most generous people Dani had ever met. Peyton, though not a vegetarian herself, always made completely vegetarian meals for Dani. She always poured Dani's drink before her own. She also made Dani laugh like crazy with some of the strange things she said and did sometimes. She was creative and smart. She was successful, and she still strove for more. Dani watched her as they all headed into the living room for after-dinner conversation.

"It really is a great script," Lennox told Jill. "I don't know how it hasn't been picked up yet, but the pilot script I only got ahold of because of my producer friend, is really good."

"Is she talking about that show again?" Peyton asked, laughing at her best friend.

"Again?" Jill asked.

"She wouldn't shut up about it when I called to invite her over," Peyton added, sitting on the sofa.

"Maybe we should watch it whenever it comes out," Dani suggested. "If it's that good, I mean. I'm not much for horror, though. Peyton can tell you that."

Dani sat next to Peyton on the sofa almost instinctually. Peyton laughed at Lennox – who'd just rolled her eyes exaggeratedly in Peyton's direction, and, at the same time, she wrapped her arms around Dani's shoulders, pulling her into her side. Dani didn't breathe for a moment. She stared at Jill, who only sat down in the chair next to the sofa. The woman lifted both eyebrows in Dani's direction, but didn't say a word. Lennox sat on the other side of the sofa, having left about a foot of space between herself and Dani.

"It's not really horror; that's the thing," Lennox told her.

"Oh, my God! Shut up," Peyton said, laughing wildly at her friend.

"What *are* we going to watch?" Jill asked, changing the subject a little as she continued to look in the direction of Peyton's arm on Dani's shoulder.

"Nothing scary because of this one." Peyton pointed in Dani's direction.

"Hey, you told me you'd protect me," Dani said back, lowering Peyton's pointing finger to her own lap. "You're just going to leave me for the ghosts now?"

"No," Peyton replied with a smirk. "I'm leaving you for the zombies." She used the hand in Dani's lap to tickle the woman's stomach.

Dani laughed. Peyton smiled and laughed along with her. Jill and Lennox looked at each other, rolled their eyes in unison, and then stood at the same time.

"I have to get up early tomorrow. I think I'll just head out," Jill expressed.

"I can drop you off on my way back to Jersey," Lennox said.

"Hey, I thought we were going to hang out." Peyton slowed her laughter, and her eyes lifted to meet Lennox's. "You're leaving, Len?"

"I'm tired. I had a great time, though. Dani, it was nice spending time with you."

Dani stood. She didn't want to leave the comfort of Peyton's touch on the sofa, but she knew she should stand and hug Peyton's best friend, as well as her own, if they were both leaving. Then, Dani wondered if maybe she should be leaving, too.

"We'll walk you guys out," Peyton offered.

Dani smiled, lowering her head to hide it. Peyton didn't want her to go. They walked the two women to the front door where they each hugged one another in turn.

"She's wonderful," Jill whispered into Dani's ear. "Tell the girl how you feel already."

"Shut up," Dani whispered in response. "She'll hear you."

Jill pulled back, winked at her, and said, "Good."

"Good what?" Peyton asked.

"Nothing," Dani answered for Jill quickly.

"I'll call you, Len."

"You better." Lennox kissed Peyton on the cheek. "Good night, you two. Don't stay up too late."

"I won't unless we watch something with zombies in it," Dani said.

"If you do, though, I have the–"

"Okay, Lennox." Jill pulled Lennox down the front steps. "Leave those two alone. You can tell me all about some new zombie show you like."

Dani watched her best friend walk off with Peyton's best friend. There was something nice about that. Peyton closed the door then, leaving the two of them alone in her house.

"I shouldn't stay too long," Dani said into the silence because she was just searching for something to say.

"Why not?"

"You have to work tomorrow."

"You don't," Peyton replied, leaning back against the door, as if trying to prevent Dani from leaving.

"No, I don't."

"What were you planning on doing?"

"Probably just buying that camera and going to take some pictures," Dani shared. "After I work out. Want to come to the gym with me before you go to the studio?"

"No way," Peyton said, walking past her back into the house.

"Come on. Why not?"

"Are you saying I *need* to work out?" Peyton asked in one of her teasing tones that Dani had picked up on and loved.

"You definitely do *not* need to work out," Dani answered, watching Peyton's hips sway in front of her. Had they always swayed like that? "You just don't want to get up early."

"I'll get up early if I'm making you breakfast, but not to go work out with you," Peyton said.

They were in the kitchen now. Peyton started to put away the glasses and extra food. Dani just watched her work, because that comment had her thinking about what it would be like – to wake up next to Peyton after they shared a night together. They would wake up naked because they had gone to sleep naked. Peyton would throw only a t-shirt on and would go down to the kitchen to make Dani one of her famous omelets. It would be delicious to eat and also to watch Peyton cook it, wearing just that t-shirt that probably didn't cover much below her hips.

"I'll help you clean, and then I'll go," Dani said after clearing her throat.

"I'd have to call you another car, since Len and Jill ran off with the one that brought you here."

"Where's the one that brought Lennox?" Dani asked.

"I don't know." Peyton laughed. "I don't keep tabs on them. They're not all my SUVs. It's a company. You know that, right? Lennox has the app and a link to my account. She just called it up before we went into the living room."

"Why don't I get the link to your account?" Dani asked.

"You want the link to my account?" Peyton smirked at her.

"Depends… What do I have to do to get it?" Dani squinted at her as Peyton approached her side of the island.

"Nothing." Peyton shrugged. "I'll give it to you right now." She grabbed Dani's phone off the counter. "Unlock it for me?"

"Pey, I don't–"

Peyton gave her the phone and said, "Just unlock it."

Dani unlocked her phone and passed it back to Peyton, who then downloaded something, entered some information in silence, and passed it back to her.

"Anytime you need it, you may use it." Peyton's bright blue eyes met Dani's green ones. "Do you need it right now?"

Dani swallowed at the implication of Peyton's question, mixed with the woman's beautiful eyes and her questioning expression.

CHAPTER 21

"AND SHE LEFT?" Matt asked.

"Not right away," Peyton said. "She stayed for an episode of *I Love Lucy*. We started watching it from the beginning one time. We watched one, and then she yawned a few times and said she needed to get home."

"You didn't ask her to stay?"

"No, Casanova, I didn't." Peyton strummed her guitar with purpose. "Now, can we get back to this song?"

"The song that's about the girl you're in love with?"

"Yes, okay." She grunted at him.

"Is *she* ever going to hear it?" he asked with a laugh.

"I have no idea, Matthew. I have to finish recording it first," she returned through her teeth.

Peyton's phone rang.

"I thought you kept that thing on silent when you're here."

"I do, but Dani said she–"

"Never mind," Matt replied, waving her off while laughing at her.

"Shut up." Peyton pointed at him. "Hey," she greeted Dani in a softer tone. "I'm in the studio. What's up?"

"Oh, right. Sorry. I was thinking about grabbing Thai food tonight."

"Sounds good," Peyton replied.

Dani laughed and said, "I like how you just assumed I was grabbing Thai food for you there, Peyton."

"Why else would you tell me you were grabbing Thai food?" Peyton smiled warmly. She then looked at Matt, who was laughing silently at her while strumming the notes to *I Will Always Love You* on the guitar. "Also, I may be busy tonight, murdering my producer." She glared at Matt.

"What? What did he do?" Dani chuckled at her.

"He's being a pain in my ass today."

"About a song?"

"Yes, about a song," Peyton lied and pointed at Matt to get him to stop playing that lame love song. "A love song," she added for no necessary reason.

"A love song, huh?" Dani teased.

"Thai food sounds great. Your place?"

"I'm going to, hopefully, find a new place today. But, yes, my current place around seven."

"I'll be there," Peyton said.

"Yeah, you will," Matt added for her.

"What?" Dani asked.

"Nothing. I should go. I have that murdering to get to."

"Oh, hi," Dani said on the other end.

"I think you mean bye, Dani."

"No, I…" Dani started. "Yeah, just one second. I'm talking to Peyton."

"I *am* Peyton."

"Peyton, I'm not talking to you," Dani replied.

"Who are you talking to?"

"Steven."

"Steven? Your ex-boyfriend-Steven?" Peyton asked; her heat was suddenly racing and not in a nice way.

"I just bumped into him on the street." Dani paused and said something Peyton couldn't make out. "I'll see you later, okay?"

"You'll see *him* later… Why?" Peyton asked.

"No, I'll see *you* later. I'm going to talk to *him* right now, okay? Have a good day in the studio and do *not* murder anyone. I cannot eat Thai food for two."

Dani hung up, leaving Peyton to wonder what had just happened.

"You okay?" Matt asked her.

"I don't know. She just ran into her ex on the street and hung up on me to talk to him."

"Is *he* writing her a love song?" Matt asked.

"I doubt it," Peyton replied.

"All the more reasons for you to share it with her when it's done, then."

***

"How's work been?" Dani asked him.

"Good. Busy, but good." Steven ran his hand through his hair.

"Good."

"How's your work going?" he asked back out of obligation.

"Good. I've got some covers coming out soon."

"That's great. I saw the Italian Vogue one when I was there last week," he shared.

"That was a fun one to shoot," Dani said, wondering how they'd even managed a two-year relationship when this was how they talked to one another.

"How's…" He looked around at the people moving briskly past them. "I mean, I assume you're seeing the guy you–"

"Oh, no." Dani stopped herself from adding onto that. "I'm not. I mean, I didn't just–"

"Oh, I guess that's good. I don't know… That's probably a bad thing for me to say."

"It's not. I understand."

"It's weird, not seeing you," he said.

"We hardly saw each other when we were dating, Steven."

Steven sighed and said, "I still have some of your stuff."

"I still have some of your stuff, too. I didn't want to call you since–"

"You turned down my proposal and broke up with me at the same time?" he finished for her.

"Right. That."

"Dani, I…" He met her eyes for the first time in the conversation. "I wanted to apologize to you. I thought about trying to call, but I couldn't bring myself to do it."

"Apologize to me?" Dani asked, confused.

"I messed it up," he replied. "I thought I was losing you, and I needed to do something drastic to keep you."

"Oh."

"Anyway, we were friends for a while."

"We were."

"I'm not ready for that again yet, but maybe someday, we could grab a cup of coffee or something and catch up."

"And maybe someday, I'll meet the woman you do settle down with," Dani added.

Steven smiled, laughed lightly, and said, "Sure. And I won't be at a place where I want to punch the guy that lands you."

"Right," Dani said through clenched teeth. "I have your stuff in a box, and I still have your key."

"I can send my assistant over with your stuff and your key. He can take mine."

"Okay," she replied. "Sounds good."

"I'll text you later to set it up. I've got to run to a meeting."

"Goodbye, Steven."

"Bye, Dani."

***

"You ordered meat?" Peyton asked.

"For you, yes."

"Where's your food?" Peyton pointed to the cartons that all contained meat.

"I made myself rice and tofu," Dani replied.

"Hold on… You got me Thai food but made yourself your own dinner?"

"You like this place," Dani offered in explanation. "I'm not much of a fan, but you like it."

"Dani, you don't have to bribe me with Thai food to get me to come over here."

"I wanted to do something nice for you. Sue me." Dani sat down on the sofa next to Peyton, bringing the plate with her. "Do you want to try some of this?"

Peyton glanced over at cubes of tofu on a bed of steamed rice, and said, "Absolutely not." She looked at the coffee table covered in cartons of Thai food. "And thank you."

"You're welcome," Dani said with a smile.

"So… How was your day?" Peyton asked, beating around the bush instead of asking the only question she wanted to ask.

"Good."

"Just good?"

"Yeah. How's the recording going?" Dani asked, changing the subject and taking an adorable bite of her tofu. "This is good. Are you–"

"I'm sure." Peyton picked her own plate up off the table and spied something by the front door. "What's that?" She nodded toward the box.

"Oh, that's Steven's stuff."

"His stuff?"

"You know, stuff the ex leaves at your place that they have to come pick up? When I ran into him today, it came up. He still has some of my stuff, too."

"How'd that go?" Peyton asked.

"It was okay, actually. He apologized for proposing as an attempt to keep us together. He said we might even be friends one day."

"Oh, really?" Peyton asked, taking a hesitant bite.

"We'll see." Dani smiled at her. "For now, though, he's

sending his assistant to get his stuff and drop mine. It's kind of strange, thinking that today could be the last time I ever see him. I have no idea if we'll find our way back toward friendship. I think I'd be okay if we don't. I think that's a good thing."

Peyton swallowed her bite of chicken and asked, "So, you're all good there? I mean, healed from the breakup? What about the new apartment?"

"What about it?" Dani asked.

"I don't know… It just seemed like maybe you went hunting for a new apartment as a way of coping with the breakup," Peyton suggested.

Dani laughed, lowering her plate to the table, and said, "No, Peyton. I just want a new place. My stuff is starting to outgrow this one. The timing is about the same, but that's just because now, I know I'm definitely not moving in with Steven. I'm healed." She paused and met Peyton's eyes. "I'm ready for whatever comes next."

Peyton licked her lips and asked, "Dani, come to Michigan with me?"

"What?"

"You couldn't before, but come with me now. You brought it up before we had that dinner with Len and Jill."

"I did. I kind of forgot about that."

"Come with me next weekend. Can you?"

"I think so. I need to check my calendar," Dani replied, and Peyton just stared at her. "What?"

"Your calendar is on your phone, Dani. You can check now."

"My phone is in my bedroom, Peyton. Can we at least eat dinner before—"

"Dani, I'm asking you to come away with me," Peyton said and felt the heat creep up her cheeks. "You understand what I'm asking, don't you?"

Dani gave a slight, almost imperceptible nod and said, "I'll grab my phone."

CHAPTER 22

THE LEAVES WERE yellow, red, green, and brown. Dani watched some of them fall to the ground as they walked down the trail. The air was crisp, but not cold. The sun was out, and its rays were bathing her skin in welcomed heat. When they arrived at the Bond Falls – the best waterfall of them all, according to Peyton, Dani let out the breath she had been holding in. She then turned to Peyton and smiled.

"Hey, go under the falls with me," Peyton said, nodding toward the water.

"What?" Dani asked with a laugh.

"You can't most places, but there's a section in the middle where you can get behind it and walk through the water before you run back. It's all smooth rock. And the falls are so loud, they block out all the sound from the world. You could hide back there, and no one would know, with the water as heavy as it is now."

"But we'll–"

"Get totally soaking wet, yes. Come on." Peyton pulled on Dani's hand.

Dani wasn't sure what was happening, but she followed Peyton anyway. They moved to where the falls and the ground met. Peyton removed her shoes and told Dani to do the same. They removed their socks as well, leaving themselves barefoot. Dani glanced around to see if anyone else was doing the same, but they were alone. They had been alone on their entire hike throughout the park. Come to think of it, that was a bit odd. It was a beautiful fall day, yet there was no one around, save the security team they had left in the SUV before beginning their hike.

"Peyton?"

"Yeah?"

"We're alone," Dani said.

"We are."

"*How* are we alone?"

"Oh, I kind of rent the place out whenever I come here. Not the whole state park; just a section. It's expensive, but it's worth it."

Peyton took several steps into the rushing water, holding onto rocks as she moved toward the middle of the falls. The water coated her pants and her flannel shirt instantly. Peyton yelped with the cold of it, but she kept moving. Dani followed her a little more slowly because she had never done this before. She paid attention to every spot Peyton placed her foot on; not wanting to be swept away. When Peyton arrived at the small section hidden by the water, she reached out for Dani's hand. Dani took it and allowed herself to be pulled into the space. She then met Peyton's eyes, suddenly not feeling cold at all.

"Peyton…"

"Dani…" Peyton smiled at her. "We can talk about it later, but now, I just want–" Peyton wrapped her arms around Dani's neck.

Dani stopped breathing. She wrapped her arms around Peyton's waist.

"You know what…" Peyton seemed to be having difficulty speaking the words.

Dani didn't need them. She leaned in, leaving her lips inches from Peyton's, and waited. A moment later, that felt like an eternity, Peyton's lips joined her own. It happened all at once. Dani's hands went into Peyton's semi-wet hair. Her lips parted and welcomed Peyton's between as they started to dance. Dani's hands then returned to Peyton's hips, to pull the woman against herself more fully. Peyton's hands took their turn in Dani's hair. Dani moaned into the kiss. She could have sworn they were at a waterfall, but she couldn't hear the sound of the water rushing over the rocks anymore. She could only hear the sounds of their hearts beating in time as they continued to kiss. They pulled back for just a moment. Dani's eyes met Peyton's. Dani could see Peyton was breathing just as hard as she was. Then, Peyton moved into her space even more than Dani thought was possible. Her body was pressing Dani's into the back of the smooth rock wall. Everything that had never made sense to Dani about love, finally did, because kissing Peyton Gloss was what she'd been missing in her life.

***

Dani moaned as Peyton opened her mouth to her. Dani did the same. Their tongues met, and Peyton moaned; Dani was so soft. All of her was soft. But that was the thing about Dani: not all of her was actually soft. Damn, Dani had muscles. Peyton's hands moved to Dani's abdomen. She felt the muscles contract at her fingertips and realized then how strong Dani was, too. Dani's tongue was perfect. Had Peyton ever described a tongue as perfect? Well, it was doing all kinds of things to her own tongue, to her lips, to her entire mouth. Then, it wasn't there anymore because it was on Peyton's jaw. Dani's mouth was on her neck next. Her tongue licked before her lips sucked on Peyton's pulse point.

"Oh, God," Peyton muttered, pressing Dani even more against the rocks.

"Is this okay?" Dani asked in a whisper at Peyton's ear. "Should I–"

"Stop? No, you should never stop."

Peyton's hands moved up Dani's shirt that now clung to her wet body. She stopped at Dani's bra, not exactly knowing what she should do next. As she felt Dani's lips suck on her earlobe, Peyton's legs nearly buckled beneath her. Dani turned them around, pressing Peyton against the rocks instead, as if she knew that Peyton needed that support. Dani's arms moved back to her waist. She held onto Peyton like her life depended on it. Maybe it did. Maybe Dani's life depended on holding Peyton just like this, because it definitely felt to Peyton like *her* life depended on it. Peyton held onto Dani's neck as Dani's hands moved under Peyton's shirt. They stalled – just as Peyton's had done on Dani's skin, just under Peyton's bra. Dani's lips were on her collarbone. No, they were on the other side of Peyton's neck. God, they were everywhere.

"Peyton, I–"

"I know," Peyton said when Dani couldn't finish.

She grasped Dani's face and held it between her hands, meeting Dani's gorgeous green eyes. Dani nodded. They both needed an opportunity to catch their breath because Peyton wasn't certain either of them had taken a breath since the moment their lips first met.

"What are we doing?" Dani asked as Peyton looked into her eyes.

"What we've both wanted to do since that night."

"The night we met?" Dani asked.

"Yes," Peyton replied, knowing they'd both felt this way since the moment they'd laid eyes on one another.

"Can I…"

Dani's hand met the bra clasp on Peyton's back and stilled. Peyton ran her hands up and down Dani's chest but didn't touch her breasts with any pressure. She still could feel Dani's nipples harden, and with that, Peyton looked up to meet her eyes again.

"Dani, I've written so many songs about you… And after that kiss, I feel like I could write about a hundred more."

"You've written songs about me?" Dani asked with the most beautiful smile on her face. "Really?"

"And I didn't even need a rhyming dictionary."

Dani laughed and said, "I want to hear them all."

She reached under Peyton's shirt again and ran her hands up and down Peyton's back. It was then that Peyton realized that her bra had been unclasped by the expert hands of the woman she was currently staring at.

"Dani, I want to do what I think we were about to do."

"Me too," Dani said.

"I want to, but we can't here," Peyton replied, hoping she could get this out right.

"Why not?" Dani asked, looking concerned with her arched eyebrows. "We're alone."

"God, you're sexy," Peyton said, leaned in, and kissed Dani quickly before pulling back. "All I want is for you to take my shirt off and touch me. I've thought about it so much since we met."

"Peyton, I came here with the intention of telling you how I feel; and showing you, too. I think I can safely say I've done that." Dani chuckled. "We just climbed off the plane, went to your rental, and changed to come out here. I didn't expect us to end up making out under a waterfall before we talked about what's been going on between us." She paused, took a sweet kiss from Peyton's lips, and added, "I think we should go on a date."

"A date?" Peyton laughed. "You realize that if you and I ever went on a date in public, the internet would likely explode."

"No, it wouldn't." Dani laughed.

"Dani, have you not seen the stuff that's already online about us?" Peyton asked.

"A little. They're calling us *Deyton*." Dani laughed.

Peyton found her to be perfect in that moment; and pretty much every other one, too. She moved Dani's hair behind the woman's ears and smiled. Then, she leaned in and kissed her.

"We can fall asleep next to each other tonight. Wake up next to each other tomorrow." She kissed Dani's neck. "We can have our first date here in private. I'll cook for you." She kissed Dani's collarbone. "And after that…"

"We can fall asleep next to each other again?" Dani asked softly.

"Among other things." Peyton swallowed hard at the thought of what those *other things* might be, and how good they would feel.

CHAPTER 23

DANI WAS STARING. She knew she was. She knew it was probably weird, but she didn't care. She'd risk Peyton calling her weird.

"You're staring, aren't you?" Peyton muttered against her pillow.

"Yes," Dani replied through a smile.

"You stare at me a lot, Wilder," Peyton said.

"I do," Dani offered. "But you're very pretty, Gloss. What am I supposed to do? Not look at you?"

Peyton opened her eyes.

"God, they're so blue."

"You're so sweet, you know that?" Peyton rolled over onto her back. "I knew that before, but – I don't know – you're sweeter now, I think."

"I'm just able to say what I want to say to you now, so it seems that way," Dani replied, snuggling into Peyton's side and resting her head on Peyton's chest.

"This feels good, Dani," Peyton said as she ran her hand up and down Dani's arm.

"It does," Dani agreed. "Hey, Pey?"

"Yeah?"

"I liked falling asleep next to you last night."

"I liked it, too," Peyton replied.

Dani pressed a light kiss to Peyton's neck and said, "I'm going to go downstairs and make *you* breakfast for once. Then, I'm going to take a shower. Why don't you hop in now, while I cook?"

"Why am I showering?" Peyton asked. "We can just lie in bed all day, Dani. We don't have to go anywhere until our flight back tomorrow." She pulled Dani in tighter.

"I just thought we could enjoy the outside again today. It's so beautiful out there. We can't really do that in New York without people recognizing us."

"Oh." Peyton ran her hand over Dani's arm that was on her stomach. "I guess you're right."

"And I got you something. I kind of forgot to give it to you yesterday." Dani slid quickly out of bed.

"Hey, you were warm," Peyton said loudly.

"I'll be right back." Dani chuckled, moved into the closet, and pulled out two items. She moved back into the room, placed the identical bags on the bed, and said, "One for each of us."

"Those are camera bags, Dani," Peyton pointed out, sitting up at the same time.

"And we have photography lessons coming up, Peyton." Dani lifted one of the bags and passed it to Peyton. "I picked one out for myself that had great reviews. The guy at the store said it would work well for landscape photography. I got one for you, too. There's a lot of landscape outside." She smiled at Peyton, who looked adorable with her bedhead. "I thought we could have a daylong date. Breakfast here, followed by a long, romantic hike where we take beautiful pictures, and no one disturbs us. We could have lunch, that we pack and bring with us, and the same romantic hike back. Then, we could–"

"Have dinner?" Peyton asked.

"Yes," Dani said.

"And after dinner?" Peyton lifted an eyebrow.

"I guess we'll have to see, won't we?" Dani teased.

"You bought me a camera?" Peyton stared down at the bag.

"I wanted to share something I love with the person…" Dani stopped and unzipped her own camera bag. "I thought it would be fun. I would have gotten them out yesterday, but you whisked me away the moment we got here."

"I didn't hear you complaining when we were making out under that waterfall," Peyton argued.

"Maybe if you stop being so sassy this morning, you'll get another make-out session under a waterfall today," Dani suggested.

"I'll save my shower for after the hike, then." Peyton moved to kneel on the bed, wrapping her arms around Dani's neck. "Just in case dinner goes really well." She kissed Dani's lips, pulled back, and added, "Any chance you're up to bring me breakfast in bed, though?"

"Oh, I'll bring you breakfast in bed." Dani shoved Peyton back on the bed and climbed on top of the now giggling woman.

***

With their cameras charged and lunch packed, they set off around ten for the woods behind the rental house. It was the same one Peyton had rented before, but somehow, with Dani here, it felt completely different. When Peyton had been here before, she had been lonely and worried she'd fallen for a woman who'd marry someone else. Now, she was holding Dani's hand whenever the woman wasn't taking a picture of the colorful trees, wildlife, and Peyton herself.

"Dani, stop it. That camera is for landscapes," Peyton said, holding up her hand in front of the camera Dani had aimed at her.

"There's a landscape behind you," Dani countered. "It might be blurry in the photo, though, since I'm putting the focus on you."

"Awe, isn't that sweet?" Peyton teased.

"Peyton Gloss, shut up and smile at this camera so I can get a good picture of you today," Dani ordered with a giggle she couldn't contain.

Peyton stopped complaining. She stood in front of a tree that had all red leaves. Dani clicked a few times before she looked at Peyton – no longer through the camera – and smiled at her.

"Hey, Dani?" Peyton asked.

"Yeah?" Dani asked back hopefully.

"There's a spider right behind you on–"

"Shit! What? Fuck." Dani ran toward Peyton, turning her head back as if the spider was chasing her.

Peyton laughed so hard, she felt the tears well in her eyes.

"Oh, my God. That was hilarious," she said through her laughter. "You ran all the way over here."

Dani glared at her and asked, "Was there no spider, Peyton?"

"I don't know. There are probably a million spiders out here. We're in the woods."

"I'm going to kill you," Dani said.

"It's still hilarious." Peyton continued to laugh as Dani walked away down the path they'd been on. "Wait! Dani, hold on. I'm coming." She walked briskly in an attempt to catch up.

"No, you're not," Dani said. "Not tonight anyway."

"Wait… What?" Peyton asked, stopping in her tracks.

***

"You'd never kissed a woman, right?" Dani asked her.

"When would I have kissed a woman, Dani?" Peyton asked back through her laughter.

"I don't know. I haven't known you all that long," Dani fired back.

They were sitting on the ground outside the house. The air was chilly now. Dani was sitting behind Peyton, with the shorter woman between her legs. Peyton had actually built them a small fire in the pit behind the house. They had hot chocolate, blankets, a fire, and conversation. It was quite possibly the best night of Peyton Gloss's life.

"You are the only woman I have ever kissed, Dani Wilder," Peyton replied, running her fingertips over Dani's arms on her stomach. "How many women have you had your mouth on?"

"Peyton, that sounds gross," Dani said through her own laughter this time. "I've only ever kissed you."

"That's kind of nice, huh?" Peyton asked.

"I'd hope so."

"No, I just mean that we're each other's firsts. That's nice," Peyton offered.

"Well, that's an interesting topic," Dani said.

"What is?"

"Our firsts."

"Oh, I guess it is," Peyton replied.

"What's wrong?"

"Nothing. Why?" Peyton tensed a little in Dani's arms.

"I can tell something's wrong. Plus, you just tightened every muscle in your body, Pey."

"Nothing's wrong exactly. I just realized that we still have a lot of talking to do."

"Well, yeah."

"No, Dani. We've talked a lot since we met, but these things aren't just topics that friends share with one another now. I'm crazy about you." Peyton smiled, leaned back against Dani's shoulder, and added, "That means there are things we need to talk about."

"Like, who we've been with. Peyton, I've only ever been with Steven," Dani said softly. "He and I just met when I was so young."

"And he's your only?" Peyton asked.

"I think you might be my only now," Dani said with a smile.

"That was a good one," Peyton replied with a light laugh.

"Steven is the only person I've had sex with. He was my third kiss, though," Dani offered. "I kissed a boy named

Kevin in junior high twice."

"Oh, should I be worried about this Kevin?"

"No, but maybe worry about Daryl."

"Who's Daryl?" Peyton turned all the way around then.

"The boy I made out with in high school, after prom."

"Only made out? I thought all kids lost their virginity after prom," Peyton said, facing her fully now.

"You never went to prom, did you?" Dani must have just realized. Peyton shook her head. "I'm sorry, Pey."

"The make-out session was that good?" Peyton teased.

Dani laughed and said, "Not even close. It was sloppy, at best. I ended it and went home with my friend. We spent the rest of the night talking and eating junk food."

"That sounds like fun," Peyton replied.

"It was. I'm sorry you missed out on that stuff." Dani reached for Peyton's cheek and stroked it with the back of her hand. "You're so beautiful, Peyton."

"Did you have any idea?" Peyton asked, needing to know.

Dani stared at her knowingly for a moment and answered, "I had no idea. You kind of snuck up on me."

"You snuck up on me, too."

"No, I mean you literally snuck up on me. You came up from behind me at the party."

"Oh." Peyton laughed before she took Dani's hand and kissed the palm. "I told Lennox that I wanted to meet you. I didn't know why at the time. After I performed, I went backstage. I planned to just go home. I was exhausted. Lennox was only in town for a bit, and I wanted to spend as much time with her as I could. Then, I saw you." Peyton stared into green eyes that had reds, oranges, and yellows from the fire dancing in them. They reminded her of the trees surrounding them in the backyard. "I had to meet you."

"Why?"

"I had no idea." Peyton laughed. "I knew who you

were. I've seen the commercials, the pictures, the damn billboards, Dani. That one where you're in lingerie in the middle of Times Square is particularly memorable. I'm not going to lie to you… It kind of sucks that the entirety of New York City has seen you in your underwear and I haven't."

"Well, you have," Dani began. "I mean, you saw the billboard."

"Did Daryl get to see you in your underwear?" Peyton asked with a lifted eyebrow.

"No. But he did get to see me in a bright pink prom dress with ruffles up top."

"Oh, I need pictures."

"No way. I want you to *want* to be with me."

"No chance in changing that," Peyton told her. Then, she smiled and added, "I wanted to meet you that night, Dani. I don't know – I was compelled to approach you. I saw you in a flash after I went backstage. I told Len I wanted to grab something to drink really quick. She warned me that I might have to take pictures or answer questions if I didn't just leave, but I had to talk to you. Then, you and I were talking, and that was it. I don't think I stopped smiling until I dropped you off at your place after Hawaii."

"Why'd you stop smiling then?" Dani asked.

"Because you were going to see him. You had a boyfriend." Peyton shrugged her shoulders.

"Pey, I'm yours now. I think I have been since we met."

Peyton ran a finger along Dani's jaw.

"I've been with more than one person, Dani."

"I guess we're going back to that," Dani replied and watched Peyton's finger as it slid down to her collarbone. "Oh."

"You probably knew that already. My relationships haven't exactly always been private."

"You don't have to–"

"Three guys. I've been with three guys." Peyton

followed the movement of her own fingertip as it slid down to the space between Dani's breasts. "I was nineteen when I was with Wallace Hollowell. That didn't end well. The tabloids went crazy when we broke up, but he was on the number one TV show at the time. When I was with Michael, his career was just taking off. We met on tour when he was opening for me. It was fun at first, and then it was nice to just have someone on the road with me like that. He cheated on me with one of his backup singers. That ended that." Peyton paused as she tugged forward on Dani's T-shirt a little with that finger. "And you know about Trevor."

"I do," Dani said and swallowed so hard, Peyton could feel it.

"None of them have ever made me feel like what I feel when I'm with you, Dani." Peyton tugged again. "Dani, I want you. I want to be with you."

"I want that, too."

"I want you now," Peyton said, meeting Dani's eyes. "If you want to wait, we can wait. We can go inside and fall asleep next to each other. But, Dani, I wanted you at the waterfall yesterday. I wanted you last night, when we were making out in bed. I wanted you today, when we were on our hike, and then again, when we stopped to eat lunch, and we sat there for a while just like this. I want you now."

Dani didn't say anything for a minute. Peyton worried she had said something wrong. Maybe she was taking things too fast. She should slow them down. She could wait for her. She *would* wait for her. What she felt for Dani was worth everything to her. Dani didn't say anything in that moment where Peyton's heart almost pounded out of her chest. Instead, she just lay down on the blanket and reached for Peyton.

CHAPTER 24

DANI WATCHED AS PEYTON moved on top of her. They'd been in this position before. Last night, Peyton had climbed on top of her in much the same way. They had held one another and kissed one another, but both of them knew nothing else would happen. They had agreed that tonight would be their first official date. What a date it had been. They had spent the entire day together. They had shared another dinner at a table with candles Peyton had packed with her. After that dinner, they'd opted to come outside and enjoy the night air and the fire. Dani knew they were about to take a step that neither of them had ever taken; that neither of them had ever thought they would take. Peyton hovered over her. She licked her lips. Dani licked her own subconsciously in response.

"Are you sure?" Peyton asked softly.

Dani nodded, wrapping her arms around Peyton's neck.

"I thought about doing this at the waterfall," she admitted in a whisper.

Peyton smiled and said, "Me too."

"Really?" Dani asked back. "I wasn't sure if you'd actually go through with it."

"I would have, but we started talking. And I think it's possible that that's going to happen now, unless I stop it by kissing you because I really, really want to kiss you right now, Wilder," Peyton said all that very quickly before she lowered her lips to an inch away from Dani's.

"Then, shut up and kiss me, Gloss."

Peyton connected their lips. Dani felt the same thing she felt every time she kissed Peyton. She had never felt that in any of the kisses she had shared with her long-term boyfriend. She thought, in the back of her mind, as Peyton's tongue slid into her mouth, that she should probably think about how that had happened. She had always considered herself to be a straight woman. But, God, the way Peyton touched her without actually touching her, had Dani rethinking that theory.

Her hands were not hesitant. They were searching. They were searching with determination. They slid under Peyton's shirt, unclasped her bra as if she'd done that a million times, and rubbed up and down Peyton's back quickly because she couldn't wait to feel that expanse of skin. It dawned on her then that she probably had undone a hundred bras or bikinis for other models when they'd had to do quick changes at runway shows. Dani smiled through the kiss at that realization. Peyton pulled back for a second.

"What?" Dani asked.

"You're smiling," Peyton said.

"You're beautiful," Dani replied, choosing not to bring up what she had really been thinking about.

Peyton leaned back down and reconnected their lips. Dani sucked Peyton's tongue into her mouth, earning a light moan from Peyton that she barely heard from the crackling fire behind them but knew it had happened because she'd heard that same moan last night when they'd made out for hours. Peyton's lips moved to her neck. Dani knew Peyton had already left a mark there – she had noticed it this morning when she had looked into the bathroom mirror, but Peyton was working the same spot in an attempt to make it even darker. She was claiming her. Peyton Gloss was claiming Dani as hers. There was something very sexy about that. Dani grew wetter at the sound Peyton made when she pulled back. It was almost a guttural moan at the same time as Dani's hand slid up the front of Peyton's shirt and cupped her breast under her bra.

Dani squeezed lightly, watching Peyton lift up to straddle her. Peyton pulled off her own shirt. Dani watched the movement; she watched Peyton toss it beside their blanket. She also noticed that her hand was still cupping

Peyton's breast. It was then that it really hit her: they were about to have sex. She was about to touch another woman in her most intimate places. Peyton was going to do the same. And by the way Peyton was reaching for Dani's sweatpants, Peyton was going to do it first.

"Peyton, hold on a second," Dani said through rapid breathing.

Peyton stopped trying to pull Dani's pants off instantly, met her eyes, and said, "Do you want to stop?"

Dani smiled up at her and replied, "No, I just want you to take your bra off first."

Dani removed her own hand and pulled Peyton's already unclasped bra off the woman's body. She then looked up at Peyton's breasts for the first time. Dani had seen a lot of breasts in her time. She had been modeling for as long as she could remember. She had seen them at various stages of development. Never before had she wanted to touch them, taste them, and explore them. She reached for Peyton's hips, pulling Peyton more firmly into her, sat up, and kissed the space between them. Her lips tingled a little. She was sure that was partly out of pleasure, but also out of nervousness. She had never done this after all. What was she supposed to do now?

Peyton's hands moved into her hair, which Dani had left down after she had showered and dried it. Dani's lips connected over and over with Peyton's skin, but in the same spot. Peyton lifted Dani's face up to get Dani to look at her. She leaned down and kissed her. Then, she lowered Dani's head to her breast as if knowing Dani needed that from her. Dani's mouth opened, and she sucked a hard nipple into her mouth.

"Oh," Peyton let out. "That's…" Dani sucked harder. "Yes," Peyton whispered.

Dani knew she was doing something right then. She moved one of her hands to Peyton's other breast and squeezed tentatively. Peyton made a few more sounds, causing Dani to reach with her free hand for Peyton's sweats. She tugged on them, pulling them around Peyton's thighs, wanting all of Peyton at once. Peyton reached down to her own pants and continued to push them down her thighs until they were at her knees.

"Peyton…" Dani muttered when she pulled back to look at the woman kneeling in front of her.

Peyton was topless. Her pants were down as far as they could go without her having to move. Her underwear was slightly mussed but still covered her skin. Dani met Peyton's eyes then. Peyton looked vulnerable yet determined at the same time. Her eyes were dark. Her lips were swollen. Dani lay back down and reached for Peyton. She pulled her down by the neck, begging silently for the woman to take her. Peyton worked against Dani for only a moment to pull her pants off entirely before she lowered back on top of her, clad only in her underwear. Dani wasn't sure if they were a pale color or just white. The light outside was gone, save the porch light several yards behind them. The fire on the other side wasn't offering her any clarity, but the feel of Peyton on top of her like this, made that little fact completely unimportant.

Peyton's hands slid under Dani's shirt. She lifted it up high. Then, she pushed the cups of Dani's bra up over her breasts. Peyton's mouth was on the right nipple in an instant. Dani held back the sound she wanted to make. It would have been too loud. They were alone, but practically screaming at Peyton's first touch to her breast might cause Peyton to rethink the rest of this night entirely. Peyton sucked. She licked. She played using her teeth. Then, she moved to the next breast to repeat the action. Dani wanted her shirt off. She wanted that bra gone. She maneuvered up enough to remove both before lying back down. Peyton lowered her lips to her side. She kissed down it slowly while squeezing Dani's breast. She moved to Dani's abdomen. Dani watched as she kissed over the rigid muscles there. Peyton smirked up at her before she licked around Dani's belly button. Dani wanted to scream again but held it in.

Peyton lowered her lips further until she reached the waistband of Dani's sweats. Without looking up, she pulled down on them, removing them entirely, and tossing them on top of her own. She moved back on top of Dani and pressed their bodies together.

"Jesus, Dani," she said. "What is this?" she asked, kissing Dani's forehead, her nose, her lips, and her jawline. "I can't get enough of you. I've never wanted this so much."

"Me neither." Dani pulled back to look at Peyton. She then looked up into those perfect blue oceans and said, "Take them off."

"Whose?" Peyton asked with a short laugh, knowing Dani was talking about underwear.

"Take everything off, Peyton. Make love to me." She watched Peyton's expression turn serious again. "Please."

Peyton nodded, kissed her, and moved to kneel in front of her. She ran her fingertips over Dani's skin before she reached for the underwear that was the final barrier between them. She removed Dani's first, dropping them onto the growing pile. Without looking down, she stood and removed her own, placing them on top of that same pile. She knelt again. Then, she looked.

"Oh, wow." She sighed as she reached for Dani's knees, which Dani had bent and pressed together out of nervousness. "Can I see you?"

Dani nodded. Peyton spread her legs with ease once Dani's tension released at the feel of Peyton's fingers on her skin. That first time they'd touched at the party, Dani had known Peyton would be someone that would both excite and calm her at the same time. She had no idea how she'd known that then, but as Peyton moved to settle on top of her, Dani knew she'd been right. She knew this woman on top of her was right. Her nerves wouldn't go away. This experience wasn't just the first time she would sleep with a woman. It was, quite possibly, the first time she'd make love with *her* person.

Peyton kissed her. She slid her tongue over Dani's

bottom lip, followed by the top. She slid it inside then, and Dani almost moaned. Peyton nibbled on Dani's lip. She lowered her mouth to Dani's neck again, content in taking her time. Dani wasn't sure she had any time left. Peyton's hips were slowly starting to rock into her. With Dani's legs spread, she could feel Peyton's center pressed into her own. She could also hear Peyton's little gasps, sighs, moans, and small squeaks that were adorable. Then, she heard Peyton grunt slightly as her hips rocked a little harder. Dani felt Peyton's wetness that had coated the coarse blonde hair between her thighs. Dani knew she was wet as well. She wasn't sure how much longer she could take the feeling – as good as it was, without Peyton touching her.

"Pey, I need…"

Peyton reached between them, cupping her. Then, she spread Dani's lower lips, just knowing that was what she should do, apparently, in that moment. Dani had no idea what *she* was supposed to be doing. She felt Peyton rock harder after she spread her own lips. They were touching. Every single part of their bodies, of their minds, hearts, and souls were touching. It was the most truthful moment of Dani's entire life. She looked up past Peyton into the stars she wasn't entirely sure were real. She was definitely seeing stars, though, because Peyton's wetness was mixing with her own. Dani's clit was touching Peyton's, and Peyton's was hard. Damn, Peyton's clit was hard, she realized.

"Dani, I want…"

"Anything," Dani replied, holding onto the back of Peyton's head.

Peyton looked down at her, nodded a tiny nod, kissed her, and rocked harder.

"I might…"

"It's okay," Dani said.

"No, I want you to come. I want to come with your hands on me."

"Okay," Dani replied. "Can you stop doing what you're doing?"

"I don't want to. I want all of it," Peyton said, rocking harder.

"Oh, hell." Dani pressed down on Peyton's ass, cupping her cheeks and encouraging her to continue.

"That's not helping," Peyton said.

"Yes, it is. Come like this. I *am* touching you, Pey. All of me is touching all of you."

Peyton then reached down between them. She began stroking Dani. Two of her fingers were running along either side of Dani's clit. Dani wanted to scream, but she held back.

"Come with me," Peyton said.

"Okay," Dani replied.

Peyton stroked her fully now. She stroked her fast, slow, fast again, and then harder. When she moved one finger inside, Dani held back another scream. Peyton continued to move her hips, but Dani realized she had lost her friction since she'd focused her attention on stroking Dani. Dani reached down and stopped Peyton's hand. She pulled it up and moved her own between them. She stroked Peyton twice before she reached to spread her lips. Peyton took the hint and lowered herself again. Dani spread herself wider for her. Peyton rocked. Dani was ready to burst. She wanted to do this always. She wanted to watch Peyton take her pleasure and to bring Dani to the brink always.

"Oh, God," Peyton said as she came.

Her hips thrashed, to the point Dani wasn't certain anything was actually touching anything. But watching this woman come above her, made it impossible for Dani not to come. Her own clit was hard and aching and ready. She came when Peyton kissed her lips hard. Then, Peyton was moaning against her lips with the intensity of her orgasm. Dani moaned back loudly, not able to keep it in. When Peyton's mouth pulled back, Dani finally screamed.

CHAPTER 25

"ARE YOU COLD?" Peyton asked moments later as she lay next to Dani, stroking her stomach slowly and staring at the beautiful nude woman beside her.

"I'm okay. Are you cold?" Dani asked back.

"No," Peyton replied. "It is getting kind of chilly, though. The fire's dying."

"Do you want to go inside?"

"No," Peyton said and noticed Dani was staring up at the night sky. "Are you okay?"

Dani's head turned immediately as she said, "Yes. Are you?"

"You've had a lot of major life events happen in the past few weeks. Well, most of them were just this weekend. I want to make sure you're okay."

Dani rolled onto her side and placed a hand on Peyton's cheek. She leaned over and kissed her. Then, she rolled a smiling Peyton onto her back and climbed on top of her.

"I'm okay, Peyton. What we've experienced since the moment we met, is something I couldn't deny anymore."

"And you liked what we did tonight?" Peyton asked, risking the possibility of a negative response but needing to know.

"I *loved* what we did tonight, Peyton. It's us." Dani ran her fingers up to Peyton's still hard nipples and stroked them. "I'm going to like what we do next, too."

"Yeah?" Peyton asked with a sly grin.

"Definitely," Dani said. "But, please don't worry about everything else, okay? At least, not tonight. Tomorrow, we can talk or try to figure this whole thing out, but tonight is just for us to be together this way."

Dani leaned down and sucked a nipple into her mouth. Peyton let go that little bit of tension she had been holding onto since they had both come down from their first orgasm. Dani tortured her slowly, but Peyton loved every minute of her soft touches. Some were hesitant, like, when Dani kissed just below her belly button. Others were firmer. Then, Dani nipped at the skin around Peyton's hip bone. When Dani's lips lowered still, to just on the inside of her thigh, Peyton wondered if Dani planned to stay down there or would, again, turn hesitant and return to kiss her lips.

Dani spread Peyton's legs with both hands. She stared down at Peyton's center that Peyton knew was still wet. She had come down from her first orgasm, but her body craved another. Dani touched her just enough to spread her lips and met her eyes for a moment. She then looked down again. Peyton watched as Dani lowered herself, spreading Peyton's legs further. That was when Dani's mouth met Peyton's center, and Peyton Gloss saw God.

"Dani… Oh! Wow!"

Peyton lifted her head, placing her arm under it in order to watch Dani Wilder go down on her. Dani's mouth was hesitant only for a moment. Then, her tongue moved around Peyton's clit. Her fingers kept Peyton spread wide enough so she could suck on her clit. Peyton could only keep her eyes open for another moment before she removed her arm from behind her head and, instead, placed it on the back of Dani's, encouraging her to continue. Dani did continue. She continued to take Peyton even higher than she had gone moments before. She sucked on her clit until Peyton's hips lifted higher and higher, and Dani had to reach over Peyton's stomach to lower her back down to the ground. Peyton came hard. She rocked against Dani's flat tongue, pressed to her clit, and then her hips crashed back to the ground.

Dani kissed her clit. She kissed the inside of Peyton's thighs. Then, she slid back up Peyton's body. She kissed Peyton's lips, sliding her tongue inside Peyton's mouth and allowing Peyton to taste herself. Peyton could hardly catch her breath, but she knew she needed to touch Dani again. She reached down between Dani's legs, and just as she had done earlier, she slid one finger inside her. Dani, caught off guard, detached her lips from Peyton's. Peyton stared up at her. She pulled her finger out, and recognizing Dani could handle more, pushed two inside her. Dani allowed her body to take Peyton in. She sat up, straddling Peyton, and slowly started to move.

Peyton watched as Dani rocked from side to side, forward and back, and then, she did this figure-eight thing that had Peyton mesmerized. Dani started rocking harder the moment Peyton used her thumb against Dani's clit and her free hand on Dani's nipple. Dani's green eyes were open; staring down at her. Peyton stared back, imploring Dani to feel good at her touch. Dani's eyes closed as she started to climb. Peyton sat up then. She took Dani's nipple into her mouth and used her free hand to hold Dani in place against her. She needed that closeness as Dani came again, screaming Peyton's name into the night.

"We have to go inside now," Peyton said several minutes later.

"Why? It's so nice out here. This is where we made love for the first time," Dani replied, holding onto Peyton.

"I know. I was there," Peyton said.

"Do you want to put more logs on the fire? We've run out of wood. We could ask one of the security guys to go scavenge for us, but I don't like the idea of them seeing us naked, and I don't want to put clothes on," Dani replied.

"Well, I do like the idea of you not putting clothes on," Peyton replied and snuggled more into Dani's side. "Just a little longer?"

Dani sensed there was something more to Peyton's desire to stay outside. It was pretty chilly now that the fire had all but died. They had a blanket over them and their body heat, but Dani's feet were sticking out of that blanket, thanks to her 6'1" height, and she was starting to forget what her toes felt like.

"Is everything okay?" she asked.

"It's just magical out here," Peyton replied. "We had this perfect day, Dani. I woke up with you in my bed. We went hiking through the woods. We were all alone. No one asked me for an autograph or a picture. Security could back off because of it. We made out in the woods and held each other after a picnic." She chuckled softly against Dani's skin. "And we came back here, made a meal together, ate it, and came out here to sit by the fire and talk."

"We did more than talk," Dani said, kissing the top of Peyton's head.

"And all of it was so perfect."

"You're worried if we go inside, it will be less perfect?"

"I'm worried the world is going to get us." Peyton sighed. "We left our phones in there for a reason, remember?"

"Peyton, we said we'd talk about all that stuff tomorrow."

"It is tomorrow, technically."

"It's late. We've had a long, amazing day. Let's go inside and get some sleep. We can have breakfast in bed again when we wake up late. We can talk more about all this stuff."

"Just a little bit longer out here, okay?" Peyton requested.

Dani kissed the top of her head again and replied, "Okay."

***

Thirty minutes later, Dani finally convinced Peyton that it was time to go inside the house. They stood, still nude and trembling from the cold, and ran inside the house, laughing as they went. Dani caught Peyton at the back door, pressed Peyton against it, and kissed the woman senseless through her laughter. That laughter died down when Dani's thigh pressed between Peyton's. It disappeared altogether when Dani stroked between her legs, coaxing yet another orgasm from her. It returned later when they were lying in bed, looking up at the ceiling which had, at some point, been painted and repainted. They pointed out the splatter spots and gave them names. It was ridiculous. It was the perfect end to a perfect day.

When Dani fell asleep that night, it was nude and pressed to Peyton's back. It was also while listening to Peyton's soft, comforting breathing that Dani thought, sometimes, love was like a dimmer switch. It had been with Steven. It was a slow process of realizing she wanted to be more than friends with the man. It took time for them to even get to the point where they could talk about going on a date. It had taken years. With Peyton, love was like a light switch. It was switched on for them by some unknown power above. It was bright all at once. It was intense and fluorescent. Dani never wanted to go back into the dark again.

***

Dani stared at Peyton for the second day in a row. She smiled at the softness of the woman's sleeping face. Peyton appeared to be at peace; happy. Dani couldn't resist. She reached for her phone, opened the camera app, and prayed that she had disabled that stupid camera sound in her settings. She clicked the photo, heard the sound, hated herself for a moment, dropped the phone, watched as Peyton's one eye opened and then closed again, and then laughed.

"That better not end up in the clouds, Dani Wilder," Peyton muttered against the pillow.

"The clouds? Like there's more than one of them?" Dani asked through her laughter.

"I don't know how many of them there are," Peyton replied, rolling onto her back. "There could be a dark cloud somewhere where people store their blackmail pictures. I am a musician; not a computer engineer."

"You are so cute sometimes," Dani said.

"Not when I've just woken up, I'm not," Peyton argued.

"Well, I've only woken up next to you a few times, but I'd say you look pretty cute to me. This may be the cutest so far." Dani reached for the sheet and pulled it down. "Or the sexiest. Actually, it's both. You're both the cutest and sexiest woman I've ever seen."

"Says the model," Peyton teased.

"Says the pop star," Dani argued back.

"Not even close to the same thing." Peyton rolled onto her side. "I make music."

"You're also a model, Pey. You might have more magazine covers than me at this point," Dani said.

"Please, I'm a singer-songwriter, Dani."

Dani climbed on top of her, straddling her thighs, and said, "You are mine. That's what matters most, right?"

"That I'm yours?" Peyton asked softly, reaching for Dani's hips.

"You are, though, right?" Dani asked back just as softly.

"You're asking me that *now*?" Peyton laughed. "Not last night, before you had your lips down there?" She glanced down her body.

"I told you we would talk about this stuff today. Last night was about last night," Dani said with a smirk. "And I'd like to put my lips back down there at some point, but if you don't answer my question soon, I might have to hop off you and go make myself an egg white omelet."

"Don't get crazy," Peyton replied, squeezing Dani's hips. "I'm yours, Dani. Have been since we met. Are you mine?"

"All yours." Dani smiled down at her. "Now, may I continue?"

"Please do," Peyton answered with a smirk.

CHAPTER 26

"THESE ARE GOOD, DANI," Gibson Shaw told her. "Peyton, you might try a different angle on something like this."

"Mine's good, but yours needs work." Dani winked at Peyton from their spot behind their instructor for the day, Gibson Shaw

"All he said was that I *might* try a different angle." Peyton glared at her. "*Might.*"

"It would open up your shot," Shaw said.

"It would. He's right," Dani agreed.

Peyton smiled at Dani, reached around Dani's back, and pulled her into her side. Gibson couldn't see the movement, but he heard Dani's squeal of surprise at the action.

"She's never gotten positive feedback on her pictures before. She's pretty excited," Peyton offered in explanation.

"You're a promising talent, Dani, but you could definitely benefit from training. Have you ever considered going to school for photography?" he asked, turning around in his chair to face them.

"Never had the time," Dani replied, shifting away from Peyton.

"It's hard work, but if you're really interested in photography, you have to put in the time." He stood and moved to the printer. "This one could use some editing, but it's a great shot all on its own." He took the glossy print from the printer and moved back over to them. "Your subject does a lot of the work for you, but the way you framed her with that post on one side and the sun on the other, is what really turns it into a stunning photo."

Dani took the picture from Shaw and glanced down, wondering which one he was talking about. She smiled when she saw Peyton in the photo. Peyton looked at it with her, smiled, and looked back up at Shaw.

"We had just gotten done with a hike. I hardly think I look—"

"Beautiful. You looked beautiful. That's why I took it," Dani interjected. "Thank you for this. I'm going to frame it."

"Frame it?" Peyton asked her. "God, why?"

Dani ignored her by rolling her eyes and looked at Shaw to ask, "Are any of Peyton's photos here frame-worthy?" She smirked at his expression.

***

Peyton had Dani right where she wanted her. Dani wrapped her arms around Peyton's neck and pulled her more on top of her. Then, Peyton kissed her slowly and greedily at the same time. She had missed those lips. She had missed everything about this woman. They had only been apart for two days while Dani had a commercial to shoot in Los Angeles, but those two days had been the longest days of Peyton's life. Dani had flown back in that morning. They had initially planned to meet at her place and drive to the session with Shaw together, but Dani hadn't flown on Peyton's plane. Her flight had been late. They'd had to meet at his studio instead.

The entire session, Peyton stared at Dani whenever she got the chance. If Shaw was looking through a lens or talking to Dani, Peyton's hungry eyes were on Dani's breasts, her hips, her legs, her lips, and her crazy intense eyes. They had squared off in a strange competition, with Shaw as the judge over their best photos. Dani had clearly won. What Dani didn't know, though, was that Peyton was incredibly competitive. She, it appeared, was also incredibly turned on by competition.

Peyton's hands were greedy. She reached for Dani's shirt before realizing she would need to stand up in order for them both to get naked. Peyton did so, then removed her own shirt, bra, pants, and underwear after she kicked off her shoes. She pulled Dani's off, along with her pants, while Dani worked on her own shirt and bra. Peyton climbed back on top of her. They settled onto the bed. Peyton kissed her breasts, sucking Dani's nipples into her mouth one at a time, paying equal attention to each.

"You missed me, huh?" Dani teased.

"Yes. All of you. I've had one thing on my mind the entire day," Peyton replied.

Dani watched as Peyton lowered herself into the space between Dani's legs. They hadn't done this yet. Well, Dani had to Peyton, but Peyton hadn't reciprocated with this act. They'd had one amazing weekend; then, one night together in the city before Dani had had to leave. Peyton hadn't yet given Dani what she was about to. Everything else between the two of them had felt so amazing, all the emotions and sensations were more than enough to sate Dani. Peyton knew that, but here Peyton was anyway, sucking on the inside of Dani's thigh as her hand snaked up to cover Dani's breast. She knew she wasn't doing this for Dani. She was doing this for herself, because she had really been thinking of just this act since the moment she'd woken up that morning.

Peyton hesitated for just a moment and knew Dani had noticed. She looked up at Dani first. Then, she descended. Then, she took. She took Dani's clit between her lips. She took her tongue and slid it up and down fast and slow. She took her time bringing Dani to the edge. She took pleasure in supplying Dani with pleasure of her own. She took Dani over the edge.

"Wow. That was…" Dani said moments after Peyton slid back on top of her.

"Yeah?" Peyton asked. "I've wanted to do that all day." She kissed Dani's lips. "Phone calls are not the same, Dani."

"No, they're not. But, Pey, we're both busy. As happy as I am to see you, we won't always be able to make these surprise trips to see one another when we're working." Dani ran her hands through Peyton's hair. "I'm still supposed to be in LA. We're just lucky the commercial wrapped early. If it hadn't, I wouldn't have been back until after you went to visit your family. We wouldn't have been able to see each other until next week."

"I know. But you could do it this time, so you did." She kissed Dani again. "Now, I'm starving. Are you hungry for dinner yet?" Peyton rolled off Dani and moved to lie beside her.

"I'm sorry. Did you think we were done?" Dani asked, rolling on top of her. "You don't get to make me come like that and just eat dinner with me after."

"No?" Peyton smirked up at her.

"No. I will order us some dinner after I'm done with you."

"That's a plan I can get behind," Peyton replied.

***

"Peyton?"

"Yeah?"

"Peyton, your phone."

"What?"

"Pey, your phone is ringing."

"Oh," Peyton muttered, lifted her head, opened her tired eyes, and saw the phone on her bedside table. "Hello?" she greeted.

Peyton felt Dani's front press into her back. She exhaled deeply at the feel of Dani's soft, naked skin pressed to her own.

"I'm going to hop in the shower," Dani whispered into

her ear, kissed just behind it, and moved to climb out of bed.

"This better be good, Em," Peyton scolded her sister.

"It's after nine. I didn't think you'd still be asleep," Emily said.

"I was. I went to bed late."

"Working?" Emily asked.

Peyton rolled onto her back and watched Dani's long, lithe form head into the bathroom.

"Not exactly," Peyton said.

"Lizzy wanted to know if we could use the plane."

"*Lizzy* wanted to know?" Peyton asked, heard the water turn on, shook her head at the thought of Dani in her shower, and tried her best to return her attention to her sister. "What does she need it for?"

"Her boyfriend's family lives in Portland. She wants to spend Thanksgiving with them, but he can't afford a plane ticket. He's going to take the bus, Peyton. A bus. It's like a thousand-hour trip by bus."

"I have so many questions," Peyton said, sitting up in bed and letting the sheet fall to her waist. "First of all, shouldn't Lizzy be spending Thanksgiving with Mom and Dad and you guys?"

"She said she'd be here for Christmas."

"Okay. Second. Why isn't *Lizzy* asking me this?"

Peyton knew the answer. She knew she shouldn't have a favorite sister, but she did. Emily was the nicest of the triplets. She was also the one the other two usually elected to ask Peyton for something they wanted, for that very reason.

"He's *her* boyfriend, Em," Peyton added.

"I told her I was going to call you for something else, and that I'd just ask for her," Emily replied.

"What did you want to ask me, then?"

"Oh," Emily replied and then promptly paused. "Can you come home for Thanksgiving instead of the upcoming visit?" she asked.

"I *was* planning on coming for Thanksgiving," Peyton replied, wondering in that moment what Dani would be doing for Thanksgiving.

"I thought you were doing that friends' thing you do sometimes," Emily said.

"I did that last year in LA because everyone could come. But I didn't plan anything for this year because Mom and Dad said you guys would be at home this year."

"Lizzy won't be, but Erica and I will."

"But you don't want me to visit this week?" Peyton asked.

"Erica, Lizzy, and I don't want to come home yet. We want to stay at school until Thanksgiving break."

"I'm not forcing you to come home just because I'm visiting," Peyton said. "And I'm only visiting because Dad asked me to."

"Because Grandma and Grandpa are going on their cruise before Thanksgiving, so they won't be able to see you if you do come then."

"Emily, just ask me whatever you want to ask me. I'm going on, like, no sleep here, haven't had caffeine yet, and have better things to do than to try to translate this conversation first thing in the morning."

"Mom and Dad want us to come home if you're there. If you're not there, they won't be mad at us if we choose to stay on campus."

"So, you want me to cancel my trip so that you guys can stay on campus?"

"It's college, Peyton. There's something new here practically every week. We only have four years to enjoy it. Mom's guilt-trips are killer; you know that."

"I do." Peyton laughed. "I'll talk to Mom." She thought for a moment that she could skip this trip and just go for Thanksgiving. She had Dani now, and they were only just starting. She would make good use of this extra time with her. "And Dad, too."

"Thank you," Emily replied. "And the plane?"

"Have Lizzy text me the details, but only if Mom and Dad said it's okay," Peyton said.

After they exchanged their goodbyes, Peyton got up, stretched, and moved toward the bathroom where she could still hear the water in the shower running. Peyton smiled at the sight of Dani in her shower, running her hands through her hair to remove the shampoo.

"Are you going to join me or just watch?" Dani asked.

"Is joining an option?" Peyton asked back.

"It's a requirement if you're planning on touching me before your trip home. I'm about to get dressed and head to a meeting at the agency. I have a dinner tonight I can't get out of, and you leave–"

Peyton climbed in behind her, wrapped her arms around Dani's body, and said, "I'm not going."

CHAPTER 27

"WHAT DO YOU MEAN you're not going?" Dani turned in Peyton's arms, rubbing the soapy water from her eyes.

"I thought you'd be happy to have me here a little longer. Now, we *can* rush, but we don't have to." Peyton slid a thigh between Dani's legs.

"You were looking forward to this trip home."

"I'm going again in a few weeks anyway."

"Peyton, what happened?" Dani asked, sliding her body away from Peyton's.

"Nothing happened."

"That was your sister on the phone, right?"

"Emily, yeah."

"Did she ask you not to come again?" Dani asked her.

"That was just because it was parents' weekend at school, and the trips didn't want a spectacle. I am a bit of a spectacle, Dani." Peyton reached for Dani's hips.

"They're your family, Peyton. You're not a spectacle to them."

"But now, I get to spend more time with you." Peyton shrugged. "Here. Let me get your back for you."

Dani turned around reluctantly as Peyton washed her back for her. She tried to determine how best to handle the situation. She really didn't want Peyton to go home. She wanted them to have as much time together as possible, with their relationship being so new. She also knew that Peyton's grandparents wouldn't be home for Thanksgiving this year and had requested a visit from their oldest granddaughter before they set off for a month-long cruise.

"Pey, as much as I want you here, I don't want you to miss out on being with your grandparents because of me."

"Well, it's not because of you. It's a special request from the trips," Peyton replied.

"They do that a lot, don't they?" Dani asked.

"Do what?"

"Make special requests of you."

"I'm the big sister."

"Pey, do you want to go home?" Dani asked her seriously.

"Yes, I'd like to see my grandparents off and spend some time with my parents and my sisters. I mean, I'm going home for Thanksgiving this year, but that day is always so hectic. I get in Wednesday night. The trips are already there, and they're just excited to be off from school for a few days. They fill us all in on their lives. Then, we go to bed early. Thanksgiving itself kicks off early because my mom needs help cooking for all of us. My aunt and two uncles come over with their families. It's about fifteen people. I help where I can, but it's not really a fun day. It's cooking and cleaning mostly. We all eat. Then, everyone goes home. I typically fly out on Friday or Saturday at the latest, because I have work or an event. I was kind of hoping to have a nice, low-key visit before all that."

"Babe, you should go," Dani said, cupping Peyton's cheek. "Screw your sisters."

Peyton smiled at her and replied, "It's always kind of been like this. It's not a big deal. I'm used to them not wanting me around. Ever since my career took off, and they grew out of the phase where they idolized their big sister, it's been this way."

Dani wrapped her arms around Peyton's neck and said, "Peyton, visit your family."

"I will, on Thanksgiving. I actually realized with Em's call that I don't know what you're doing that day."

"I'll be with my family, as usual." Dani moved into Peyton's body, feeling the water rush over both of them. "Now, don't change the subject. I'm not that easy to trick, Gloss."

"I tricked you into liking me." Peyton winked at her.

"No, you didn't." Dani pressed her lips to Peyton's softly. "You were just you. That's why I liked you."

Peyton sighed and said, "It really is just easier to go for Thanksgiving. I have fought with my family before about stuff like this, and it's never been worth it."

"Is it weird, being an older sister of triplets?" Dani asked. "You guys aren't exactly close in age, either. I imagine it's weird a little bit."

Peyton didn't say anything for a long moment. She pulled Dani into herself more. Then, she rested her head against Dani's shoulder and allowed the water to spray into her face. Dani held onto Peyton. It took a moment for her to realize that Peyton was crying. The woman was in tears. Even the sound of the shower couldn't cover the sobs now coming out of Peyton. Dani squeezed her more tightly and cooed into Peyton's ear, not wanting to ask any questions at that moment. Peyton's fingernails pressed hard into Dani's back, but Dani didn't let go. She held on until Peyton pulled back, opened the shower door, climbed out, and covered herself with a towel before leaving the bathroom entirely.

"Pey?" Dani asked softly when she emerged from the bathroom, clad in her own towel.

"I'm sorry." Peyton was sitting cross-legged on the bed; the towel not exactly covering everything. "I didn't mean to–"

"Hey," Dani began, sliding beside Peyton onto the bed. "Peyton, you can cry on my shoulder anytime. That's one of the benefits of being with someone."

Peyton wiped her eyes, turned to Dani, and said, "It's not supposed to be like this in the beginning, though. I'm still supposed to be showing you how amazing I am and how we could be together; not sobbing in the shower over something so stupid."

Dani removed the towel from her own body, lied down, and welcomed Peyton against her chest. They lay like that for a few minutes, with Peyton's sniffles as the only sound between them.

"Do you want to tell me what happened?" Dani asked, running her hand along Peyton's back.

"It's kind of a long story."

"I'm not going anywhere," Dani replied.

"You have a meeting at–"

"This is way more important than that," Dani said.

"I don't want to make you miss something, Dani."

"Peyton, I'll call them and reschedule." She kissed the top of Peyton's head. "It really isn't a big deal. Just talk to me."

"When I first started out in music – like, really started out, things were good. The trips were young and annoying, but all little siblings are." She laughed against Dani's chest. "They've always had their own language, the trips. I'm five years older. I don't know what it's like to be a multiple. I didn't share their language. My parents never discouraged them from being exactly who they were – which is a good thing. But it definitely makes someone who doesn't belong, feel just like that; like they don't belong."

"They're your family, Peyton."

"It's easier to say than to believe, sometimes," Peyton said so softly, Dani almost didn't hear it.

"Because of the triplets being a pain in your ass?" Dani asked.

"Because I'm adopted, Dani," Peyton said, and Dani remained still as she let the words wash over her. "I know; it's a lot."

"I didn't know."

"No one does. I mean, my family does, obviously. Outside of that, it's only Lennox."

"You never told…"

"No one I've ever dated has known." Peyton lifted herself up and leaned over Dani on her elbow. "I trust you, Dani."

"Good. I'd never tell anyone, anything you told me in confidence, Pey." Dani ran her hand through Peyton's still wet hair. "Is that why you feel like an outsider in your own family?"

"Sometimes." Peyton nodded. "It didn't feel that way when I was a kid, of course. My parents always made me feel like I was their child. Once the triplets came along, though, things changed a little. It wasn't just that they'd had their own birth children. They had multiples. So, I was the adopted kid, and then I was the adopted kid with three younger sisters, who had each other and that special relationship only multiples can have."

"What did your parents say?"

"About what?" Peyton asked.

"When you told them how you sometimes feel, babe."

Peyton smiled again and said, "I don't really like to bring it up."

"Why not?"

"What's the point? I'm an adult now. I've lived on my own for years. I go home and visit when I can, but I'm okay."

"You just cried in the shower, Peyton. Your sisters asked you not to come home again, and you cried because you want to see your family, babe."

Peyton smiled for a brief moment before the smile disappeared. Dani's experiment had worked. She'd noticed recently that every time she called Peyton that nickname, Peyton smiled, despite the topic of their conversation.

"I'll see them on Thanksgiving."

"Peyton, do you want to go home tomorrow? I mean it. Answer the question. Don't just say that it's okay or that it's no big deal. And don't make it about spending more time with me, either."

"Fine. Yes. I want to see my dad. I haven't in a while. And I want to see my grandparents."

"Then, you should go home and talk to your family."

"Dani, it's fine. I'm okay. I just had a moment."

"Okay. If our roles were reversed, and I was the big-time rock star with some family issues I needed to work out, and I'd just cried on your shoulder in the shower, what would you tell me to do, Peyton?" Dani asked.

"That's a low blow, Wilder," Peyton replied, squinting her eyes at Dani.

"Maybe. But you know the answer." Dani shrugged.

"Fine. I'll go. But I'm not guaranteeing I'll bring anything up. I'm only going because I want to see them."

"Now, you're just being stubborn." Dani laughed at her.

Peyton climbed on top of her then, losing the towel entirely. She stared down at Dani, kissed her forehead, her nose, her cheeks in turn, and then her lips.

"I'm going to miss you," Peyton said.

"I'll miss you, too. But I'll be here when you come back."

"Is it okay if I don't tell them about us just yet?" Peyton asked.

"What? Of course, it is." Dani ran her hands over Peyton's back. "I don't expect you to tell anyone until you want to."

"I want to. It's not that. I want everyone to know. I mean, look at my ridiculously hot, supermodel girlfriend." Peyton smirked, glancing down Dani's body. "I get to see her naked."

It was Dani's turn to smile at the word Peyton had used.

"Oh, yeah?"

"Well, she's naked right now, and I'm seeing her."

Dani looked at the woman above her. Peyton's

beautiful blue eyes had a puffiness around them now, along with those red lines that came with tears. Dani ran her hand along Peyton's cheek, wanting so badly to tell the woman exactly how she felt. She swallowed.

"I'm proud of you," she said instead.

"I haven't done anything yet." Peyton kissed Dani's lips again.

"You've done so much already." Dani kissed *her* this time.

CHAPTER 28

"W̲E̲'̲R̲E̲ G̲L̲A̲D̲ Y̲O̲U̲ came home, honey," Peyton's father said after pulling away from the hug. "But, are you sure you can't stay a few extra days?"

"No, I have to get back to work, Dad."

"Pey, tell Mom you told me it was okay to use the plane for Thanksgiving," Lizzy said.

"Mom, I said it was okay for Lizzy to use the plane for Thanksgiving," Peyton repeated in her mother's direction as she and Lizzy entered the living room.

"Lizzy, you've been dating this boy for a few months. We're your family. You should be having Thanksgiving here with us."

"Peyton doesn't always have Thanksgiving with us."

"Peyton's twenty-five years old, lives on her own, and doesn't rely on us for college tuition," her mother rebutted.

"Please, like you and Dad are paying for our school. We all know Peyton's really paying for it," Lizzy fired back.

"Excuse me," Peyton said. "I'm not paying–"

"You paid off the house for them and grandma's medical bills. That gave them the money to–"

"Elizabeth," her father warned. "Be careful with what comes out of your mouth next."

"What's going on in here?" Erica asked, entering the living room with a bowl of what looked like melted ice cream.

Peyton hadn't ever liked the concoction, but the

triplets had always stirred ice cream in bowls until it was basically soup. Then, they would pour in some root beer or whatever soda they had lying around. It was weird. And it was yet another thing she did not share with them.

"Mom doesn't want me to go to Portland for Thanksgiving," Lizzy said.

"Mom's right." Erica sat on the sofa next to her father. "You've known Kenneth for, like what, four months? You've known us your whole life."

"We literally came out of the same womb together," Emily added as she entered the room, carrying an identical bowl of ice cream. "Don't be mad at Mom because she wants you with us on a *family* holiday."

"You guys just don't like Kenneth," Lizzy said as she flopped into the chair next to the sofa.

Peyton stood in the room, watching the usual episode unfold. She had been on her way upstairs for the night when her father had stopped to ask if she could stay a little longer. Peyton had had a nice few days with her parents and her grandparents. Her mother's guilt-trip had worked, and all trips had grumbled through the visit. Peyton had been excited at the thought that she might make it through an entire trip home without one of these events. It happened every time. One of her sisters would be upset with one of her parents or, sometimes, one of her other sisters. There would be an argument. Peyton would stand or sit off to the side and listen. Then, when she would disappear up the stairs into a different room or outside, no one would even remember she was there. She sighed loudly at Dani's words to her that last morning in her apartment. Dani had been proud of her. And she felt unworthy of that pride so far.

"Lizzy, shut up," Peyton said loudly enough for the room to hear. "You should be here with your family for Thanksgiving. But if you insist on spending it with your boyfriend, you two can take the plane only if you're back Friday. Mom, since grandma and grandpa are gone, and, apparently, it's just us this year…"

"I asked for a year off from the big production." Her mother nodded at Peyton.

"Lizzy, you have to be back with Kenneth no later than Saturday morning. We'll do Thanksgiving then as a family."

"You can't just–"

"Do you want to use the plane or not?"

"That's not fair," Lizzy argued.

"Fair? You want fair, Lizzy?" Peyton moved more into the room. "You've never had to work a day in your life; not like Mom or Dad or me. Mom and Dad made it possible for me to have my career. And yes, that career makes it possible for you three to share in the benefits. But *I* work hard for what I have. Nothing was given to me. You could be a little more grateful."

"Fine. I'm sorry." Lizzy shrugged. "I just wanted to meet my boyfriend's family and–"

Peyton looked at Emily in that moment and added, "And you three can't just pick and choose. I'm not the famous sister you can bug for stuff one minute, and then the one you don't want near you another. I'm either your sister, or I'm not. You either take me for who I am and what I bring with me, or you don't. I'm tired of getting told not to be somewhere because I might bring press or security or fans. You don't get to borrow a plane one day and then tell me you wish I was normal another," Peyton said.

"Honey," her mother interjected softly. "What's going on? Are you okay?"

"No, Mom." Peyton's tears began to well. "I've been here for days, and this whole trip has been about the triplets and how they're doing in school. It's been about grandma and grandpa's trip, and Dad's new workbench outside."

"Pey, we talked about you at dinner," Erica said, sincerely believing it.

"Erica, the three of you talked about my upcoming tour and the vacation in the south of France you guys want to take during it. It's not the same thing." Peyton let a tear fall. "Mom, you haven't even asked me about Dani."

"Dani? Who's Dani?" her father asked.

"A friend of Peyton's." Emily placed her bowl on the coffee table. "I've seen the pictures online."

"She seems nice, Pey," Erica added.

"Sweetie, I'm sorry. Things have been a little busy around here, with all four of you being home and your grandparents staying, too. I've had a full house. But you're right, I should have asked."

"Asked what?" her father pressed. "Who is Dani?"

"She's my girlfriend," Peyton answered loudly, wiping a tear away.

"Girlfriend?" Lizzy whispered. "As in…"

"No," Erica said, shaking her head. "As in that way all of Peyton's famous friends call each other."

"No, Erica. Dani's my girlfriend, and we're a couple. We're together. I'm in love with her." Peyton smiled at the memory of Dani calling her 'babe' repeatedly and just how good that felt. "I love her."

"That's fantastic, Peyton." Her mother stood and wrapped her arms around Peyton. "I'm so glad you told her. I should have asked you about it. I'm so sorry."

Peyton wrapped her arms around her mother's waist and pulled her in, smelling that all familiar smell of home.

"You have a girlfriend?" Emily asked.

Peyton nodded but continued to hold onto her mother.

"That's awesome, Pey," Lizzy said. "You're in love?"

Peyton nodded again.

"I hope she's better than Trevor. That guy didn't deserve you at all," Erica chimed in.

"He was a prick," Lizzy agreed.

"Dani seems so nice," Emily said, standing up. "I've seen a few interviews she's done, Pey. Can we meet her the next time we're in the city?"

"At Thanksgiving," Lizzy suggested. "Bring her to Thanksgiving, Pey."

"She has Thanksgiving with her own family," Peyton said, finally pulling away from her mother.

"Yeah, on Thursday. But you just demanded I come home for Saturday so that we could do Thanksgiving together. I'll bring Kenneth. You bring Dani."

"I can't, Lizzy."

"Why not?"

"I don't know Kenneth. I'm sure he's a nice guy, but I can't trust that he wouldn't say anything accidentally or otherwise. I don't want anyone to know about Dani and me just yet. We're still very new, and you know what happens when people find out who I'm dating."

"Your fans are going to shit bricks," Erica said.

"Erica!" her father exclaimed.

"I'll leave Kenneth in Portland," Lizzy shared. "I can trust him, but I get it, Peyton. I wouldn't do anything to jeopardize this for you if she makes you happy. Bring her. It'll just be us." Lizzy looked around at her family; at Peyton's family.

"You don't have to do that."

"Yes, she does," her father said, standing. "I want to meet this Dani." He smiled at Peyton. "I've already met Kenneth. It's time I meet my oldest daughter's girlfriend."

"Dad…"

"I want to meet her, too, Pey." Emily moved toward Peyton. "And I'm sorry we're such assholes sometimes."

"Me too," Lizzy said.

"Me three," Erica added in their customary triplet-style apology.

"Yeah, well, me four." Peyton smiled at Emily.

"Did Pey just have a total breakdown in our living room?" Erica asked, winking at Peyton.

"I think she almost did, yeah." Emily reached for Peyton, pulled her in, and hugged her. "And I love you, big sister."

"I love you, too." Peyton hugged her back.

"I'm sorry," Lizzy said when it was her turn for a hug.

"I'm kind of a jerk."

"Just remember that and try to prevent the jerk from coming out in the future, okay?" Peyton laughed at her.

"I'll try to remember that you're my sister and not just ask you for things all the time, Pey. I really am sorry. I didn't realize—"

"It's okay."

Peyton hugged Erica after Lizzy. Then, her father stood in front of her, reached out for her, and pulled her in for a hug.

"You are my first child," he whispered in Peyton's ear so that only she and her mother could hear. "I love you more than life, Peyton. If I don't show it the right way or enough, I am so sorry, baby." He kissed Peyton's cheek. "Remember this and never tell those three," he began. "Your mother and I *chose* you. We chose you because you were our daughter the moment we laid eyes on you. We love all of our girls. We want you all to be happy."

Peyton let a few more tears fall before she said, "I love you, too, Dad." She then smiled over at her mom, who still had a hand on Peyton's back.

When Peyton finally pulled away, she stared out at the living room full of people who loved her. She didn't feel all that alone anymore.

"So, when you say *girlfriend*, you mean a girl you…" Erica tried.

"Make out with?" Emily added.

"And have sex with?" Lizzy finished.

"And on that note, your mother and I will leave you four to gossip until Peyton has to leave tomorrow," her father said.

Her parents bid them all goodnight and retired to their bedroom. Peyton had no doubt that her father was asking her mother questions about Dani and what it meant for Peyton. He'd probably ask Peyton those same questions in time. But, for now, she was content in knowing her mom could handle it. She thought about going upstairs herself, but her sisters had a different idea. They pulled her down to the sofa and hammered her with questions.

"You've kissed her, right? What's it like, to kiss a girl?" Emily asked.

"She's her girlfriend, Em. I'm sure they've done more than kiss. Is it good? I mean, I assume you like it, because you're with her... But what's it like?" Erica asked next.

"Is she good to you?" Lizzy asked.

Peyton turned to the youngest of the triplets and smiled at her. She then ran her hand through Lizzy's dark brown hair.

"She's very, very good to me."

CHAPTER 29

"I WAS HONORED you called," Jill teased. "You've been so busy with your new girlfriend lately, I've hardly seen you."

"You've been in another country since she and I got together," Dani argued while laughing at her friend.

"I'm happy for you two," Jill said with a wink.

"Thank you."

"Where is she, though? I thought you said she was back from visiting her family."

"She is. She's actually hanging out with Lennox today."

"Oh."

"She told her family about us," Dani revealed. "Well, most of them. She's telling Lennox today."

"She told her family already?"

Dani nodded and picked up the TV remote.

"They took it well, according to her. They want me to come for Thanksgiving."

"You're not doing it with your family?"

"Peyton's family is doing it on that Saturday so her little sister can be with her boyfriend's family on the actual day and so I can do the same."

"That's nice of them," Jill said, snagging a few of the vegetarian nachos on the plate in her lap. "These would be better with meat."

"Then, make your own nachos." Dani laughed at her. "And eat them fast because we have to be there in two hours."

"Why are you dragging me to this thing? You have a

girlfriend now, who has to at least pretend she likes the things you do so you have sex with her again."

"She's busy. I just told you," Dani argued, taking a nacho off the plate. "And she does like photography. Well, she likes that I like it. She went last time."

"Fine. I'll go *this* time. But only because I need more juicy details of that little trip to Michigan."

***

"You two are together?" Lennox asked excitedly.

"We are," Peyton replied, smiling at her friend. "Since Michigan."

"Please, since that night at the party. I knew it."

"You knew it?"

"Yes. You two were all over each other."

"No, we weren't." Peyton laughed at Lennox's choice of words. "We hardly touched that night."

"You didn't need to touch her to be all over her, Pey. And she was all over you, too."

"Fine. Fine. Since that night."

"Except for the whole her having a boyfriend thing."

"Don't remind me," Peyton requested.

"Where is she?"

"With Jill. They're doing that second photography lesson together today."

"We should all hang out again," Lennox suggested.

"You should find someone for yourself so that we could all hang out as couples. Jill's married. Dani and I are together. What about you, Len?"

"I'm working on it." Lennox shrugged. "Not a primary concern. It'll happen when it happens, I guess."

"It will." Peyton smiled at her best friend.

"So, things are good with you guys?" Lennox asked.

"I love her, Len."

"Obviously."

"No, Lennox. I've said that to you before about

someone I was with, but I don't mean it in the same way."

"Then, how do you mean it?"

"She's the one." Peyton lifted a shoulder. "She's the person I'm supposed to be with."

"That's great, Peyton."

"I told her about the adoption, about the family stuff, and she made me feel so much better just by being there." Peyton paused. "She'd suggested I talk to them about how I was feeling, and I did. I told them all about it. Then, I told them about her."

"You told your parents about Dani?"

"I did. My mom had already known how I felt about her, but I told them all that we're together. They're happy for us, Len. None of them care that Dani's a woman or that it might be a big deal if we ever decide to tell the world about us."

"Will you?"

"Will we what?"

"Tell the world?"

"I have no idea." Peyton laughed. "Right now, we're keeping it between us because it's new. It's the beginning. I want to have that with her without any interference more than I want anything in my life."

"More than another platinum record?"

"More than anything, Lennox," Peyton told her friend seriously.

Lennox smiled affectionately at her best friend and said, "I'm really happy, then."

"Me too."

***

"What do you think?" Peyton asked.

"I've never been in a recording studio before," Dani said. "Well, I've had to record audio for a few commercials and stuff, but I've never been in this kind of studio."

"It's not bad," Matt shared. "I've seen better."

"You have not," Peyton argued while laughing at him. "And are you about ready?"

"I'm ready. Are you?" he asked.

"What are you recording today?" Dani asked, sitting down on the sofa behind the table.

"The anthem track," Peyton said, opening the door to the room she would go into to record her vocals.

"I thought we were doing the ballad today," Matt said. Then, his eyes got big. "Shit... Did I get my info wrong?" he asked, glancing at his computer. "You're right. Sorry. Anthem today."

"Ballad?" Dani questioned, glancing at Peyton.

"There's always a couple of those on my albums," Peyton said sheepishly. "I thought you would like to watch us lay down what will likely be the first single."

"Is the ballad an option, though?" Dani asked, leaning forward. "I don't want to throw you guys off. Maybe I could come back on a day you record that, too."

Peyton looked over at Matt, who had made a genuine mistake, and glared at him anyway.

"We're set for the anthem," he offered.

"I can just come back on–"

Peyton inhaled and exhaled deeply before she said, "No, it's fine. Matt, can we change the schedule up a little?"

"Are you sure?" Matt checked.

"I'm sure." Peyton nodded at him, felt her own cheeks redden, and looked at Dani. "Just... I mean, keep in mind that the songs are always works-in-progress until they're released, okay?"

Dani smiled at her and replied, "I understand." She nodded with that same wide smile.

As Peyton made her way into the recording room, closing the door behind herself, she knew that she was making the right decision. Then, they got started. When the background music started playing in Peyton's headphones, she stared into Dani's eyes through the glass and sang to her and her alone.

People say it's cold and gray
My past always felt that way
I've been living in-between
I met you, and I saw green

Before that night, I thought I'd lived
Before that night, I'd given all I could give
But now, all I want is you at night
Now, I want you all the time

Whenever I can't seem to find my words
I think of you, and my heart, it stirs
My pen hits the blank page, and I arrange
Why is it those three words can be so hard to say?

Before that night, I thought I'd lived
Before that night, I'd given all I could give
But now, all I want is you at night
Now, I want you all the time
Now, I love you all the time
I know I'll love you my whole life

I used to see gray
Now, all I see is green
Your eyes are all I see
Yours is all I want to be

When Peyton finished running through the entire song for the first time, her eyes opened. They met Dani's. The gorgeous green of the woman's eyes nearly made Peyton lose her footing. The tears welling in them made her wonder if she'd gone too far. The smile that followed next made her think she'd gone just far enough.

Peyton removed the headphones, knowing they would need to record again and again but not caring about that right now. Matt must have picked up on it, too. He flipped some switches, stood, and said something to Dani that

Peyton couldn't hear. He then opened the door and left the room. Peyton opened the door. Dani was standing in front of the sofa.

"So, that's the ballad," Peyton said softly because she didn't know what else to say.

"It's my ballad, isn't it?" Dani asked, moving toward Peyton.

"One of them, yes."

Dani held onto Peyton's waist and pulled her in to whisper, "Can you say it again?"

Peyton met her eyes and replied, "A whole song about you wasn't enough? I have more. I can show them to–"

"I love you, Peyton," Dani interrupted.

Peyton's heart started racing. Her eyes went wide. Her arms went around Dani's neck to pull the woman in closer.

"I love you, too," she whispered against Dani's lips.

CHAPTER 30

"WHAT ARE YOU looking at?" Dani asked.

"Plans for the house in London." Peyton stared at her laptop.

Dani moved to lie down beside her and glanced over at it.

"Blueprints?"

"I bought it knowing I'd need to remodel. These are the plans from the architect I hired."

"It looks nice. I'm not good at reading blueprints, though, so what do I know?" Dani laughed.

It had been two weeks since they said they loved each other for the first time. Dani wasn't sure her feet had hit the ground since then. She had insisted Peyton give her a copy of the unfinished song she had written for her. Dani had played it nearly a thousand times. She had also gotten a sneak peek at some of the other lyrics the woman had written on random pieces of paper and in her notes app on her phone. Dani knew she would never be able to write Peyton a love song, but she also knew she would do everything she could to make sure Peyton knew how much she loved her.

"You have many other special skills," Peyton said, looking over at her girlfriend. "Hey, do you want to go?"

"To my place? I thought I was staying here tonight."

"You're so cute," Peyton said, smiled, and moved her laptop off to the side. "You *are* staying here tonight." She moved to straddle Dani. "And I plan to take full advantage of those other special skills you have."

"You do?" Dani asked, moving her hands into Peyton's hair. "Well, if you weren't talking about tonight, what were you talking about?"

"Picking up on my hints about wanting to touch you right now isn't one of your special skills, is it?" Peyton smirked.

"I guess not." Dani laughed into Peyton's kiss.

"And I was talking about going to London."

"London? Why?" Dani asked, kissing Peyton's long neck.

"Because I have a house there, and it would be nice for us to get away."

"We just got away. Remember Michigan?" Dani pulled Peyton's shirt down in order to kiss between her breasts. "Not that I don't want to go away with you."

"Work?" Peyton asked.

"No, I'm okay for the next couple of weeks. I didn't think you were, though."

Peyton sighed and said, "I'm not. You're right." She pulled away from Dani and resumed her previous position lying down beside her. "We're wrapping up recording here, and I am prepping the tour. It's easier since we've already done the US side, but I still have too much work to do to get away. I guess it was just wishful thinking."

Dani lay back down as well. Her mood suddenly changed at the mention of the tour Peyton would soon be undertaking.

"Right. The tour is coming up, huh?"

"I was thinking about going to check out the house in person the weekend before I go. You could come with me. We could have a little going away party with some of my friends that live there. I know you have a bunch there, too."

"I do," Dani confirmed.

Peyton rolled onto her side, facing Dani, and asked, "What do you think? We could have a night with our friends and then a couple just for us before I fly out for the Asia leg."

"I think I'm going to miss you like crazy," Dani said softly.

"Oh." Peyton slid over a little closer. "I'm sorry. I keep forgetting that while I've done this part a million times, it's still new to you."

"My girlfriend leaving for eight months? Yeah, that's pretty new."

"Steven went away a lot, though, right?"

"I'm sorry… Did you just compare yourself to my ex-boyfriend that I broke up with?" Dani lifted an eyebrow at her. "Pretty much so I could be with you…"

"I was just making a point that you've had to deal with someone traveling a lot for work before." Peyton ran her hand under Dani's shirt over her back.

"Peyton, what I feel for you and what I once felt for him aren't even close." Dani pressed her forehead to her girlfriend's. "I love you. I don't want to be without you for eight months."

"You won't." Peyton rubbed Dani's back. "We haven't done this yet, but we should get our calendars out and find times when you can meet me on tour or when I can come see you wherever you are. It'll be hard, but we'll make it work, Dani."

"We should. You're right." Dani kissed Peyton gently. "Eight months is such a long time for a new couple, babe."

"Like I could go eight months without seeing you, Dani. I don't even like going eight hours without seeing you." Peyton kissed her lips.

"I don't want to go to London, Peyton. I want to stay here, in this bed with you, and never let you go." Dani squeezed Peyton then, entwining their legs together.

"We'll stay here then. I'll check on the progress in between the Asia and Australia tours. It's no big deal." She kissed Dani's shoulder. "And I want you on tour with me, Dani. Whenever you can get away, I want you there."

"I won't get in the way of all your other suiters?" Dani asked.

"Did you just say *suiters*?" Peyton asked through a wide smile. "Babe, I love you. You are the only person I want to be with. I don't care about any other suiters." She laughed a little.

"Why do you seem kind of okay with this, and I'm just now realizing that I might fall apart when you leave?" Dani asked.

Peyton rolled them over, climbed on top of her, and sat up straddling Dani's legs.

"Dani, I am absolutely going to fall apart the moment I get on the plane and leave you here." Peyton slid her hands under Dani's shirt, resting them on the woman's stomach. "I've had to leave people to go on tour before. But this will be the first time I've left the person I'm spending the rest of my life with. You know that, right? That I want my life to be with you?"

"I remember some lyrics that alluded to that fact, yes." Dani smiled up at her.

"So, you'll plan it with me? Join me whenever you can? I promise I'll try to meet you places, too. It won't just be on you."

When Dani's phone rang, she reached for it, winking at Peyton to give her a moment to take care of it.

"Hey, Joan."

"Hi, Dani. Listen, there's a new listing that won't be on the market long. I'm talking hours, at most. It's in your price range and has what you want. Can you take a look at it today?"

Dani's realtor had continued to find her listings. With Dani's work and her new relationship taking up the majority of her time, she had only had the chance to see a few more places since she and Peyton went that first day. She had actually made an offer on one she liked, but it wasn't accepted. Truthfully, she had known it wouldn't be when she made it. Joan had been pressuring her to at least make an offer on it. Had it been accepted, though, Dani wasn't sure she would have ended up going through with it. Dani stared up at Peyton, who was running her fingertips over Dani's stomach and watching them as they moved. Her hair was down, framing Peyton's face. Her shirt was slightly bunched at her hips. Her shorts had snowmen on them, for some reason. They made her seem even more perfect to Dani.

"I don't think I can make it today," Dani told her.

"Dani, I emailed you the listing. You should at least check it out. Three bedrooms, two and a half bathrooms, a terrace, and a brand-new kitchen with stainless steel appliances and marble countertops. It's all hardwood, too. It's the best you're going to get."

"I've already found the best," Dani replied.

Peyton looked at her, gave her a quizzical glance, and returned her attention to her hands.

"Can I call you back later? I have to talk to someone about something first."

"Oh, okay. But, Dani–"

"I know, Joan. It'll be gone soon. I understand the risk. I'll call you later, okay?"

"What risk?" Peyton asked when Dani hung up. "Everything okay?"

"She had a listing she wanted me to check out."

"We can go if you want," Peyton offered.

"I don't want." Dani reached for her hips again. "I want you to keep doing what you were doing."

"New York real estate is intense, Dani. If she has a listing, you should at least check it out."

"You are not good at taking hints, either, when I'm trying to touch you." Dani sat up, pulled Peyton's shirt over the woman's head, and lay back down. "Are my intentions clear enough now?"

Peyton laughed, looked down at her bare chest with a lifted eyebrow, and met Dani's eyes.

"Are you sure you don't–"

"Pey, I don't care about the listing. I don't care about finding a new place anymore."

"What? Why not? You said your place is too small and you wanted–"

"My life to be with you now," Dani interjected. "You and I are together, Peyton. I don't know… It just seems like finding a house should move down on my priority list."

"Because of me?"

"Because of us, babe." Dani sat up, removed her own shirt, and again, lay back down. "You know those things I didn't want with Steven? The house, the wedding, the kids?"

"Yeah."

"I want them with you."

Peyton lowered herself, settling between Dani's legs as Dani spread them wide for her.

"I want them with you, too," Peyton said.

"Then, I don't need to buy my own place right now." Dani wrapped her arms around Peyton's neck. "You already own, like, fifteen houses. I'll just move into all of them one day." She smiled up at Peyton, kissed her nose, and giggled when Peyton tickled her sides.

"You want to live here one day?" Peyton asked.

"That's the plan."

"You should move in."

"What?" Dani asked. "Peyton, not now. I mean later, once we've been together for a while."

"I don't care when you do it as long as you do it." Peyton kissed her lips.

"Right now, I want to do something else."

"You mean you don't want to move into my house right now?" Peyton teased as she kissed Dani's neck.

"Peyton?"

"Yeah?" Peyton kissed her neck again.

"I want to touch you while you're on top of me like this."

"You do?"

"Yes," Dani whispered into Peyton's ear.

"And what am I supposed to do while you're doing that?" Peyton asked softly.

"Let me."

Peyton lifted herself up and looked down at her girlfriend. She then climbed off Dani, slid her own shorts along with the panties off, reached for Dani's to do the same, and climbed back on top of Dani, straddling her hips once more.

"You can do whatever you want, Dani Wilder. I'm yours."

CHAPTER 31

"YES, THERE," DANI SAID. "There. Oh, that's…"

Peyton was on her knees in front of her standing girlfriend. Dani had her hand in Peyton's hair, making a complete mess of it – which wasn't a good thing because they were guests.

"Dani, quiet," Peyton said against Dani's center before she dragged her tongue through it and gripped Dani's ass, pulling Dani more into her mouth.

"I can't help it," Dani said just a little quieter. "That feels so good."

Peyton sucked Dani's clit into her mouth. She knew Dani was close to coming. They'd been together enough times now, for Peyton to recognize the signs. Whenever she went down on Dani, Dani came fast. It was why – when they'd rushed into Peyton's bedroom because they'd both needed to touch the other – she'd immediately lifted Dani's dress, removed her panties, and knelt in front of her. Dani's hand gripped Peyton's head, pushing Peyton into her more. Then, she uttered an expletive or two, rocked her hips against Peyton's mouth, and released.

"Wow," Peyton said, wiping her mouth and standing up to kiss her girlfriend.

"I'm supposed to say that," Dani replied. "I cannot believe we just did that in your childhood bedroom."

"I couldn't help it. You've looked so sexy in that dress all day." Peyton ran her hands up Dani's sides, kissing the woman's neck.

"Your family is downstairs, Peyton. What if they heard me?"

"I told you to be quiet." Peyton pulled back to smirk at her. "Besides, you knew what I had in mind when I told you I needed something from my room."

"What are you talking about?" Dani laughed, wrapping her arms around Peyton's neck.

"You were giving me those sexy eyes."

"I was not." Dani laughed.

"Yes, you were, Dani Wilder. Trust me, I know your sexy eyes by now."

"Oh, yeah?"

"Yes. And if you didn't want it, you sure didn't do anything to stop me. Your panties are currently around your right ankle."

Dani reached under Peyton's dress, tugged at the woman's underwear, sliding them down Peyton's thighs to her knees, and then allowed them to fall.

"So are yours," she said.

"What are you going to do about that?" Peyton asked in a husky voice that she knew gave her own need away.

***

"You two can stay here. You know that, Peyton. You didn't need to get a hotel room."

"I know, Mom. It's just easier." Peyton shrugged at her mom.

"We wouldn't have a problem with Dani sleeping in the same room. We know you two are together," her mother said. "You've never brought anyone home before. We were hoping we'd get to spend more time with her; with the two of you."

"Dani has to work on Monday. She has an early shoot,

and then she flies to Miami for a commercial. I leave for the tour soon. We don't have all that much time together, so I thought a night in a nice hotel would be–"

"I understand." Her mother held up her hands. "You'll be by for brunch tomorrow before you fly back to New York, though, right?"

"I don't think I have a choice. The trips are obsessed with my girlfriend. I've had about ten minutes alone with Dani all day today." She didn't mention what they'd done during those ten minutes.

"She's a supermodel."

"They've met my other model friends."

"Those friends were not your girlfriend, Peyton."

"No, they're not."

"You two seem happy, honey," her mother said as they made their way into the living room, where the rest of the family had retired after the dishes had been done.

"We are. I mean, I am. I think she is."

"She is."

"You can tell?" Peyton asked.

"Every time she looks at you," her mom replied. "And every time you look at her."

"She's beautiful, isn't she?" Peyton asked softly as she caught sight of Dani on the sofa between Erica and Lizzy.

"You both are." Her mother patted her back. "And you're beautiful together."

"Thanks, Mom." Peyton crossed her arms over her chest, leaned against the doorframe, and watched Dani laugh at something Lizzy said. "I'm going to marry her one day, Mom."

"You are, are you?" Her mother chuckled.

"Yes, I am." Peyton met her mother's eyes. "So, I hope you like her, because she might be your daughter-in-law one day."

"I like her plenty." She laughed again. "And when that day comes, your father and I will be there, happy that our daughter is happy and in love."

"Do I have to make the trips bridesmaids?" Peyton asked, lifting an eyebrow at her mother. "Because I don't think I could handle all of their opinions on our special day."

"I guess that's up to you and Lennox, but I've always assumed Lennox would be your maid of honor, and if you wanted to include the girls, you would."

"Len would be my maid of honor." Peyton turned back to Dani. "This is stupid. I shouldn't be talking about all this right now. I'm about to go on tour. I need to focus on keeping her while I'm away."

"Honey, that girl isn't going anywhere. She's head over heels in love with you."

"It's eight months, Mom."

"You'll see each other when you can. You'll work at it when you can't. When the tour is over, sweetie, you two will come out of it as a stronger couple."

"I hope you're right." Peyton moved into the living room, stood in front of Dani, and held out her hand. "You ready to head out?"

"Sure." Dani nodded.

"It's still early, Pey," Emily said from her spot on the floor.

"It's after ten, Em. We're ready for sleep," she said of her and Dani.

"Sleep, huh?" Erica teased. She then stood, reached for Peyton, and pulled her in for a hug. "Didn't sound like a lot of sleep earlier, when I walked past your old room."

Peyton cleared her throat, squeezed her sister, and replied, "You heard nothing."

"You couldn't wait for the hotel?" Erica asked in a whisper.

"Have you seen my girlfriend?" Peyton finished the embrace. "One day, you'll understand."

"Understand what?" Lizzy asked, hugging her big sister next.

"I'll tell you later," Erica said for Peyton.

***

"Here's another one," Dani said.

"Why are you reading those?" Peyton chuckled at her. "We agreed we wouldn't worry about stupid rumors."

"Babe, the rumors are true – we are a couple." Dani held out her phone to Peyton. "This one claims I'm pregnant with your child. I mean, why is it just assumed that I'd be the pregnant one?"

"You're more nurturing," Peyton replied, sliding into bed. "And they're just rumors. No one really knows we're together. And as far as I know, you are *not* pregnant with my child."

"I wouldn't mind it in the future, though." Dani locked her phone and placed it on the table by the bed. "Your sisters asked me that, actually, after dinner."

"They asked you about our kids?" Peyton asked a little louder than she had intended. "We just got together."

"I don't think they expected us to pop them out now, Pey. They saw the stupid article and thought it was funny."

"Do they bother you?"

"Your sisters?" Dani asked.

"No, the articles." Peyton stared at Dani intently.

"No, babe. I couldn't care less about some article speculating about our relationship."

Peyton wrapped an arm around Dani's waist, moved into her, and rested her head on Dani's chest.

"One day, we'll have to tell people we're really together."

"Probably."

"There are some fans that still think I'm with Trevor. I've never actually commented on my relationships. People just take pictures of me with the people I'm dating, and when they stop getting the photo ops, they assume we've broken up. There's actually a group of people who think I'm secretly still dating Michael and that Trevor was only a friend."

"Are you worried I won't be able to handle it?" Dani asked, kissing the top of Peyton's head.

"I just want to make sure that we protect this." Peyton pressed her hand to Dani's heart. "I don't care about rumors or pictures or stupid articles. I only care about us." She paused, kissed Dani's collarbone, and added, "And I want us to tell people only when we're ready."

"I'm ready to tell my family. I want them to meet you, but I know the tour's coming up. It's hard, because I want as much time with you as possible. I don't want to share you with anyone." Dani squeezed Peyton. "Some people still think I'm with Steven, Peyton. Neither he nor I have ever commented on our relationship publicly."

"Do you want to now?"

"What? Tell people he and I aren't together anymore? No, not really. I don't care who knows what about me. I'm with you. That's all that matters. Steven can say what he wants if he feels like it. But if I do, it might open us up to more rumors. I don't want that. I just want to have a couple more weeks with you before you leave."

"How about you bring your family to New Zealand?" Peyton suggested. "You're coming out there for a couple of weeks anyway. We can fly them in for a week or so. I'll see if my family can join, too. We'll introduce the in-laws." She laughed.

"In-laws?" Dani asked, running her hand through Peyton's hair.

"If you think I could have fallen this hard for you without thinking about the day we tie the knot, Dani Wilder, you're nuts." Peyton pinched Dani's arm.

"Ow," Dani yelped and then laughed. "I'll talk to my parents about New Zealand."

"And your brother, too."

"Really? He's kind of annoying. Are you sure?"

"I'm sure." Peyton chuckled against Dani's breast. "About all of it."

CHAPTER 32

"DANI, I'M SERIOUS. I think you'd really like it," Gibson Shaw told her.

"I'm sure I would, but I have no experience."

"Yes, you do. You're gaining experience every time you grab your camera and take pictures. From what I've seen, that's happening a lot lately."

"It has been," Peyton confirmed. "She takes it with her everywhere now."

"I have one slot open. If you want it, it's yours." Gibson closed his laptop. "You've had three lessons, and I've already seen development in your work."

"Thank you."

"What about *my* work?" Peyton asked then, and Dani smiled at her competitive girlfriend.

"You could use another lesson or two," he teased.

"I'll settle for just knowing this one here, I guess." She pointed at Dani.

"You're pretty good as a subject, though, Miss Gloss," he said. "Half her pictures are of you, I think."

"Not half."

"About a third," Dani joked.

"Well, you make a good subject."

"Thank you," Peyton said through a laugh.

"That slot, though, it's really available? And you'd consider me for it?" Dani asked him.

"I already am. It's a six-week course. It's five days a week, and it's work outside of the workshop. I expect commitment from my students when I do these things."

"I understand."

"Before, you said you didn't have time for school. You would need to make the commitment that you would have time for this. It's not a four-year program; only six-weeks."

"Can I think about it?" Dani asked.

"It starts next week. Call my assistant by the end of the day tomorrow. I have other people who want the slot."

"I will. Thank you." She shook his hand.

Gibson Shaw then left the fairly deserted coffee shop. Peyton sipped on her coffee as Dani stared out the window for a moment.

"A six-week workshop, huh?" Peyton asked.

"It starts right when you leave."

"I know."

"I can't do it, though." Dani shrugged a shoulder. "I'm supposed to join you in Hong Kong for the weekend in a couple of weeks."

"That's true," Peyton replied.

"Plus, he told me about it during the last lesson I had, too. It's six-weeks, but that's the beginner course. If he thinks I'm good enough, there's an intermediate eight-week course that starts a few weeks later. The advanced one is another four weeks after that, but that's only if I got in."

"You researched it?" Peyton asked.

"The other night, yeah. I was prepping for the final lesson with him." Dani took a drink of her own coffee. "You ready to go? There are a couple of cameras out there. It's only a matter of time before more show up, and we're swarmed."

"Dani, famed photographer Gibson Shaw just hand-picked you for one of his rare workshops."

"I know. But there will be more."

"Did you miss the word *rare*?" Peyton asked with a sideways grin. "If I wasn't going away, would you do it?"

"I don't know. Maybe."

"Dani, we can arrange something else for us."

"I don't want something else." Dani pouted.

"Yes, you do. You want the workshop, and that's okay. I want it for you."

"We shouldn't do this here." Dani glanced back out the window. "There's more every minute," she said of the photographers.

"Leaving here won't prevent the conversation, Wilder. It'll only delay it until we're in the SUV."

"Peyton…"

"Dani…" Peyton rolled her eyes at her girlfriend. "I love you. You love me. Postponing our time together while I'm on tour won't change that. Do you want to do this workshop?"

"If I do, that's six weeks I couldn't travel."

"I know."

"What about New Zealand?"

"We can still do it. I'll work it out with the tour if I have to. It'll just be a couple of weeks after we'd originally planned."

"A couple more weeks of not seeing each other," Dani added.

"A couple more weeks of missing each other like crazy, yes; but also, a couple more weeks of you getting to do something you love. We can look at all the great pictures you take when we're on FaceTime. You can text them to me or upload them in those clouds." Peyton smiled at the memory of their previous conversation about that very topic. "I'll look at them every day."

"But you're my best subject. What if I suck if I'm not taking pictures of you?"

"I'm pretty sure your talent has nothing to do with me," Peyton replied.

"It's a long time without seeing you, Pey."

"You'll see me. I'll just be on your iPad."

"It's not the same thing."

"Oh, Dani, I know that." Peyton leaned forward. "I know what it's like to not be able to touch you. It's torture. I don't want it any more than you do. But this is my music. I can't skip out on a tour. And it's your passion. You can't skip out on it any more than I can. You told me when we first met that you wanted to be a photographer."

"Yeah, later, when I'm old and can't model anymore."

"Please, you'll be modeling walkers with tennis balls on them when you're eighty, and you'll still be hot." Peyton chuckled more at Dani's exasperated expression than her own joke. "You don't need to wait if you love it now. And I think you do. Besides, it's not like you ever *have* to work again, Dani."

"Not all of us are rock stars with royalties rolling in, Pey. I have money, but not—"

"Remember that thing about me wanting to spend my life with you? That means you share what I have, babe. It's our stuff now. That all started the moment I laid eyes on you."

"Like I'm ever going to be your housewife." Dani winked at her and took a drink.

"Like I'd ever want that from you," Peyton replied. "You know the one thing I do want from you, though?"

"Orgasms?" Dani asked.

"Dani!"

"Sorry, was that out loud?"

"You just took a really sweet moment and turned it into something completely different." Peyton laughed.

Dani laughed as well and said, "Okay. Sorry. Ask again. Ask the question."

"You know the one thing I do want from you, though?"

"What?" Dani asked.

"To be completely and totally happy in everything that you do."

"So, we're back to orgasms?" Dani teased.

"Oh, my God." Peyton couldn't help but laugh.

***

"I cannot believe you watch this show. It's for teenagers, Lennox."

"It's for everyone, Peyton."

"It's actually pretty good. You missed a great episode," Dani said. "Also, hello."

Peyton leaned down and kissed her girlfriend sweetly. Dani was lying on the sofa with Lennox at the other end, allowing Dani's legs to be placed in her lap.

"Hello," Peyton replied. "And you watched it with her, I see."

"We watched it together," Lennox answered for Dani. "You were supposed to be here an hour ago so that we could all hang out on my last night in town before you go."

"I know. Sorry. We had some last-minute stuff to iron out before we leave," Peyton said. "Should I be worried about you two?" she motioned to the feet in Lennox's lap.

"Nope. I'm yours. I'm just tall." Dani moved her legs and stretched. "Want to snuggle with me and watch another episode?"

"Another one?" Peyton sat down next to Dani.

"We're binge-watching the first season since Dani hasn't seen it."

"I'll need something to keep me occupied when you're gone." Dani rested her head on Peyton's shoulder.

"Fine. I'm in. Should I make a snack?" Peyton asked.

"I've got it. You two look pretty comfy." Lennox stood and stretched. "Pey, remember that actress I mentioned to you one time?" she asked as she headed toward the kitchen.

"Len, you *are* an actress. You talk about other actresses all the damn time."

"Kenzie," Lennox said.

"Bless you," Peyton mocked.

"She means Kenzie Smyth." Dani smacked Peyton's thigh. "She's the star. You'd like the show if you give it a chance."

"Dani, nachos?"

"Yes, please," Dani told Lennox.

"I want nachos, too," Peyton said.

"You're an asshole. I'm bringing you a tiny box of raisins."

"Hey, I'm sorry I'm late," Peyton said, kissing Dani on the top of her head.

"It's okay. I know it's coming up. You have a lot of work to do."

"Did you call Gibson?"

"I did."

"And?"

"And I'm going to do it."

"That's great, Dani." Peyton kissed Dani's lips when Dani lifted her head to look up at her with those bright green eyes Peyton loved so much.

"It is."

"Then, we'll go to plan B; unless you get selected for the intermediate one, too. If so, we'll figure something else out."

"Not necessary," Dani told her. "I'm just doing the beginner one."

"What? Why? Did he think you couldn't—"

"No, he didn't say anything. I'm going to do the six-week workshop, visit you, and do the intermediate one next fall when he offers it again. The truth is, I barely have time for the beginner part. I can make it work, though. After that, I have to focus on my career."

"And visiting your girlfriend?" Peyton asked, hopeful.

"And visiting my girlfriend. I've worked it all out. I have a plan I'll show you once Lennox heads out tomorrow."

"Yeah?"

"Yeah."

"And you're sure you're okay with her staying tonight when it's one of our last before I go?"

"She's your best friend, Peyton. She can stay as long as she wants to." Dani kissed Peyton's lips. "Besides, I think she's exhausted from all the interviews she had to give today and her flight. She'll crash soon. Then, you and I can…"

"Watch more teenage television shows?" Peyton asked.

"Not exactly what I had in mind."

"What *did* you have in mind, Miss Wilder?" Peyton lifted an eyebrow.

Dani leaned in and whispered, "Licking you… everywhere."

"Hey, wine or just water?" Lennox asked, reentering the room.

"Water." Peyton licked her lips. "A lot of cold water."

Dani laughed at that.

CHAPTER 33

THIRTEEN HOURS. That was all Dani had left of her time with Peyton for the next six weeks. Things had been a little awkward between them all day. They'd woken together at Peyton's house, shared breakfast in bed, lay around, and watched some reality TV mainly for Peyton's benefit. Then, they'd shared lunch, reviewed their calendars for the hundredth time to make sure they hadn't missed any opportunity to see one another during Peyton's tour, and watched a movie. They'd held onto one another throughout the entire day, and they had found excuses to touch each other as much as possible. Peyton held her hand after they'd finished up dinner and headed in the direction of the bedroom.

"Can I show you something?" Peyton asked.

"Sure."

She pulled Dani toward her music room, opened the door, and let her inside. She moved them over to the shelves and pointed.

"I added a few pictures to my collection," Peyton said, pointing at three new additions.

"Oh, Pey." Dani rested her head on Peyton's shoulder.

On the shelf, there were three newly framed photos. One was of Dani in Michigan in front of the waterfall. Peyton had taken it with her phone after they'd run through the water. Dani was sopping wet, but she was laughing. She recalled how happy she'd been that day after they had finally shared their first kiss. The second picture was of the two of them the following day, on their hike. Peyton had her head on Dani's shoulder. They both looked so content just to be near the other. The third picture was the one Dani had taken of Peyton. Gibson Shaw had printed it for them. Dani had left it at Peyton's and decided when she couldn't find it later, she'd just print it herself and hang it up at her place.

"Do you like my choices?" Peyton asked.

"I wondered where that one went," Dani said, pointing at that picture. "You look so beautiful in that one."

"I didn't put it in here because it's a picture of me. I put it in here because *you* took it. I love it because of that. I wanted you in here, Dani. This is my most special place in the world, and you're my most special *person* in the world."

Dani kissed her cheek and said, "I love you."

"You have a key, Dani. You can stay here whenever you want, you know that, right?"

"I know."

"Maybe save the moving in until I get back, though." Peyton kissed Dani's cheek this time.

Dani chuckled and replied, "Weren't you all about me moving in, like, yesterday? Sick of me already?"

Peyton turned to her, placed her hands on Dani's hips, and said, "You can give up your apartment tomorrow, for all I care. I'm in this, Dani. I know what *this* is. This is it. I want this to be *it* for me. I say save it until I get back only because I want us to do all the steps together. I don't plan on doing much manual labor; there are moving companies for that. But I want us to plan what this place will look like with your stuff and my stuff together. I wouldn't mind us working on the place in London together, either, since that work is really just beginning. All my places are your places now."

Dani pressed her forehead to Peyton's and said, "We only have thirteen more hours."

"No, we have our whole lives, Dani." Peyton kissed Dani's lips ever so softly. "Come to bed with me."

Dani nodded. Peyton took her hand again and pulled her into the bedroom. All at once, Dani felt the need to go incredibly slow and incredibly fast. She wanted to give Peyton as much pleasure as possible in the hours they had left, but she also wanted to touch every single part of Peyton's body, to memorize her skin, and worry about breaking an orgasm record another time.

"Why am I nervous?" Dani asked through nervous laughter.

"You're nervous?" Peyton asked back, reaching for Dani's neck to pull the woman into herself.

"We've done this before."

"Not enough if you ask me," Peyton offered, pressing her forehead against Dani's again. "It'll never be enough, Dani."

"Your fingers are just playing with my hair right now, and I have goosebumps."

"I like that I give you goosebumps," Peyton whispered. "I hope I always do."

"You whisper, and I get goosebumps," Dani said back, her cheeks turning red.

"*When you whisper*… That sounds like a great song title," Peyton whispered against Dani's lips. "*When I kiss you* does, too, though."

Peyton leaned in, pressing their lips together gently. Dani's arms went to Peyton's waist and pulled her in. Peyton's tongue toyed with Dani's, causing Dani to smile. Her nervousness dissipated with the realization that this was Peyton, *her* Peyton. She loved her with her whole heart and wanted to be with her forever. Dani's hands slid under Peyton's soft t-shirt, caressing her back and earning a small moan in the process. Peyton pulled back to remove her own shirt entirely and toss it aside, revealing her bare breasts with already peaked nipples to Dani. How was it that Dani had seen so many women topless throughout her career, but only the sight of Peyton's breasts made her wet with need?

Peyton removed Dani's shirt next. She leaned back in

and kissed Dani's neck in just the spot she knew Dani loved. She nibbled on Dani's skin as her hands slid up Dani's abdomen and cupped the woman's breasts. Dani gasped when Peyton played with her nipples. She reached for Peyton's waistband and tugged until her shorts were at her knees. Peyton shook them down her legs at the same time Dani was pulling down Peyton's panties. Once Peyton had kicked them both off her body, Dani moved into her, backing Peyton up against the bed.

Peyton sat on the end of it and reached for Dani. She pulled Dani's pants down, her underwear after, and moved Dani into her body, kissing her stomach and between her breasts. Dani held onto the back of Peyton's head, keeping the woman in place. The touches Peyton was applying were amazing, but keeping Peyton there was about more than just the touches. Peyton belonged with her. Their bodies had always belonged together. It was why they'd never been able to keep their hands off each other even when they weren't a couple.

Dani cupped Peyton's face, lifting her girlfriend's lips to her own as she bent down to kiss her. She then lowered Peyton onto the bed, kissing her neck, and lowering her own lips to Peyton's collarbone and her breast. She sucked on Peyton's nipple, earning another sexy moan. She repeated the action on her other nipple before she lowered her lips to Peyton's stomach. She kissed every inch of Peyton's skin, using her tongue around the woman's belly button. Peyton's hips began to lift on their own as her legs still hung over the side of the bed. Dani knelt, lifted Peyton's legs over her own shoulder, leaned in, and kissed her thighs.

Peyton lifted her head to watch Dani's tongue slide over her left thigh. When Dani's eyes met the blue ones that were looking down at her, her tongue slid into Peyton's folds. She loved doing this to Peyton; she had ever since the first time she'd touched her this way. She had no idea what that meant, because never in her life had she thought she'd do this to another woman. But it didn't matter when it felt this good. Peyton's hand moved to the back of Dani's head. Her head went back. Dani watched Peyton's back arch slightly as she entered the woman with her tongue. She listened to Peyton's moans, gasps, and shouts as she brought her to orgasm. She stayed on her knees, kissing, sucking, and licking Peyton until she climbed again. When Peyton was about to climax, Dani slid two fingers inside her. Peyton arched, allowing Dani to slide further inside. Dani loved the feeling of sliding inside her girlfriend. She sucked Peyton's clit hard as she moved to curl her fingers. Peyton yelled Dani's name when Dani began thrusting. Then, she came.

Dani watched Peyton. She wanted to always remember this moment – what it looked like when Peyton came on their last night together before their longest time apart. When Peyton's arm went over her eyes as if she was spent, Dani moved her legs together, climbed on top of her, and straddled her hips. Without warning, she took Peyton's hand and slid it between her own thighs. Peyton's eyes opened. Her other arm moved to Dani's hip, and she held onto it as she slid her fingers inside Dani. Dani gasped at the sensation of being full in every way.

Peyton sat up slightly as Dani began to lift herself up and down, crashing on top of her long fingers. Peyton's thumb moved to Dani's clit, causing Dani to jerk forward into Peyton's embrace. She rocked her hips. She grasped Peyton's face, bringing it to her own, and kissed her. Dani knew Peyton could taste herself on her lips. She loved that fact. She rocked harder as her orgasm built. Peyton's mouth slid down to Dani's neck again. When Peyton bit softly into her pulse point, Dani came. She came hard. She rocked even harder, wanting more of her girlfriend.

Peyton recognized the need. She gripped Dani's waist and rolled Dani onto her back. She hovered over the woman now, kissing her lips, sliding her fingers deep inside, and carrying Dani all the way through her orgasm. Then, Peyton slowly removed her fingers, allowing Dani to come down entirely. When Dani looked up at her girlfriend, Peyton was standing up fully. She was naked. Her chest was heaving. Her eyes were dark. She was not done. Dani slid to the top of the bed, watching Peyton follow her until Peyton's entire body was pressed to her own.

"I love you, Dani Wilder," Peyton whispered into Dani's ear.

***

For the first time in her entire career, Peyton didn't want to go on tour. She loved her job. She loved touring. Sure, it got tiresome sometimes. It was a difficult way to live. The bus became her rolling home. There were different cities every night. The repetition could make some days boring. She wouldn't give it up for anything, though. Well, almost anything. As she sat in the SUV, with Dani glued to her side, she knew then that she would give it all up to be with her. She wouldn't have to; Dani would never ask that of her. Still, Peyton knew she would have, in a heartbeat. The way it felt just being in the same orbit with this woman, was better than writing the best song she would ever write, creating just the right string of notes for a hook, or performing on the world's largest stage.

"We should say goodbye in here. The windows are tinted," Peyton told her the moment the driver exited the SUV once they were parked next to her plane.

Dani lifted her head up, showing Peyton her watery eyes.

"Hey, you're going to have the best time, babe. You get to take photography lessons from Gibson Shaw. You won't even miss me." Peyton winked at Dani as she cupped the woman's cheek.

"I know you're trying to make me feel better, but that's ridiculous, and you know it," Dani replied.

"What I do know is that I love you. I love you so much, I don't even want to get out of this car." Peyton's eyes welled with tears as well. "Saying goodbye to you is the hardest thing I've ever had to do."

"I know your tour is going to be amazing and that you love your job, but… God, Peyton, this is hard." A tear ran down Dani's cheek, and Peyton wiped it away for her. "I wish I could just come with you."

"No, you don't." Peyton wiped her own tear away. "You have your own career, Dani. You love your job. You want to do that. You don't want to spend eight months on the road with me." Peyton chuckled.

"I'd settle for just more time before you had to leave. We've only had a few months since we got together."

"We've had five months. We got together the night we met." Peyton kissed Dani's nose.

Dani chuckled and replied, "Except for that pesky boyfriend thing."

"You have always been mine, and I have always been yours." Peyton kissed her lips. "And we will always belong to each other."

"Eight months will fly by." Dani wiped her own cheeks and tried to take a deep breath. "I love you."

"I love you." Peyton kissed her softly. "You are the love of my life, Dani Wilder."

"You're mine." Dani sniffled, cupped Peyton's face, kissed her again, and pulled back just enough to say, "I don't want you to go."

"I love you," Peyton repeated. "And I have to. The plane's waiting."

"I know. I know." Dani pulled back, releasing Peyton's face. "I'm not a sap. I can pull myself together." She wiped her cheeks again.

Peyton laughed at her girlfriend, leaned over, and kissed Dani's cheek.

"I'll call you when I land."

"FaceTime me?"

"Whatever you want."

"I want you here." Dani looked at her.

"I will be." Peyton pressed her hand to Dani's chest. "Always."

"God, you're such a damn songwriter," Dani said with another nervous chuckle.

"It's what I do, baby," Peyton teased.

"Shut up." Dani leaned over. "Kiss me one more time."

"Always," Peyton repeated.

EPILOGUE

"THESE ARE GREAT, DANI."

"Thanks, Lennox."

"They're alright," Peyton teased her girlfriend.

"Those lessons with Shaw paid off, huh?" Lennox told Dani, ignoring Peyton.

"I think the landscape of New Zealand is what made the pictures good. I just held the camera." Dani shifted on Peyton's lap.

"You two look good together," Peyton's friend and an actress, Quinn Harris, said as she pointed at them; she seemed to contemplate their relationship all in one glance. "Dani, your new, lighter hair is on point."

"Thanks," Dani said, leaning her cheek against the top of Peyton's head. "It was for a shoot. I don't know if I'll stay blonde or not."

"What's your girlfriend think about it?" Bobby Jane asked.

"She thinks it's hot," Peyton confirmed. "And would have no problem if Dani decided to keep it."

"Oh, yeah?" Dani asked, looking down at her.

"Oh, God… Please don't start making out again. I already caught you guys in the pool earlier," Jill said, sticking her finger down her throat as if she might vomit if they make out in front of the group.

There were about twenty women in various stages of

dress and drunkenness at Peyton's Hamptons' estate. Well, Peyton *and* Dani's now. It was Peyton's annual Fourth of July party. She had invited all her girlfriends that could make it and many of Dani's as well. It had all gotten started that morning when the majority of them had arrived and claimed the guest rooms they wanted in the large vacation home. They'd had lunch by the pool, dinner on the beach, and were now sitting around the fire, catching up with one another.

Dani and Peyton had made it through her tour. Dani had gone to New Zealand. Peyton had gone to Paris. Dani had gone to London. Peyton had gone to Rome. They'd made the most of their time together and their time apart. They had come out stronger, just as Peyton's mom had suggested they would. They had only recently told their friends that they were a couple. Peyton had wanted them to be able to be themselves on this trip to The Hamptons. She wanted to be able to touch, kiss, and be with Dani in the only way she knew how: as the woman who loved her like crazy and still got goosebumps every time they touched.

As the fire died, and some of their friends jumped into the cold ocean, while the others sat on blankets on the sand, strummed guitars, and sang along to Davica's number one hit or Lynn Erickson's new single, Dani sat on Peyton's lap, running her hand through the soft hair that had lightened a little already thanks to the summer sun. Peyton would look up at her every so often. She kissed Dani's lips, her neck, her jaw, her cheeks, and held her lips just beyond Dani's ear.

"I love you," she whispered.

Dani leaned down, kissed her, and said, "I love you, too."

"Inside?" Peyton asked with a nod toward the house.

Dani nodded her reply. They stood quietly, not wanting to draw any attention to themselves, and turned to head inside the house.

"Good night," Lennox offered with a wink. "I'll keep them occupied for a while."

Peyton smiled at her best friend, held onto Dani's

hand, and they moved to the back of the house. Dani grabbed a bottle of red wine and two glasses from the kitchen. They made their way up the stairs, still holding hands, and into the master bedroom, which had a terrace that overlooked the beach and their crazy friends.

"I think they need a chaperone," Dani said, watching a few of them jump into the water without clothing. "They're going to get arrested."

"They'll be fine," Peyton returned, standing right behind her. "Come to bed."

"What if–"

"Dani, we haven't been together in over a month," Peyton said, kissing the woman's neck, as she wrapped arms around Dani from behind to undo the button on her jeans.

Dani's hand covered Peyton's and encouraged her to unzip them as well as Dani closed her eyes.

"I hate our busy schedules sometimes," she replied.

"Me too."

For the past month, they'd been missing one another. Whenever Dani had been in New York, Peyton hadn't been. If Peyton had a chance to be there, Dani had been on a photo shoot somewhere else in the world. Peyton hadn't touched Dani in four weeks. She craved those touches, those sounds Dani made when she was just starting to get turned on; and especially, the sounds Dani made when she was coming.

"Come to bed," Peyton repeated.

Dani reached for the curtains, pulling them together but leaving the sliding glass doors to the terrace open so they could still enjoy the ocean breeze. She turned around to face her girlfriend, reached for Peyton's t-shirt – which she removed, and then undid Peyton's bikini top, letting it fall to the ground on its own. Peyton took Dani's hand and walked them over to the bed. Next to it, on the bedside table, was a picture Dani had taken of the two of them in New Zealand. Well, it was one of the many pictures she took of them in New Zealand. She had been showing a few of them on her phone to Lennox outside, before Peyton had started that neck kissing thing that she did that made Dani want her naked.

On her side of the bed, Dani had a picture of just her girlfriend that she had taken and used as a part of her project for Gibson Shaw. He had loved how she'd edited it, asked her to join the intermediate workshop, and had been very disappointed when she had declined. She would go the following fall, or maybe even the next year. As much as she loved taking pictures, Dani loved her career right now, and she loved her girlfriend. Her heart was full.

Peyton laid her down, removing Dani's clothing as she did. Then, she pulled her own capris down her legs along with her bikini bottoms, climbed on top of Dani, breathed in Dani's scent, and kissed her. Dani's arms were around Peyton's back, encouraging Peyton's hips to lower and press into her. Peyton did. She kissed Dani's neck first, lowering to take her nipple into her mouth right after. Dani's hips bucked. Peyton reached between them. She parted Dani's lips, parted her own, and pressed them together in the same way she had the first time they'd touched this way.

"How'd you know?" Dani asked.

"I didn't. I just missed this."

"Me too," Dani replied, pressing Peyton's ass down with both hands. "Don't stop."

"I have no intention of stopping," Peyton muttered against Dani's lips before she kissed her girlfriend deeply.

"I missed you."

"I *love* you," Peyton said.

"I love you, too," Dani replied.

"Then, come for me." Peyton rocked harder against her.

Dani did come. She came hard. In part, because it had been a while; and in part, because Peyton always made her come hard. Peyton came soon after, rocking even harder against Dani. When she came down, she lowered herself entirely on top of Dani, and Dani held her. She held Peyton because she loved her so much. She held her because she'd never wanted to hold someone more than this woman. She held her because she knew Peyton Gloss was supposed to be held by her. Nothing else mattered in that moment. Their friends, playing on the beach outside, didn't matter. The world that still didn't know they were a couple didn't matter. The people that would, undoubtedly, have a problem with them being a couple when they did tell the world, didn't matter. Only they mattered in moments like this. Dani knew it now like she knew it always. There would be no after Peyton Gloss for her.

***

"It's not even over yet, and you're already thinking about next year?" Dani asked Peyton the following morning as she lay in bed. "And they're all still out there. I think they've slept out there," she added as she walked from the terrace back to the bed and slid in next to Peyton.

"It takes a long time to plan week-long parties like this, Dani. There's an art to it." Peyton stared at the computer screen in her lap. "I want to do something different; something special."

"This is pretty special," Dani commented, laying her head on Peyton's shoulder. "Also, do you want breakfast? Everyone is crashed out there. We should eat before they all wake up and walk into the kitchen, hungover like zombies."

"Zombies are, apparently, Lennox's area; not mine," Peyton teased her friend.

"That joke only works if she's here to hear it, babe."

Peyton smiled and replied, "Then, pretend like I said it for the first time later."

"Will do." Dani kissed her naked shoulder.

"I was thinking about doing more than just a beach party next year."

"Private island party?" Dani suggested. "Igloo party?" she added, laughing at herself.

Peyton glared at her, kissed Dani's nose, and returned her eyes to her laptop.

"Igloo party is the best idea yet. How does one rent a giant igloo?"

"I think part of the event is *making* the igloo. Then, we get to party in it."

Peyton continued her search with a smile, thinking about how cute Dani Wilder was sometimes. Then, she came across something that sounded so ridiculous, it might be just what she was looking for.

"Huh…" she said mainly to herself.

"What?" Dani asked, glancing up at her screen.

"Summer camp," Peyton replied.

Made in United States
Orlando, FL
18 November 2021

10508542R00142